COURAGEOUS
LOVE

By the Author

New Beginnings

Courageous Love

Visit us at www.boldstrokesbooks.com

COURAGEOUS LOVE

by

KC Richardson

2016

COURAGEOUS LOVE

ISBN 13: 978-1-62639-797-2

THIS TRADE PAPERBACK ORIGINAL IS PUBLISHED BY
BOLD STROKES BOOKS, INC.
P.O. BOX 249
VALLEY FALLS, NY 12185

FIRST EDITION: DECEMBER 2016

CREDITS
EDITOR: CINDY CRESAP
PRODUCTION DESIGN: STACIA SEAMAN
COVER DESIGN BY JEANINE HENNING

Acknowledgments

I want to thank Radclyffe, Sandy Lowe, and the rest of the Bold Strokes Books staff for welcoming me into this incredible family. Being a Bold Strokes author has been truly a high point in my life. To my editor, Cindy Cresap, thank you for teaching me the art and skill of writing. Your patience with me is greatly appreciated.

Thank you to my readers who have reached out to let me know you wanted to read Alex's story. It means so much to me that you liked her and wanted to know more about her. I appreciate all your emails and Facebook posts, and especially your support.

Thank you to my beta readers, Andrea, Penelope, Dawn, and Maya, for helping me write a pretty decent first draft.

Thank you to Carrie, Kris, and Christopher for your expertise in police, paramedic, and ER matters. I hope I did your professions justice. You are the real-life heroes.

Thank you to my best friend, Nicki, for Alex's "counseling session" and for helping me brainstorm this story. I'm forever grateful for becoming friends with you way back in our college days. Your support, friendship, and love over the past couple of decades mean more to me than I could ever express. I love you, little bear.

A very special thank you to my good friend Shannon, who was gracious enough to share her journey with me. Shannon, you are one of the bravest women I know and a true hero to me. I love you greatly.

Thank you to my family and friends for your unwavering support. Having you all cheer me on and seeing your excitement for my new journey really keeps me writing.

Most importantly, thank you to my wife, Inger, for your support and encouragement to finish this story. There were times where it was emotionally difficult to write, but you were there every step of the way and I was able to finish it because of you. There is no one else I'd rather take the difficult journeys with. I love you.

Finally, this story was important for me to write because too often, pre-menopausal women think breast cancer won't happen to them. I ask of you to listen to your body and fight for it. Do your self-exams, get your mammograms, and if you detect a lump or other possible sign, get tested. Early detection could be the difference between life and death.

To my grandmother, my friend Shannon,
and everyone who has bravely fought breast cancer.

CHAPTER ONE

A lex had finished a busy shift at the ER and was excited to start her long weekend. She jumped into her car and pushed the phone icon as she pulled out of the parking lot of County Hospital.

"Hey, it's me. I'm on my way over and was calling to see if you needed me to pick up anything."

"No, I think we have everything."

"How's my boy? Is he ready to see his auntie?"

"Yep. He's already in his swim diaper and is just waiting for you to take him swimming."

"Wonderful. I'll be there soon." Alex hung up and checked a quick text message she had received before turning off her phone. She swerved before she could cross into the lane next to hers and decided to pay attention.

The blue and red lights that flashed in her rearview mirror brought Alex's breathing to a halt. She wasn't doing anything wrong. Well, not really. She was driving only ten miles per hour over the speed limit. Surely, she wasn't being pulled over for speeding. She flicked on her blinker, turned to look over her shoulder, and safely pulled to the shoulder of the road. The police car pulled in behind her, and the officer remained in his car. Damn! This day held such promise.

She was off work from the ER for the next few days and ready to have a good time. She had been on her way to her best friend Jordan's house for a pool party and barbecue. She had hoped to meet a single woman at the party that she could maybe spend the next couple of days having fun with. Getting pulled over was not how she imagined this day would go.

The officer finally got out of his car and started to approach. Alex looked in her side mirror and watched him—wait a minute—*her* carefully draw near with her hand placed near the butt of her gun. Alex's pulse sped up as she sized up the officer. She was a little taller than average with olive skin and short, dark hair. Alex couldn't tell what her body looked like due to the vest under her uniform top and her duty belt, but she had a feeling it would be spectacular. The officer had a confidence to her gait, more like a swagger, as she arrived at the passenger side window. She had a stern look to her face and mirrored black Oakley sunglasses. Alex wondered if these sunglasses were standard issue for cops. She saw enough officers in the emergency room wearing the popular style.

The officer gestured for Alex to roll down the window. Alex looked at the officer's name tag and gave her the most flirtatious smile she could. "Is there something I can help you with, Officer Greco?"

"May I have your license, registration, and proof of insurance, ma'am?"

Alex felt her eyebrows shoot up her forehead. *Ma'am?* "Officer, I'm sure—"

"It's Sergeant, ma'am."

"Okay, Sergeant," Alex drew out, "I'm sure you have better things to do than waste your time on me. How about you let me get on my way and you can go back to protecting the streets?"

"I can't do that, ma'am. Now, let me see your license, registration, and proof of insurance."

Alex blew out a breath in frustration. "Fine." She rummaged through her purse and removed her license and insurance card from her wallet, then leaned over and opened the glove box to get her registration. She reluctantly handed the items over to the sergeant.

"I pulled you over for speeding and failure to use a hands-free device, Ms. Taylor," Sergeant Greco said after scanning the license. "The speed limit is forty miles per hour, and I clocked you doing fifty. It's also against the law to talk on your cell phone while operating a vehicle if you're not using a hands-free device. Wait here, please."

Alex watched her retreat to her cruiser. If she hadn't been so embarrassed or angry, Alex would have appreciated the toned ass that even the polyester uniform pants couldn't hide. As time dragged on, Alex became more miffed. She could feel her blood begin to boil and took some deep breaths to calm herself down before Sergeant Greco returned. She checked the rearview mirror and saw the officer returning to Alex.

"Here you go, ma'am." Sergeant Greco handed the items back to Alex, along with a speeding ticket. "Be safe, stay off your phone while you drive, and slow it down a little."

"Sure thing, *Sergeant*," Alex mumbled under her breath as the officer left. "Thanks a-fucking-lot."

Alex put her blinker on and waited for a break in traffic to pull back onto the road, resisting the urge to peel out and spray dirt and rocks on the officer's car. She thought of the handsome sergeant on the drive to Jordan's. Under different circumstances, Alex could have imagined spending time and getting to know her better. Alex never had a "type" that she preferred. She had been with butch and femme women, and everything in between. She tended to gravitate toward a woman who could spark her interest. A woman with self-confidence. Sergeant Greco displayed that in spades.

There was definitely a commanding presence to the sergeant, not only in her demeanor, but her face as well. She had a strong, square jaw and Romanesque nose. Even though she never removed her sunglasses, Alex could imagine the intensity in her eyes. Oh, well. Alex hoped never to run into the commanding Sergeant Greco again.

Alex pulled into the driveway behind Jordan's car and took a few more deep breaths. She was about to spend the day with three of the most important people in her life, and she wasn't going to let that damn officer ruin the rest of her day.

She knocked on the front door and let herself in. She felt all of the stress fall away into thin air. Her godson Aiden's blue-green eyes twinkled as he toddled his way to Alex and tried to say her name. He got the "A" part down, but that was it for now. The "lex" would come soon, she was sure. She scooped him up, nuzzled his neck, and inhaled the sweet scent of his baby shampoo and powder. The giggles that came from Aiden made Alex want to continue tickling him.

Aiden leaned back from Alex, put his little hands on her cheeks, and moved back in for a sloppy kiss. This was new for him, and Alex felt the tears sting her eyes. "Jordan, go pack Aiden's clothes. I'm running away with him and never bringing him back."

Jordan chuckled as she greeted Alex. "You can borrow him

anytime you want, Al, but you have to promise to bring him back. You do not want Kirsten hunting you down." Alex accepted Jordan's kiss hello and turned her attention back to Aiden. Jordan had been Alex's best friend since their first year in college. They'd seen and helped each other through really great times and really bad times. Alex was an only child, but Jordan was the sister she had always wished for.

Jordan's avoidance of relationships ended when she met her now-wife a little over three years ago. Alex loved Kirsten as much as she did Jordan, and when they asked her to be Aiden's godmother, it solidified her place in their family. She longed to find a woman who would complete her life as Jordan and Kirsten completed each other's. Who knew? Maybe she would meet her today.

❖

Sergeant Francesca Greco was relieved her shift was finally over. It had been a relatively quiet day—well, as quiet as it could be for a patrol supervisor on a Saturday day shift. As she drove back to the station, she recalled her last stop. She had only twenty minutes before she headed back to the station to clean up and meet some friends. She put her car into gear and started to pull up to the stop sign just ahead when a car sped past her going westbound. Frank went in pursuit of the bright yellow Volkswagen Beetle. By pacing the car, she estimated the driver was going about ten miles per hour over the speed limit. She observed the driver holding what appeared to be a phone up to her ear and was weaving slightly. There were enough cars on the road that this could be a potentially unsafe pursuit. She flipped on her lights as she gained ground on the speeding vehicle. When the driver signaled to pull over, Frank offered up a silent thank you to the police gods.

Frank radioed dispatch with the make, model, and license plate and waited for the information. The dispatcher came back. "Vehicle registered to Alexandra Taylor. No warrants."

"Copy that." Frank exited her vehicle and approached the passenger's side. She was normally a very even-keeled woman, but she couldn't help the quickening of her pulse whenever she approached a vehicular stop. In her ten-plus years of experience, domestic calls and vehicular stops were always unknown and could be very dangerous. As she approached the car that reminded her of the brightly shining sun, she had a feeling this would be a routine stop, but was cautious nonetheless. She tapped on the window and the driver lowered it. Frank noticed the gorgeous woman sitting behind the wheel with the thick chestnut brown hair, high cheekbones, the nose that curved up oh-so-slightly, and the full, luscious lips. If only they had met under different circumstances. She asked for the woman's ID, insurance, and registration. No, this stop definitely wouldn't be routine.

Frank had considered letting Alex off with just a warning when she was so apologetic, but then Alex had to go and ask Frank if she could just let her go. In her opinion, people who asked to get out of a ticket were only sorry they got caught and weren't really looking to change their driving habits for the better. At least with a ticket, they might think about what they did and not look to do it again.

"Wait here, please." Frank took the items back to her patrol car and called the dispatcher again with the license information. After the dispatcher notified her that the driver did not have any warrants, Frank began writing the ticket. She studied Alex's picture on her license a little longer than necessary. Although the picture was small, Frank could see the warmth emanating from her chocolate brown eyes. She sighed and thought another time, another place. Frank completed the information on the ticket and made her way back to Alex's car.

"Here you go, ma'am." Frank handed Alex's items and ticket to her. "Be safe, stay off your phone while you drive, and slow it down a little." Frank got into her cruiser and waited for Alex to safely return to the road. She let out a deep breath, disappointed in the way they met. The chatter over the radio as she headed back to the station was white noise as she thought about Alex. She second-guessed her actions in giving her a ticket, and thought if she had let her go with a warning, maybe there would have been a slight chance to get to know her better if they met again. Frank knew she blew that chance when she saw in her eyes the, what? Anger? Disappointment? Whatever it was told Frank it was a done deal.

When she returned to the station, she dropped off her keys and headed to the locker room and the showers. Once she was dressed in tan cargo shorts and a black polo shirt, she spiked up her hair with a little gel and shook her head a few times to give it a bit of a wild look. Frank grabbed her backpack out of her locker, headed to her black Dodge Ram pickup, and drove to the party she had been invited to. She parked her truck on the tree-lined street and hiked half a block to the house. She noticed a bright yellow Beetle in the driveway and took a sharp intake of breath, then laughed at herself. *Just a coincidence. There are a few hundred of those cars that same color driving the streets of Southern California.* But like most cops said, she reminded herself, there were never coincidences.

She knocked on the front door but when it opened, her breath hitched when she saw Alex Taylor. Alex narrowed her eyes before slamming the door in Frank's face. Frank stood there stunned, sure she should turn around and leave, but she couldn't make her feet move. The door opened again, and she saw her friend Jordan standing in the doorway, looking as bewildered as Frank felt.

"What the hell was that all about?"

Frank shook her head. "Um, I think I should go, Jordan. Thanks for the invite." She turned to leave when she felt a hand grab her.

"Not so fast there, Frank. Come in and have a beer so you can tell me why my best friend slammed the door in your face, then hurried past me while swearing under her breath."

Frank barked out a laugh. *Best friend. Just great. This day just keeps getting better and better.* She felt herself being pulled by Jordan and was too shocked to resist. Jordan led her to the kitchen and introduced Frank to Kirsten, Jordan's wife.

"Frank, this is my wife, Kirsten. Baby, this is my friend I told you about, Frank Greco."

"I'm so happy to finally meet you, Frank. Jordan's told me so much about you. I can't believe you two used to play basketball against each other in college. How did you become reacquainted?"

Frank thanked Jordan for the beer and took a drink. "I hurt my knee during training, and the doc sent me to Jordan for PT. We recognized each other and laughed at fate bringing us back into each other's lives." She wanted to laugh again at fate. What were the chances of running into Alex again so soon? And her being Jordan's best friend? A wave of disappointment slashed through Frank like a knife. Jordan must have noticed.

"Hey, baby, would you excuse us for a moment? I need to talk to Frank privately."

"Sure, love. I'll be out at the pool with our guests." Kirsten turned to Frank and smiled. "I hope you brought your appetite and suit. I look forward to talking with you more."

Frank and Jordan watched Kirsten's retreating form, and Jordan turned back to Frank. "Okay, let's have it."

Frank took a deep breath. "I think your Alex hates me."

Jordan looked concerned. "Why would she hate you?"

"I gave her a speeding ticket about two hours ago."

Jordan broke out in laughter. "Was she speeding?"

"Yep. And talking on her cell phone while driving."

Jordan laughed again. "Good. I'm glad you gave her a ticket. I'm always telling her to slow down, so now maybe she will. That phone call must have been to me to let me know she was on her way. I wonder why she wasn't using her Bluetooth."

"She said the battery died. I don't know, Jordan. Maybe I should have given her a warning."

"Uh-uh. You did exactly the right thing. Alex is a very safe driver with the exception of her speeding. You were doing your job."

Frank finished her beer and was grateful for Jordan's understanding, but didn't feel like she should stay. She didn't want to ruin the party for Jordan or Alex. "Thanks for the beer, but I'm going to take off. Please say good-bye to Kirsten for me."

Jordan stopped her again. "Forget it, Greco. You're staying. Alex might be a little pissed now." Jordan laughed when Frank raised her eyebrow. "Okay, a lot pissed off, but she'll get over it. She's really great once you get to know her."

Frank hesitated. "I don't know…"

Jordan threw her arm around Frank's shoulder and led her to the sliding glass door. "C'mon, it will be fine. There are plenty of other women here to talk to, and if you're not enjoying yourself in another half hour, I won't stop you if you want to leave. What do you say?"

Frank shrugged. "Sure, okay."

Jordan squeezed her shoulder. "Great. I want you to meet our son."

❖

Alex relaxed on the chaise lounge with Aiden sitting in her lap. After seeing Sergeant Greco at the door looking all kinds of yummy in her black shirt, tan shorts, and spiked hair, Alex panicked and slammed the door in her face. She acted like a petulant child, and it embarrassed her that she behaved that way, but she just couldn't help it. The fact that she wanted to grab her and kiss her breathless shocked her more. She took Aiden from Jordan's arms as she stormed past her out to the backyard. She ignored the questioning look on Jordan's face as she wrapped her arms around Aiden. She inhaled Aiden's scent, and his giggles calmed her. She spotted Jordan and Frank as they headed her way.

"Alex Taylor, I believe you've met my friend, Frank Greco." Jordan smirked as she took Aiden from her arms. "Frank, this is my best friend, Alex, and this handsome little man is my son, Aiden."

Alex watched the exchange between Aiden and Frank and felt her anger start to dissolve. The transformation from tough cop to the woman who was cooing with Aiden surprised Alex. Frank held Aiden on her left hip and extended her hand to Alex.

"Ms. Taylor." Frank smiled at Alex. "It's nice to see you in more pleasant circumstances."

Alex could feel her mouth tug into a grin but tried to remain aloof. "Sergeant Greco."

Alex noticed the amusement in Jordan's eyes, having seen it many times in the years they'd been friends. She made a mental note to get revenge later. Jordan took Aiden from Frank and called out over her shoulder as she went to Kirsten's side. "You ladies play nice." Alex thought she heard Jordan snicker but couldn't be sure.

Alex rolled her eyes as Frank looked anywhere but at her. It was when Frank looked down at her feet that Alex decided to lighten up. She indicated the empty chair next to her. "Would you like to sit down?"

Alex almost laughed at the look of relief that swept over Frank's face. "I'd like that, but I'm going to grab a beer. Can I get you anything?"

"A beer would be great, thanks."

Alex watched Frank saunter over to the cooler with her confident swagger back in place. Alex found this much more attractive than the tail-tucked-between-the-legs look Frank was just exhibiting. The warmth infusing her body was testimony to that, along with the sight of Frank's ass as she bent over to retrieve two beers out of the ice chest.

Frank returned, and after twisting off the cap, handed the beer to Alex and took the vacant seat.

Alex took a drink that quenched the dryness of her mouth she'd been experiencing since Frank went to get their beers. "So, how do you know Jordan?"

"We played basketball against each other in college. We weren't exactly friends, but we knew each other. A few months ago, I got hurt and Jordan was my PT. We got to talking and hit it off."

Alex smiled. "That's how she got together with Kirsten. She was Jordan's patient, but after she was discharged, they became friends and eventually fell in love."

Frank laughed and shook her head. "Well, I'm happy with us being just friends." She took a pull from her beer. "What about you, Alex? Do you think we can be friends?"

Alex raised an eyebrow and eyed her suspiciously. "I don't know, Sergeant. Are you allowed to be friends with a criminal?"

Frank leaned closer and lowered her voice. "I won't tell people you're a criminal if you don't. It can be our little secret."

Did she just flirt with her? *Damn, she's sexy when she loosens up.* Alex crossed her finger over her heart. "I promise."

Frank leaned back against the chair and assumed a relaxed pose. "What do you do for a living? Besides breaking the law, I mean?"

Alex couldn't help but laugh. She was beginning to appreciate Frank's sense of humor. "I'm a nurse in the ER at County Hospital."

"Really? Why haven't I seen you before? I'm there at least a couple of times a week tending to calls. I definitely would have noticed you."

Yes, most definitely flirting. This could be fun. "I just transferred over from Fountain Hills Regional a few weeks ago. But I'll be sure to warn my new colleagues to look out for you."

Frank's eyebrows shot up her forehead and made Alex laugh. "Warn them? About what?"

"Not to speed when you're on duty," Alex said with a sly grin. *And to look out for the devastatingly good-looking Sergeant Greco.*

Frank tipped her nonexistent hat. "Just trying to keep the streets safe, ma'am."

Alex again raised her eyebrow suspiciously. "Uh-huh. How long have you been a police officer?"

Frank relaxed and leaned back against the chair. "A little more than ten years. I got my degree in criminal justice and entered the police academy shortly after I graduated college."

Alex was ready to ask another question when Jordan came over. "Hey, ladies, food's ready. Grab a plate and help yourselves."

Frank stood and offered her hand to Alex. She looked at Frank and smiled. *A gentlewoman too.* She took her hand and contemplated keeping hold of it, but that idea was nixed when Frank let go. Instead, Frank placed her hand on the small of Alex's back and gently guided her ahead.

"After you."

They gathered in the kitchen where Jordan introduced Frank to some of her friends. A few of the women were from Jordan's recreation league basketball team, and when they discovered Frank played against Jordan in college, they invited her to play on their team when league started back up. Alex's pulse raced when she saw Frank's face light up with excitement. Damn, Frank was attractive. If Frank decided to play, it would give Alex one more reason to attend more games.

They grabbed their food and headed back to the lounge chairs. They hardly spoke as they devoured their burgers and potato salad. When they finished eating, Alex held out her hand for Frank's empty plate. "Do you want more food, or can I take this to the trash?"

"No, I'm stuffed, but I can throw it away."

Alex grabbed the plate from Frank's hand. "I got it. Do you want anything to drink?"

"Just some water. I need to be going soon."

A wave of disappointment rushed through Alex as she went to throw away their plates. She thought she and Frank were getting along okay. She tried to brush away the regret and plastered on a smile she knew didn't reach her eyes. She handed the bottle of water to Frank, and when their fingers touched, Alex felt like her insides caught fire. Frank must have felt it too judging by the look on her face. Just as quickly, the connection was broken when Frank took the bottle from Alex's hand. Her voice sounded huskier when she said thanks. Yep, Frank must have felt it too.

Frank gulped the water down quickly and fiddled with the water bottle. Alex wondered what was going through Frank's mind because her confidence was now replaced with a look of uncertainty.

"So, Alex, I was wondering if I could call you sometime and, um, maybe ask you to dinner."

As attracted as she was to Frank, dating her didn't seem like a very good idea right now. She wasn't sure why exactly, but the warning bells going off in her head told her to politely decline. "I'm sorry, but I don't think that would be a good idea."

A frown was quickly replaced by a faint smile on Frank's face. "Sure, okay." Frank stood and offered her hand to Alex. "Good to meet you, Alex. Maybe I'll see you around sometime. Take care."

Alex watched Frank leave with her shoulders slumped, and she felt like a jerk. Would it have killed her to give Frank her number? They could have gone out for drinks and gotten to know each other a little more, but she couldn't ignore those bells. They hadn't steered her wrong yet. Alex was surprised that Frank and Jordan both turned to her at the same time. Frank offered a weak wave and an even weaker smile, hugged Jordan, then left the party. She was unsure of what Frank said to Jordan, but it couldn't have been good judging by Jordan's determined gait and her tight-lipped mouth.

"What did you say to her?"

"Calm down, Jordan. She asked me for my number and I told her that wouldn't be a good idea."

"Why? It looked like you two were getting along."

"We were. We did. It's nothing she said or did. I just didn't think it was a good idea. She seems very nice, and I'm sure I'll see her around the ER and at your basketball games if she decides to play. I don't want any complications or awkwardness if things didn't work out for us."

Jordan laughed and shook her head. "You sound like I did a few years ago when I first met Kirsten."

Alex took Jordan's hand and held it. "I know, but just trust me on this. It's better this way."

"Okay, Al." Jordan leaned over and kissed her.

"Where's my big boy? I need some Aiden love."

"Kirsten is just finishing feeding him. I was going to snag him away so she can finally eat."

Alex stood and placed her hand on Jordan's shoulder. "Let me. You mingle with your friends, and I'll take care of the little monkey."

"Deal. But if you try to leave with him, remember, I know where you live."

Alex looked over her shoulder as she went to find Aiden. "Didn't I tell you? I moved." She could still hear Jordan's laughter as she entered the house.

Kirsten was just taking Aiden out of his high chair when he spotted Alex and squealed with excitement. All thoughts of Frank fled from her mind as Aiden practically jumped from Kirsten's arms into hers. "Why don't you go eat and I'll take Aiden off your hands."

Kirsten kissed Alex on the cheek as her face flooded with relief. "Bless you. I'm starving for food and adult conversation. Not that I don't adore this face," Kirsten said as she nibbled Aiden's cheek. His giggling made them both laugh.

"Go. I'll take him into his room, and we'll play with blocks. Come on, little man, let's build something great."

Frank couldn't get out of there fast enough. She didn't normally make the first move with a woman, but something about Alex compelled her to ask for her number. And she crashed and burned, which was exactly why she didn't make herself vulnerable. She tried a little light flirting with Alex, and she seemed to flirt back. So why wouldn't she give Frank her number? It wasn't like she was some sort of psychopath. She was a police officer, for fuck's sake. If she couldn't be trusted, who could?

Alex was a beautiful woman, and once they started talking, seemed down to earth. Frank was just starting to get to know Jordan, but couldn't imagine her being friends with a jerk. There must have been some reason Alex shot her down. There was no mention of a girlfriend. But that didn't mean she didn't have one. It depressed Frank to think she just wasn't good enough or attractive enough for Alex. All of this was making her a little crazy.

She pulled into the driveway of her home, grabbed her backpack, and went inside. She could hear the scrambling of four paws clacking on the wood floors as her two-year-old Lab mix, Bella, came to greet her. The excitement Bella displayed at seeing her erased any negative thoughts from her mind. How could anyone be sad after being greeted like this?

Bella started to jump on Frank, but she ordered her down, and

Bella sat as her tail continued to wag. Frank laughed and got down on the floor with her to give her pup lots of love.

Frank didn't know she was in the market for a dog when she went with her best friend, Katie, and Katie's girlfriend to a pet adoption event almost two years ago. She tagged along as they went to look for a cat to add to their growing family of animals. She was wandering aimlessly through the adoption area when she spotted Bella. She was just twelve weeks old, lying in her bed, seeming to take everything in that was going on around her. While some of the other dogs were barking and jumping, there was her Bella, the calm amongst the chaos. Frank filled out the application, survived a home visit, and became the proud owner of the sweetest pup she'd ever known. It had taken a few days to acclimate to her new home, but in no time at all, Frank and Bella became an instant family.

"Come on, girl, let's get you fed." Bella followed Frank into the kitchen, her tail wagging wildly, as Frank prepared her meal. She sometimes thought Bella loved mealtime more than going to the beach or park. She drank a glass of water while Bella practically inhaled her dinner.

Later that evening, as she and Bella took their nightly stroll through the neighborhood, thoughts of Alex came back to her. Pulling her over earlier in the day wasn't the most ideal way to meet. Maybe she was still pissed about that, but she had to realize Frank was just doing her job. She was sure they would run into each other occasionally with Alex now working at County.

Frank had to admit she had a good time at Jordan and Kirsten's despite how things ended with Alex. She was excited and nervous at the prospect of playing basketball on Jordan's team. She hadn't played on an organized team in a number of years, but she would occasionally take her ball to the nearest park and shoot around. Sometimes she would get involved in a pickup game or two, but that was pretty much it. She worked out regularly and ran a few miles a day, but she wasn't exactly in playing shape. She'd have to start playing more pickup games before practice started next month.

"All right, Bella. Time for bed. Grab your frog." Frank laughed as Bella wandered around the house looking for her bedtime buddy. She reappeared with the green stuffed animal in her mouth and followed

Frank into her bedroom. As Frank got ready for bed, Bella fluffed up her bed, moved around in a few circles before finally getting settled. When Frank came back into the bedroom, she smiled at the cuteness factor of Bella sound asleep with her paw thrown over the frog. "Good night, sweet pup."

CHAPTER TWO

A lex finished putting in a patient's IV and made a note in the chart. "Okay, Mrs. Bennett, try to get some rest. Someone will be along shortly to transfer you upstairs." She closed the curtain behind her and stopped in her tracks at the vision in front of her. Frank stood at the nurses' station with her forearms on the counter, leaning close as she spoke quietly to Jenny, one of the nurses she worked with. Alex quietly observed Frank. She had an almost predatory aura about her, and Alex felt her pulse speed up. She understood her visceral reaction was just physiological, but it still unnerved her. Her heart rate was just returning to normal when Frank turned her way and smiled. So much for that.

"Well, hello, Nurse Taylor." The predatory gleam in her eyes remained as she looked Alex over from head to toe, making Alex shiver in response.

Alex felt like she had been undressed by Frank's gaze, and instead of feeling insulted, as she would if someone else had pulled that shit, she was turned on, her body tingling and warming everywhere Frank's gaze lingered. She had to quickly take back control before she totally lost it. She openly admired Frank as she sauntered over, leaned one arm on the counter, and faced Frank. She quirked her eyebrow and smirked. "Hello, Sergeant. How have you been?"

Jenny looked from Frank to Alex and back to Frank. "Do you two know each other?"

"We met a couple of weeks ago…at a friend's party," Alex said as she kept her eyes on Frank and grinned wryly.

Frank gazed back at Alex as if they were the only two people in the room. "Yep. We met at a party."

With the harsh lights in the ER, Alex noticed Frank's eyes to be a light hazel, almost amber color. She had never seen eyes that color, and they were hypnotizing. Out of self-preservation, she had to find something to do, something to get her away from Frank. The ER gods were looking down on her when two paramedics rushed through the doors with an older gentleman being resuscitated on the gurney.

As they called out his vitals and presentation, Alex pointed and yelled out, "Take him to three!" She quickly followed and forgot about Frank and her sexiness. One of the things she loved most about this job was when a patient came in with a life-threatening emergency, every thought fled her mind except what the patient needed. It was almost a Zen-like state she got in where treatment became a well-choreographed dance. Every person in the room had a job to do, and if someone wasn't on their game, it could make the difference between life and death. Alex promised herself if death was the outcome, it wouldn't be because she wasn't focused.

Once they got the patient stabilized and knew he would live to see another day, Alex peeled off her gloves and gown and put them in the bin. She returned to the nurses' station and noticed Frank was now gone. She felt a strange sense of loss but quickly shrugged it off. She logged on to the computer and completed her notes. She was just finishing up when Jenny sat next to her and logged on. Jenny turned in her chair and seemed to study Alex. She smiled and turned back to the computer but could feel Jenny continuing to stare.

She faced Jenny with a questioning look. "Anything I can help you with?"

Jenny squinted at Alex. "Are you and Frank seeing each other?"

Alex wondered why Jenny would ask that. Did she feel the electricity that Alex felt hum between her and Frank? Alex thought she played it cool, but maybe not cool enough. She hadn't been at the hospital long enough to know anyone well and felt unsure of what to say. Maybe she should keep it simple since hospitals were known to be hotbeds for rumors. "No."

The look of relief that washed over Jenny's face might have made Alex laugh if it hadn't made her jealous instead. Jenny was a cute *young* woman. She also had an exuberant personality, like she was always up for a good time. If they didn't work together, Alex might have considered hooking up, but the obvious interest Jenny showed in

Frank almost made her feel like she didn't even want to get involved on any level. Alex wasn't normally a jealous woman, and she didn't like this new personality trait.

"I'm so glad to hear that. She's so hot and sexy and can really fill out her uniform. Do you think she likes me? Maybe she'll ask me out."

Alex had a flashback to junior high and wondered how old this girl was. If Jenny said Frank was dreamy, she might have to smack her. She mentally rolled her eyes. "I don't know, Jenny. Like I said, we just met the one time a couple of weeks ago, so I hardly know her."

"Well, I see her in here occasionally, but today was the first time she talked to me."

Alex thought she might throw up a little at the wistful look on Jenny's face. Thankfully, it was the end of her shift. She smacked her hand on Jenny's knee, maybe a little too hard, as a look of surprise flashed over Jenny's face. "You know what? You should totally ask her out." Alex stood. "I'll see you later."

Alex raced to the locker room, grabbed her keys and purse, and slammed her locker shut. The fact that young Jenny got to her had her frustrated beyond belief. Why should she care if Jenny and Frank got together? She didn't have any hold over Frank. Hell, she barely knew her. Alex exhaled a deep breath and hit the call button on her phone as she exited the ER. "Hey, it's me. Is Aiden up for some company?" Alex listened, then burst out laughing. "Well, it's the little monkey I really want to see, but I guess you can hang out with us. I'll be there soon." As Alex unlocked her car, she already felt her day brighten.

CHAPTER THREE

Frank often found herself thinking of Alex, and it pissed her off. Why couldn't she keep a woman who obviously wanted nothing to do with her out of her head? They hadn't seen each other since their run-in at the ER a couple of weeks ago, and it should have been a case of "out of sight, out of mind," but Frank kept thinking of Alex, wondering what she was doing and who she was doing it with. While on duty, Frank was focused on the job and her safety, but at home, all bets were off. The nurse in the ER? Jamie? No, Jenny. She showed interest. Maybe she should ask her out. No, that wouldn't do. Jenny was hot and sexy, but Frank hadn't felt any of the attraction with her that she felt with Alex. And she certainly wasn't desperate enough to try to force something that clearly wasn't there.

A call came over the radio asking for backup during a vehicle search. Frank called in her location and headed to the call. She pulled up behind the cruiser and flipped on her lights before exiting her car. Officer Jake Robbins, former college football linebacker, towered over a disheveled-looking man sitting on the curb.

"What do we have, Robbins?"

"Hey, Sarge. I pulled this guy over for an illegal lane change and he appeared suspicious. I thought I smelled something and asked him to exit the vehicle. After searching him, I found a pipe and some crystal meth. Do you want to search the vehicle or keep an eye on him?"

Frank looked over to the suspect, who was rocking back and forth and looking more than a little jittery. "You go ahead, Robbins. I'll keep an eye on him."

After a few minutes, Frank noticed the suspect getting more

agitated. He kept looking from the car to Frank. She was on full alert now, and her pulse increased after his eyes widened when Robbins called out he found something. In a split second, the guy got on his feet and bolted.

Shit! "Robbins!" Frank took off in a sprint after the suspect. Despite the fact he was handcuffed, the guy was fast, and Frank had a tough time catching up. She heard Robbins right behind her as she dove at the suspect and tackled him to the hard pavement. Robbins's football instincts must have kicked in because she felt the six-foot-three, two-hundred-and-thirty-pound man of solid muscle land on top of her, pinning her against the suspect. She felt and heard a pop in her ribs, and her breath rushed out of her lungs. "Get off me," Frank said breathlessly.

Robbins got up and pulled Frank off the suspect before putting his knee into his back, preventing him from going anywhere. "You stupid motherfucker! You thought you could get away from us?" Robbins was breathing hard and his chest heaving from the chase and probably adrenaline. Frank would give anything to be able to take in a deep breath, but the excruciating pain made it impossible. She fought hard to catch her breath, but she just couldn't.

"Robbins, call for backup and an ambulance." Her shallow gasps seemed to get his attention.

"Holy shit, Sarge! Are you okay? What's wrong? Just hold still and I'll get on the radio." He called in as Frank had requested and seemed to be torn between whether to keep the suspect pinned down or attend to Frank.

"Stay with him, Robbins. I'm okay. Just got the breath knocked out of me. You must have been one hell of a linebacker if you tackled like that."

The teasing had the desired effect, and Robbins gave her a brief smile. He returned his focus to the suspect, where it remained until backup arrived in less than two minutes. A few minutes later, the ambulance arrived and the paramedics attended to Frank. After getting her vitals, they hooked her up to oxygen, loaded her in the back, and headed to County ER. Frank winced as she felt the needle penetrate a vein in her hand when the paramedic hooked up her IV.

Frank tried to relax by shutting her eyes. She knew her breathing would worsen if she began to panic, but the inability to take deep, calming breaths scared her. The sound of the sirens and the paramedic talking to the ER did nothing to help settle Frank. She tried to block out the noise and was grateful when they pulled into the ambulance bay and the whining of the siren finally ceased. A new flurry of noise started when the paramedics unloaded the gurney and raced her through the sliding doors. It seemed all at once, medical personnel went to work as the lead paramedic updated them on Frank's status. A familiar face came into her view, and she was relieved and excited.

Alex smiled gently and brushed her fingers through Frank's hair. "Don't you think this is a little extreme as an excuse to see me, Sarge?"

Frank lifted the oxygen mask away from her mouth. "I had to do something to get you to notice me."

Alex readjusted the mask back over Frank's mouth. "Keep the mask on and try to relax. We'll take great care of you." Alex leaned down and spoke into Frank's ear. "By the way, I already noticed you."

For the first time since the accident, Frank started to relax. She closed her eyes as the nurses and doctor went to work on her. She remained alert enough to hear and understand what was going on. She felt the icy cold stethoscope move over her bare chest. She wasn't sure when she was stripped of her uniform top or vest, but figured it must have happened in the ambulance. She groggily wondered where her clothes and equipment were. Who had her service weapon? Her duty belt? She had to trust the other sergeant on duty was in possession of them and keeping them safe.

"Lungs are clear and equal bilaterally."

"Let's get a portable chest x-ray."

Frank opened her eyes to seek out the comfort she needed. She saw Alex looking down on her with caring eyes.

"It doesn't sound like you punctured a lung, so that's really good news. We're going to x-ray your chest and make sure nothing else is wrong. You're doing great, Sarge. Just hang in there, and we'll get you some pain meds right after the x-rays."

Frank nodded and closed her eyes again. She felt at peace knowing Alex was looking out for her. A while later, the doctor came and talked to her. Once the pain meds had been administered through her IV, Frank relaxed as the pain lessened. She was relieved to discover her only injury was a cracked rib, which time would heal. He gave her a prescription for pain and anti-inflammatory medications, instructed her in breathing exercises to prevent further complications such as pneumonia, and told her she would be off work for a week, but then could only be on desk duty until the rib was healed. The doctor left the exam room as Alex strode back in.

Frank smiled as Alex approached. It made her feel better to know that Alex was helping take care of her. Maybe they could be friends after all. Frank didn't think she was imagining the look of concern on Alex's face when she was brought into the ER. Alex must care a little, right? Frank's cautious nature prevented her from reading too much into it. She reminded herself that Alex was a nurse and it was her job to take care of the sick or injured. On the other hand, Alex's gentle touches and concerned eyes seemed more personal.

"Well, Frank, looks like you got lucky with just one broken rib. I talked to the brick wall that took you down." Alex laughed at Frank when she scrunched up her nose. "Officer Robbins is outside waiting for you. He told me what happened, how you became sandwiched between him and the suspect."

Now that the pain meds were in full effect, Frank found it a little easier to breathe and talk. "Yeah, Robbins is a former linebacker, and it showed today. Makes me glad I took up basketball."

Alex removed the IV needle and covered the puncture wound with a Band-Aid. Frank blushed as Alex helped her back into her uniform shirt. She hated that Alex saw her so helpless, but there wasn't really anything she could do about it. She avoided looking at Alex as she buttoned her shirt. Alex handed her a bag that contained her vest and duty belt and accompanied her to the waiting room.

"Officer Robbins went to get his car, and he's already been instructed to take you straight home." Alex pinned her with a mock glare. "Don't even think about going back to work."

Frank saluted. "Roger that, ma'am."

Alex placed her hand on Frank's arm and her face softened. "You try to stay out of trouble, Frank."

Frank felt empty and the ache in her chest returned as she watched Alex tend to her next patient.

Chapter Four

A lex sat in her car wondering what she was doing. She looked out the window at an early century Craftsman bungalow that had attractive wood siding, large picture windows, and a generous front porch. She could imagine herself sitting on the porch swing that hung to the right of the front door, drinking a cup of coffee, and waving to the early morning joggers.

She shouldn't be there. After Frank had been discharged yesterday, Alex was charting in the computer, and before she realized what she was doing, she was entering Frank's address and phone number into her cell. When her shift ended, she stopped by the grocery store, then went home and made chicken soup in the slow cooker. Initially, it was meant only for her. She could have a bowl of it for dinner and put the rest of it in the freezer to have later. But as the night went on and images of Frank lying in the emergency room with pain-clouded eyes invaded her thoughts, the more she realized she made this soup not for herself, but for Frank.

She spent the whole morning trying to talk herself out of delivering the soup to Frank. Now that she was no longer a patient, she shouldn't be of any concern to Alex. But the other voice inside her head kept telling her it would be a nice gesture and Frank would most likely appreciate it. She must be awfully sore this morning, and standing in the kitchen preparing a meal would probably make her more uncomfortable. Before the first voice could speak up again, Alex grabbed the container of soup, a box of crackers, and a loaf of French bread and headed out the door.

So there she sat in her car, continuing to look at Frank's house, continuing to wonder what she was doing there. Alex saw Frank walk gingerly in front of the window and noticed the pain etched in her striking face as she grabbed her side. Without another thought, she gathered the food, climbed up the three steps to the front porch, and knocked on the solid oak door. A series of loud, deep barks followed, obviously meant to scare away anyone who dared step foot on the porch.

Alex heard Frank command the dog to sit and the barking ceased. "Who is it?"

"Frank, it's Alex."

She heard the chain unlatch and the door opened while Frank restrained the dog by the collar. The dog that was barking was now wagging her tail. Frank's head tilted to the side, and a slow smile crept across her lips. Alex had never seen anything so fucking sexy in her life. Frank's deep voice brought Alex out of her stupor. "What are you doing here?"

Alex held up the bag. "Um, I brought you soup." *I brought you soup? That's the best you can come up with? Jesus!*

Frank tilted her head to the other side and had a near mirror image of her dog's actions, looking at her curiously. "You brought me soup? Why?"

Alex shuffled her feet, again questioning her motives. Frank asked, so she had to answer. "I wanted to check on you, see how you're feeling."

Frank quirked an eyebrow. "You make house calls, Nurse Taylor?"

The low timbre in Frank's voice made Alex stammer. "N-no, not usually. I'm sorry. I shouldn't have bothered you." Alex turned to go when she felt a restraining hand on her arm.

"Please forgive my rude manners and come in." Frank stepped to the side and allowed Alex to enter.

Alex stopped inside the entryway as Frank closed the door. She quickly observed the living room to the right that had dark oak exposed beams that matched the dark hardwood floors. There was a brown leather couch that sat in front of the large window she spied Frank in just a moment ago. Two leather Mission-style recliners flanked either end of the couch, and an oak coffee table sat in front of the couch. The walls were painted a warm sage green, and both the baseboards and crown molding were off-white. There was a large flat screen television that hung above the fireplace, and the entire room was warm and inviting. A pressure against her leg brought Alex back to attention. She looked down to the dog that sat at her side and leaned into her leg. The dog looked up at her with a sweet doggy smile.

"Alex, this vicious guard dog is Bella."

Alex felt herself relax and dropped her hand in front of Bella's face for her to sniff. When her hand was lovingly and thoroughly licked, she laughed and petted Bella's head. "She's so gorgeous." The black and white dog wagged her tail and seemed to appreciate the attention bestowed upon her. Alex looked to Frank. "You have a really beautiful home."

Frank looked around and smiled. "Thanks. So, you brought soup?"

Alex held up the bag. "French bread and crackers too."

Frank smiled, but it didn't quite reach her eyes. Alex wondered if it was from her pain or how they'd left things at Jordan and Kirsten's pool party.

"The kitchen's this way. Follow me."

Alex followed Frank into the spacious kitchen and admired the modern look. She also admired how Frank's shirt rode up her back when she reached up into the cabinet for bowls. Alex caught a brief glimpse of a tattoo scrawled across her lower back. Her fingers ached with the need to trace the design. Frank turned and caught her staring at her backside. Alex felt the heat infuse her body, could feel her face burn, and knew she was busted. She cleared her throat and busied herself with slicing the bread. She caught Frank's grin as she poured the container of soup into a pot and turned on the stove.

Frank opened the refrigerator door, then looked at Alex. "Can I get you anything to drink? I have water, regular and diet soda, or juice."

Alex thought she could really go for something a little stronger, that it might help her relax a little. "Do you have any beer?"

She saw the dark cloud that fell on Frank's face before she answered. "I don't keep any alcohol in the house. Sorry."

Alex didn't know why she asked since she had to work later and couldn't have a beer anyway. She just thought about how it would help calm her nerves. She should have requested something Frank offered, and she was mentally kicking herself in the ass. "I'll just have water."

Frank filled two glasses and carried them over to the table. Alex realized that Frank hadn't actually invited her to stay and eat with her, and was mortified that she just assumed they would eat together. This wasn't going *at all* like she imagined. She thought they could enjoy some soup and bread, fall into an easy conversation, but that wasn't the case at all. Maybe she should go. She shifted from one foot to the other as Frank tended to the meal. "I think I'm going to go. I hope you enjoy the soup."

Frank turned around with a questioning look. "Wait! What? You're not going to have lunch with me?"

Alex looked at her with apprehension. "I wasn't sure you wanted me to stay. You don't exactly look happy to see me, and I won't stay where I'm not welcome."

Frank scrubbed her face with her hands and forcefully exhaled. "Look, Alex, I'm sorry. I wasn't expecting you to come by. Hell, I wasn't expecting to see you at all except maybe at the hospital. When I asked you for your number at Jordan's and you said you didn't think it would be a good idea to see each other…well, you can imagine how confused I am that you showed up out of the blue to my home and brought me homemade soup. I guess I'm just wondering why you're really here."

Alex looked down, unable to meet Frank's inquisitive gaze, and shoved her hands in her pockets. "I'm sorry, Frank. Honestly, I'm confused too. I was worried about you yesterday and I wanted to check on you. Last night, while I was making the soup, I kept thinking about you, and I thought you would like some too."

Frank furrowed her brow. "How did you know where I lived?"

Alex mumbled, still unable to meet Frank's eyes, "I got your address when I was charting on you yesterday."

Frank cupped Alex's chin gently, forcing her to finally look into Frank's eyes. "And you did this because you were worried about me?"

The barest hint of a smile on Frank's handsome face made her relax and answer honestly. "Yes." For the first time today, Alex saw the pain dissipate in Frank's eyes.

"Well then, would you like to join me for lunch?"

Alex was flooded with relief, and for the first time since she stepped onto Frank's front porch, she felt like she was finally able to fully breathe. "I would love to."

❖

Frank's shoulders loosened as she poured the soup into two bowls and carried them over to the kitchen table where Alex was sitting. To say she was surprised Alex showed up unannounced with homemade chicken soup would be putting it mildly. She felt cautiously optimistic that they could actually end up being friends, although Frank wouldn't mind having more. Alex still hadn't revealed why she didn't want to give Frank her number, and while she was curious, she respected Alex's privacy. She took her seat across from Alex and winced from the pain in her rib. She decided this morning after she woke up feeling hung over from the pain medication that she was just going to take ibuprofen. The pain wasn't excruciating, and she didn't like the way the narcotics made her feel.

Alex looked at her across the table with a look of concern on her face. "Did you want me to get you a pain pill?"

Frank shook her head and smiled. "No, I'm not taking them. So far, the pain is manageable with the anti-inflammatories."

Alex raised an eyebrow and looked at Frank suspiciously. "Uh-huh. You're just a regular tough girl, aren't ya?"

Frank chuckled. "Hardly. I just don't like the way they make me feel all groggy."

Alex nodded her understanding. "Okay, but take one if the pain gets too bad. Promise?"

Frank felt her heartbeat quicken as she caught and held Alex's gaze. She cleared her throat and held up her right hand. "I promise."

Alex laughed and pointed to Frank's bowl. "Eat."

Frank didn't have to be told twice. The smell wafting under her nose made her stomach rumble. She lifted the spoon and blew on the hot liquid to cool it down. When the flavors exploded on her tongue, she let out an appreciative moan. This was honestly the best chicken soup she'd ever had. The variety of vegetables, the juicy chunks of chicken, and the right amount of spices made it nirvana. Frank found herself unable to stop eating long enough to compliment Alex on her cooking prowess. When she clanked the spoon in the empty bowl and finally met Alex's amused gaze, she shrugged and looked chagrined. "That was the best chicken soup I ever had. Seriously. The. Best." The look of pleasure on Alex's face made Frank feel warm all over.

"I'm so glad you enjoyed it. It has special healing powers, you know."

Frank laughed. "Is that right? Well, I better get a refill." She returned with her second helping and took her time with the second bowl. She split her time between the soup and tearing off small bites of bread. When she finished, she leaned back in her chair and placed her hands over her stomach in satisfaction. She looked across the table at Alex, who was just finishing her first bowl. "Would you like another bowl? There's some left in the pot."

Alex smiled and shook her head. "No, thanks. I'll leave the leftovers for you. I guess you liked it?"

Frank grinned sheepishly. "I did. Thank you so much. It was very thoughtful of you." She took the dishes into the kitchen and heard her cell phone alert her to a text message, but she didn't want to be rude and check it in the presence of Alex.

"I think you have a text."

"Yeah, I'll check it later."

"Don't be silly. You can check it now."

Frank grabbed her phone off the counter and read the text.

Now you can have my number.

Frank didn't recognize the number, but the smile on Alex's face made Frank realize whose number it was. "Are you sure?"

Alex walked into the kitchen and stood close to Frank. She leaned in and kissed Frank on the cheek. "I'm sorry I didn't give it to you before, but now I want you to have it."

Frank barely prevented her hand from touching the spot where Alex kissed her. "Why now?"

Alex sighed and grabbed Frank's hand. "Let's go sit in the living room and I'll tell you."

Frank's hand remained in Alex's as they retreated into the living room and sat next to each other on the couch. She really liked the way Alex's hand fit perfectly in hers like two interlocking pieces of a puzzle.

Alex turned to face her and tucked her leg under her body. "The day we met, I felt so many conflicting emotions. I was super pissed at you for pulling me over, but I was also wildly attracted to you. You looked so hot in your uniform, so confident."

Frank felt her ears get warm and knew she was blushing.

"I thought you were the biggest jerk." Alex laughed when Frank frowned. "But then I met you at Jordan's, and the gentleness you showed Aiden and the gentlemanly attention you lavished on me made me feel so confused. I didn't know what to think. Then you asked me for my number, which totally took me by surprise. I didn't give it to you then because I didn't know you well enough to trust myself. I felt my instincts were off that day, but I trust them now. I like you, Frank. I hope we can hang out, maybe be friends." Alex looked down into her lap. "Maybe go on a date?"

Frank squeezed Alex's hand and she looked back to Frank. "You want to go on a date with me?"

Alex nodded shyly and it took all of Frank's will to not lean over and kiss her.

"Then I'll definitely give you a call."

CHAPTER FIVE

"Well, that went better than I thought." Alex felt like she floated down the pathway back to her car. She had just gotten behind the wheel when her phone buzzed. She pulled it out of her pocket to see she had a text from Frank that simply asked, *When?* She looked up to see Frank standing in her living room looking at her through the big picture window.

Alex laughed and texted back. *When, what?*

When do you want to go on our date?

Alex shook her head and laughed. Anxious much? *I'm working the next three days on swing then I have four days off. How's Thursday?*

Perfect. Drive carefully.

Alex looked back at Frank and waved to her before starting her car and driving away. She had a couple of hours before she had to be at the hospital. She enjoyed her time with Frank, and she seemed grateful for the soup. The wariness in her eyes seemed to have disappeared by the time Alex left her house.

She had already experienced so many different emotions in the short time she'd known Frank, and she had a strong suspicion she would go through a lot more. One thing she knew for certain was her attraction toward Frank. Alex found Frank extremely good-looking in a rugged sort of way that made Alex want to explore every inch of Frank's body.

Once she got home, she got ready for work. When she arrived at the ER, she shifted her focus off Frank and onto medicine. Although she was fairly new to County, she had already made some friends with the staff, and they had gone out of their way to make her feel welcome.

She spotted Judy at the nurses' station. She was an older woman who had been in this department for the past fifteen years. "Hey, Judy. How're things?"

"Not too bad. Actually, it's been a little slow today."

"Shush! Don't jinx it!"

Judy laughed. "Sorry. After all this time, you'd think I'd know better. I'm about to clock out anyway, so it's not my problem."

The diabolical laugh Judy let out as she headed to the locker room made Alex chuckle and shake her head. The voice coming over the radio gave her the answer she didn't want to hear.

"County, EMS twenty-four."

Alex sighed and rolled her eyes before responding, "Twenty-four, go ahead."

"County, EMS twenty-four en route to your facility. On board I have an unresponsive male in his twenties, auto versus pedestrian. How do you copy?"

Alex grabbed a pen and paper and began jotting down notes. "Loud and clear."

"Patient was struck by sedan traveling approximately thirty miles per hour and was thrown fifteen feet. Patient found unresponsive with obvious open skull fracture, no gray matter present, open femur fracture left side, and multiple abrasions. Patient in spinal precautions, bilateral IVs started, high flow O2, and attempting intubation. Vitals ninety over sixty, heart rate one twenty, weak radial, breathing at eight per minute. If you have no further questions or orders, we'll see you in five."

"Copy, twenty-four. We'll be waiting." Alex quickly scribbled down the information she received and vowed she was going to make Judy pay for jinxing them. She quickly checked the board to see what room was open and assembled the necessary staff. The paramedics burst through the door, and Alex noted one straddling the patient administering chest compressions.

"We lost his pulse as we were pulling in, and I was unable to tube him."

Dr. Neale joined the group as they hurried down the hall. "Okay, people, let's get to work." He positioned himself at the patient's head and inserted the endotracheal tube, then attached the Ambu bag. Alex placed her stethoscope over the man's stomach then lungs.

"Absent gastric sounds, clear equal bilateral lung sounds." She slung the scope around her neck while another nurse applied the defibrillation pads.

Another nurse shouted, "Clear!" Everyone stepped away, and the nurse shocked the patient. The shock made the body rise a few inches off the table and back down. Alex looked at the monitor that showed the patient was in v-fib.

Dr. Neale barked his orders. "Push an amp of epi and let's try it again."

The nurse yelled, "Clear!" The shock was stronger, but still didn't have any effect on the patient's heart. Another nurse stepped up and resumed chest compressions.

The doctors and nurses worked valiantly for what felt like hours, but in actuality was more like thirty to forty minutes. Despite their efforts, the patient's heart never regained its rhythm and flatlined. "I'm calling it." The doctor stepped back and looked at the clock as all activity ceased. "Time of death, seventeen twenty. Thank you, everyone."

Alex watched as the staff disposed of their gowns and gloves in the appropriate receptacle. She replaced her bloody gloves with clean ones and went to work on cleaning up the patient. It wasn't uncommon to lose patients in the ER, but it really tugged at Alex's heartstrings. Even though she didn't know her patients personally, she felt the least she could do was take her time to clean them up and help them look semi-presentable when their loved ones came in to say their good-byes. She had to leave everything in place for the coroner to document that all of the treatments were actually done, but she could clean them up as best as she could.

She filled another basin with warm water and grabbed a towel. She placed the water on a table near the patient and began to wash the dried blood off his face. He was just a kid, someone's son, maybe someone's brother or boyfriend. She didn't know him, but she had a feeling he had been well loved. Her heart ached for what his family would go through, having to see his lifeless body lying on the gurney. She continued to wash his face, and once the blood had been removed, she moved on to his hands. There were bits of gravel embedded in his palms that she gently brushed away.

She dumped the water down the sink when she was finished. She went to take one final look at him before she left the room. She tried to pat down his hair as she spoke softly to him. "I'm so sorry we couldn't do anything more for you, my friend. I hope you didn't suffer too much. Peaceful journey." She left him with the sheet pulled up to just under his chin. He looked at peace, like he was sleeping, and she left him to his eternal slumber.

By the time she finished her shift, Alex was more than ready to go home. It was after midnight, and all she could think about was getting home, drawing a hot bath, and having a glass of wine. She normally felt keyed up after a shift, but after losing the young man at the start of her day, she felt as if all her energy had been drained. She would have loved to call Jordan to talk it out with her, but she knew she would be asleep. She then thought about texting Frank to see if she was still awake, but she didn't feel they knew each other well enough for a heart-to-heart talk, not when it came to losing a patient. She pulled into the driveway and couldn't get into her condo quick enough. She retrieved her wine while the tub filled with water and let out a pleasurable sigh as she sank below the bubbles.

Normally, her best remedy for cheering up after a shift like that was to think about Aiden. Just the thought of him brought a smile to her face and peace to her heart. But tonight, visions and thoughts of Frank flooded her mind. Even though their relationship was in the infant stage, Alex couldn't help imagining Frank's solid arms holding her after a shift like she just had. She pictured Frank greeting her with arms wide open, wrapping her up in a safe cocoon, taking her to bed, and comforting her through the night. That seemed just like something Frank would do. Alex looked forward to seeing how this thing between her and Frank would work out. The image of Frank's handsome face helped Alex drift off to her dreams.

CHAPTER SIX

Frank looked at the alarm clock on her nightstand through sleepy eyes as the insistent vibration moved her cell phone across the wood surface. The clock read a little after nine in the morning, and she wondered when she had fallen back to sleep. Ever since she broke her rib, sleep was continuously interrupted every time she changed positions, and it had taken a while to get back to sleep once the pain had subsided. Since she was off work with nothing to do and nowhere to be, her sleep schedule was all screwed up. She picked up her phone, saw Alex's name on the screen, and swiped to answer. "'Lo."

"Frank? It's Alex. Did I wake you?"

"Yeah, but it's okay. I need to get up anyways. How're you doing?"

"I'm good. I just wanted to call and confirm dinner for tonight."

Frank wiped her eyes and smiled. "Yeah, I'm looking forward to it, but would you mind if we had dinner at my place? My ribs are still sore, and I'm not sure if I could handle sitting in a restaurant for a couple of hours."

"That's fine. You want me to pick up something?"

Frank threw back the covers and gasped from the discomfort as she sat on the side of the bed. "No, I'll fix something. Maybe grill some steaks?"

"Don't even think about it. Let me bring the food so we can relax. How's Thai?"

"That sounds great. I really appreciate it, Alex."

"No problem. I'll see you around six tonight."

Once they hung up, Frank shuffled to the bathroom and looked at herself in the mirror. Her hair was sticking up at odd angles, and she had dark circles under her eyes. She turned on the shower in hopes it would help wake her up. The hot water helped ease her sore muscles, and she felt a lot better when she stepped out and dried herself off. She was feeling halfway human again. She got dressed in a white tank top and bright green board shorts before heading to the kitchen. The sight of Bella lying in front of the back door, looking at her with sad puppy dog eyes, made her heart melt.

"I'm sorry, girl. Mama's not feeling too good, but Julie's coming over later to take you for some exercise."

Bella's tail wagged at the sound of her dog walker's name. Julie had been referred to her by the rescue Frank got Bella from when she had told them she sometimes worked long hours. On the days Frank worked, Julie would come get Bella and take her for runs or to the dog park to play with her doggy friends. Julie and Frank became friends, and she was grateful that Bella could get some exercise since she physically wasn't up to it. Frank unlocked the dog door for Bella to go outside, then went to start the coffeepot and get Bella's breakfast together.

The knock on the front door sent Bella scrambling across the wood floors and she slid into the door with a thump. Frank laughed and shook her head as she reached the frantic canine. "Bella, sit." Once Bella obeyed, Frank opened the door to find Julie standing there holding a bag of bagels. "Hey, perfect timing. Coffee's ready."

Julie stepped inside and gave Frank a gentle hug. She handed over the bag of bagels before kneeling down to get kisses from Bella. "Hey, Bella. How's my girl?" Bella whined and wagged her tail, making Julie and Frank laugh.

"Don't let her fool you. You'd think she'd be content to have her mama home, but I think she's bored. I tried throwing the ball for her, but my ribs aren't ready for that."

"Poor baby," Julie said as she patted Bella's head. "Are you feeling any better? I have to tell you, you look like hell."

Frank smirked. "Thanks." They returned to the kitchen and Frank winced as she reached into the cupboard to retrieve a couple of plates and mugs. "Actually, the pain is manageable during the day as long as I don't make any sudden movements. Sleeping is a whole different story. The pain wakes me if I roll onto my side. Needless to say, I haven't been sleeping well."

Julie looked to Frank after she finished slicing the bagels. "I guess that's why there're dark circles under your eyes. Is there anything I can do?"

"You've been a great help by exercising my girl. It's just going to take some time for the injury to heal."

"I can bring you some dinner tonight if you want. Lisa is having a work dinner so I don't have any plans."

Frank grinned and shook her head. "Thanks, but I have kind of a date tonight."

Julie looked up from her plate. "Really? Who?"

"Her name is Alex and she's an ER nurse at County. She's bringing Thai food."

"Tell me about her. How'd you two meet?"

Frank chuckled. "I pulled her over for speeding and gave her a ticket."

Julie nearly spat out her coffee when she started laughing. "And she agreed to a date? You sure she's not going to poison your food?"

Frank's eyes widened. "God, I hope not." She laughed. "Actually, she's my friend Jordan's best friend. A few hours after I gave her the ticket, we met again at Jordan's pool party and we got to talking. I've run into her at the ER a couple of times, and the day after I broke my rib, she brought me soup. We were going to go out to eat, but I asked if we could eat here and she agreed."

"That's great, Frank. Maybe the four of us can hang out sometime."

"We'll see. It's just our first date. She may decide I'm not her type."

Julie placed her hand on Frank's shoulder. "She'd have to be blind."

Frank raised an eyebrow. "What do you mean?"

"I mean, if I wasn't married and totally in love with Lisa, Alex would have some serious competition from me."

Frank blushed and looked down at her plate, unable to meet her eyes.

"I'm sorry. I didn't mean to make you uncomfortable. I just meant you'd be a great catch to any woman available. You're good-looking, kind, honest...shall I go on?"

Frank felt the heat engulf her face at Julie's compliments. She tried to live her life as a kind and honest person, but to hear someone actually say that to her left her with unfamiliar feelings. Her parents never took the time to say anything positive to her. The only time they paid her any kind of attention was if they needed something from her. Her twin sister was the only one she could rely on to tell her the truth. She was Frank's greatest supporter and they could only rely on each other. But now her sister was gone, and she wanted nothing to do with their parents. She had a few really good friends, her brothers and sisters in blue, and that's all she needed. The two people who made her and her sister were no longer considered family.

"Come on, Bella. Let's go before I embarrass your mama anymore." Julie proceeded to the laundry room with Bella hot on her heels. Julie fastened her harness and leash, and called over her shoulder, "We'll be back in a couple of hours."

It took the two hours of alone time to clean the house and make it presentable before Alex arrived. When Julie returned Bella nice and tired, Frank sat on the couch to watch some television while Bella napped on her bed. She closed her eyes for just a moment before she heard a knock on the door. Frank looked at her watch and discovered it was six o'clock. She had wanted to dress in nicer clothes than what she had on for her dinner with Alex, but she guessed changing would have to wait. She looked over at Bella, who barely opened her eyes before closing them again. Frank shook her head at Bella's lack of energy as she went to answer the door. She felt her heart stop for just a moment as she took in Alex dressed in a black sheer blouse with a black camisole underneath, and black jeans that fit her like a second skin. Frank really felt underdressed.

When Frank answered the door in her white tank and lime-green board shorts, Alex's pulse raced and her mouth became dry. Frank's olive-toned skin and muscular shoulders and arms looked tantalizing in the white tank top. The tribal tattoo that covered her right deltoid just added more yumminess to the mix. Alex knew she was staring and her mouth was probably hanging open, but damn! Frank was just sexy as hell. Her deep voice brought Alex back to the present.

"Hey, I'm glad you could make it."

Alex finally got her voice to work. "I'm glad we decided to eat here tonight. You look really good."

Frank looked down at her extremely casual clothes. "I meant to dress nice, but I guess I fell asleep on the couch. I can go change quickly."

Alex placed her hand on Frank's hip and kissed her on the cheek. "Don't change. I meant it when I said you look really good."

Frank took the bag of food from Alex and returned a kiss to her cheek. "You look beautiful."

The way Frank was looking at her made her stomach flip, and she had to give herself a little room, otherwise they might not eat until much later. Bella slowly ambled up to Alex and looked at her with sleepy eyes. She laughed and scratched behind Bella's ears.

"What did you do to her? She looks exhausted."

"My friend Julie took her to the dog park for a couple of hours today and ran her ass ragged. Bella, go back to bed."

Bella stood and slowly made her way to her bed, turned around three times, collapsed, and let out a deep sigh before closing her eyes, which made Alex and Frank laugh harder.

"It's funny, but being so young, she doesn't have much stamina. She plays hard for an hour or two, and then she passes out for the rest of the day. But come morning, she's ready to go again." Frank took Alex's hand in hers and led her to the kitchen. "The food smells great. What can I get you to drink?"

Alex started removing the food from the bag and recalled Frank didn't keep alcohol in the house. "Water will be fine." She pulled two plates from the cupboard and scooped the food onto them. They brought the food and drinks to the table and dug in.

"So, how are you feeling?"

Frank finished chewing a bite of her pad Thai before she answered. "A little better. Still a little sore, but feeling better every day. My only problem is sleeping. Rolling onto my side is enough to wake me and keep me up for a while, which is why I keep taking naps. I'll be glad when I can sleep for more than two hours at a time."

"Any other problems besides sleeping?"

Frank smirked. "No, Nurse Taylor. As long as I don't cough or sneeze, I'm fine."

Alex eyed Frank suspiciously. She knew too much about these tough-girl types. They always seemed to downplay how much pain they were in. "Okay. If you say so."

"How was your week?"

Alex recalled the young man who had been hit by a car and ended up dying in the ER. Alex didn't want to bring it up. Not tonight. This was her first date with Frank, and she hoped there would be second. She wanted to keep tonight nice and easy. "It was fine. I'm really glad I transferred to County. The people I work with are really cool and fun to be around. Besides, there's never a dull moment."

That made Frank laugh. "Yeah, I bet. It always seems to be busy when I've been in."

Alex really loved Frank's smile. The pearly white teeth and her full reddish-brown lips that curled at the corners made her criminally attractive. Alex had dated a lot of women, but never clicked enough with anyone to make it long-term, but there was something about Frank that made her feel very interested in seeing how far this could go.

When they finished eating, Alex observed Frank as she carried their dishes into the kitchen and moved gracefully, despite her injury, in cleaning the dishes and putting them away. Alex thought Frank liked a tidy house, as did she, and that was a check in the positive column Alex was mentally tallying. The only negative she'd come up with so far was that Frank didn't seem totally and completely open. Alex was reserving judgment on that until they knew each other better. Frank seemed to slowly relax around Alex, but still seemed closed off.

"Do you want some coffee and dessert?"

"Coffee is good, but I'm too full to think about eating anything else. I take it black."

Frank led Alex to the living room where Bella was snoring. She turned on some soft jazz and dimmed the lights before joining Alex on the couch. Alex kicked off her shoes and pulled her feet under her while she cradled the warm coffee mug in her hands. Frank sat next to her with her ankle crossed easily over her knee and her arm spread across the back of the couch. Alex scooted closer until she was pressed against Frank's uninjured side. "I'm really glad you agreed to have dinner with me."

Frank's hand moved until it rested on Alex's shoulder. "Thanks for bringing the food. All of it was delicious." Frank kissed the top of Alex's head, which was now resting on her shoulder. "I hope we can go out again."

Alex lifted her head and kissed Frank on the lips—long enough to ensure her of more kisses to come. "I'd really like that." After a little while, Alex felt Frank begin to relax a little more. She really liked how she fit so well against her. Frank's arm remained around her shoulder, and to her surprise, Alex didn't want to be anywhere else at that moment. A soft snore came from Frank, and Alex looked up to see a relaxed face and a slight grin tugging at Frank's lips. Alex was content to just watch her sleep, but felt it would be best to leave so Frank could go to bed. She gently kissed Frank on the mouth, which startled her awake.

"Oh, man, I'm such a loser falling asleep on the couch while I have a beautiful woman sitting next to me. I promise I'm usually much better company."

Alex smiled against Frank's lips. "You are definitely not a loser, but I think I should go so you can go to sleep." Alex kissed her again, this time tracing her tongue across Frank's lips. Frank allowed Alex's tongue to enter, but when Frank tried to put her other arm around and embrace Alex, she broke the kiss with a gasp.

"Oh, Frank, are you okay?"

Frank grimaced in pain. "I'm so sick of this injury. Please say I'll get another chance at this when I have less pain."

"Oh, don't worry. I think you're going to have a lot of chances with me," Alex said in a sultry voice. "Come on, Sarge. See me out."

Alex held Frank's hand as they walked to the door. She was disappointed their evening was ending so soon, but she didn't want to risk hurting Frank even more, and there was no guarantee that she would be able to slow things down if she stayed there. The way Frank explored Alex's mouth made her crave more of Frank's tongue, her touch. The inherent need to explore Frank's body from head to toe made Alex continue to the door. She picked up her purse and dug out her keys then placed her hands on Frank's hips. "I'm off the next couple of days, so if you feel like hanging out, give me a call." Alex kissed Frank chastely, not wanting to fan the flame that was still burning hot. "I'll see you later."

Once Alex was safely inside her car, she looked back to Frank's house and saw her standing in the doorway. She waved before driving off and smiled as she recalled the softness of Frank's lips, the insistence of her tongue. Oh, yes, there would definitely be more kissing.

CHAPTER SEVEN

Frank was going stir-crazy being cooped up in the house. It had been almost a week since her injury, and enough was enough. She was determined to take Bella out for some exercise and get some fresh air. She had slept better last night and felt better rested. She had a nice time with Alex the night before, and Alex had mentioned she had the next few days off. Maybe she'd be interested in coming over and going out with them. She dialed Alex's number. The phone rang three times before Alex finally answered.

"Hello."

"Hey, Alex, it's Frank."

"Hey, yourself. What's going on?"

Frank brushed her fingers through her hair and let out a frustrated sigh. "I have cabin fever and I need to bust out of this joint. Care to join me?"

"I'd love to, but I just got off the phone with Jordan and she's allowed me to take Aiden off her hands for a couple of hours."

Frank felt more than a little disappointed. She really wanted to see Alex today, but she guessed it would have to wait. "That sounds like fun. Maybe we can get together some other time." The last thing Frank wanted was to sound desperate.

"Wait. Why don't you go to the park with us? I was going to push him in the stroller. The park is just down the street from Jordan and Kirsten's."

"That would be great. Would it be okay if I brought Bella?"

"Sure. I don't think Aiden's ever been around a dog before. It'll be fun to see how he reacts. Meet me over at their house in about an hour."

"All right. See ya then."

Frank got dressed and gathered the necessities for Bella. She shoved everything in the cargo pockets of her shorts and knelt next to Bella to clip her leash. "We're going to visit with Alex and Aiden today. Aiden's a very little boy, so you have to be very gentle with him." Bella placed her paw on Frank's arm as if to acknowledge she understood.

Frank drove over to Jordan's, all the while replaying the kisses she shared with Alex the night before. Damn her ribs. She was sure they would've spent more time together, kissing, and maybe doing a little more if the ache in her chest hadn't made her stop. She really liked Officer Robbins, but right now, she wanted to kick his ass for tackling her and the suspect. Alex's lips were so full, so soft, that she wanted more. Just the thought made her blood rush hot through her veins.

She pulled up behind Alex's car and waved to Jordan as Alex placed Aiden in his stroller. Kirsten came down the walkway a moment later with Aiden's hat. Frank grabbed Bella's leash and met the group. "Hey, ladies. What? No one works on Fridays anymore?"

Jordan gave her a hug that made Frank's breath catch.

Alex held up her hand to Jordan. "Easy. She has a broken rib."

Jordan stepped back and looked at Frank, then Alex. "Oh, shit. I'm sorry. What happened?"

Kirsten stepped up to Frank and kissed her on the cheek instead of giving her a hug.

"I got sandwiched between a former college football linebacker and a tweaker." Frank laughed at their expressions. "The football player is a cop, and the tweaker tried to bolt. I broke a rib and was taken to the ER where this fine woman took good care of me." The look of affection Alex gave her made Frank smile. The whining at her leg made her look down. "Sorry. Where are my manners? Jordan and Kirsten, this gorgeous girl is Bella."

Bella waved her paw in the air as if to wave hi, making them laugh.

Aiden stuck his arm out of his stroller and reached for the dog. "Easy, Bella," Frank said. Bella walked over, sat next to the stroller, and allowed Aiden to pat her head. "Good girl." Bella licked Aiden's face, which made him giggle hysterically.

"So, you never answered why you two are home today."

"After Aiden was born, Kirsten and I decided to take Fridays off to spend with our boy. The three of us usually have an outing to the beach or we go hiking."

Frank looked to Alex then to Jordan and Kirsten. "Oh, man. Do you want us to go?"

Jordan wrapped her arms around Kirsten and looked to Frank. "Nope. I want you two to take him away for a couple of hours so I can have some time alone with my wife."

Alex laughed and Frank turned red from embarrassment. "Come on, Frank, let's go before they start groping each other out here on the sidewalk."

"Funny, Al. If you're coming back before the two hours, give me a heads up, huh?"

"Sure thing, Jordan." Alex started to push the stroller as Aiden waved. "Have fun, you two."

Frank and Alex strolled to the park with Bella heeling. "They sure make a great couple."

Alex smiled. "Yeah, they really do. I've never seen Jordan happier, especially since they had this cutie." She pointed to the stroller.

Frank looked to Alex. "How about you? You ever been that happy?"

Alex shook her head. "I haven't found the one yet, obviously. Otherwise I wouldn't be single. But I'm certainly ready for her to come along. How about you?"

Frank shook her head too. "No. I thought I did. We were together for a year and a half, but in the end, she decided she didn't want to be with a cop. You know, the danger, the long hours. I haven't had a serious relationship since her, about three years now."

Alex nodded. "Our work schedule can be hard to take for someone who works banker's hours. Even though I'm not putting myself in danger when I go to work, I see some pretty nasty shit. It's hard to talk about that with someone who doesn't work in our fields. They can be sympathetic, but they won't completely understand."

They arrived at the park, and Alex placed Aiden in the baby swing, gently pushing him, which made him giggle.

Frank took the tennis ball out of her pocket and pointed to the grassy area. "I'm gonna try to throw the ball for Bella."

"Um, dogs aren't supposed to be off leash here."

Frank smirked. "Are you going to call the cops?"

Alex gave her a swat on the butt. "I just might, smartass."

"C'mon, Bella, let's get some running in before the po-po arrive."

Alex continued to push Aiden in the swing for a few minutes, but the gentle back and forth was putting him to sleep. She pulled him from the swing with little fuss and placed him in the stroller, reclining the seat so he could lie flat. She pushed the stroller over to where Frank was throwing the ball for Bella and spread a small blanket under a tree. She watched the dog retrieve the ball, drop it in Frank's hand, and sit while she waited for Frank to toss the ball again. Frank was unable to throw it far, probably because of the pain in her ribs, but Bella didn't seem to mind too much.

She took in a deep breath and closed her eyes. The smell of the freshly cut grass and the chirping of the birds in the tree above her gave her such a sense of peace. It was a perfect day. She had her favorite kid asleep in the stroller, an attractive woman throwing the ball for her incredibly sweet dog. She felt life couldn't get better than this very moment. So what was that dread that just appeared that seemed to be knotting up her stomach? As Frank and Bella returned, she tried to push that feeling aside. "You tired already?"

Frank looked at her incredulously. "Me? Psh, no. I told you Bella has no stamina."

On cue, Bella turned around three times before lying down next to Aiden's stroller and closing her eyes. Frank sat next to Alex and leaned back on her hands.

"How do your ribs feel?"

"Not too bad, just a little sore."

"Why don't you lie down and put your head in my lap?"

Frank turned her body perpendicular to Alex's and lay down, resting her head in Alex's lap. Alex wiped a few beads of sweat from Frank's forehead and started running her fingers through Frank's short, thick locks. She was beginning to really like Frank and was looking forward to getting to know her better. Frank grabbed Alex's hand and brought it to her lips. She kissed every fingertip then sucked on the tip of Alex's index finger. A wave of arousal shot through Alex, and her clit began to throb. She closed her eyes and gasped in sheer pleasure. She nearly lost control when Frank began to swirl her tongue around Alex's finger.

Alex pulled her finger away and tried to calm her racing pulse.

Goddamn it for timing. "You start something like that, Sarge, you better be ready to finish it."

Frank looked at her with pure lust and Alex felt light-headed. "Believe me, when I'm recovered, I'll be more than happy to finish it."

Aiden began to fuss and sat up in his stroller. Frank sat up too so Alex could pick him up. *Thank God he woke up, otherwise we could've been in real trouble here.* "How's my sweet boy?" She sat down with Aiden cradled against her chest and started to rock back and forth while humming a lullaby. Frank looked at her with what appeared to be admiration. She smiled at her and closed her eyes.

"You're so good with him. Do you want kids of your own?"

Alex opened her eyes. "I do, but if it doesn't happen, it'll be okay. I've been with this little guy since he was born. I've fed him, played with him, rocked him to sleep, comforted him when he cries, and changed more diapers than I can count. I don't think I could love him more if he were my own. In a way, this might be better. Who do you think he's going to come to when he's pissed at his moms?" Alex and Frank laughed, then Alex continued, "We have a very special bond that will last a lifetime. He's as comfortable with me as he is with his moms."

"Do you have any brothers or sisters that will give you nieces or nephews?"

"No, I'm an only child, but Jordan's my sister from another mister, so he's like my nephew. How about you? Any brothers or sisters?"

The smile fell from Frank's face, and her eyes became cloudy with pain. Frank just shook her head. Alex reached for her hand, but Frank stood and turned away from Alex.

"We've been gone for a couple of hours. We should probably get him home," Frank said brusquely.

Bewildered, Alex didn't know what to say, so she agreed. "All right."

Frank folded up the blanket, then she grabbed Bella's leash. They wandered back to Jordan and Kirsten's in silence and waited at the front door. Jordan opened it, looking fresh from a shower with her wet hair hanging past her shoulders.

"Hey, ladies. Did you have a good time?" Jordan scooped Aiden out of the stroller and held him high above her. She blew a raspberry against Aiden's belly, making him squirm and laugh.

"We did. Monkey got to swing. Frank threw Bella the ball. It was a nice day."

Frank nodded in agreement but didn't say anything.

"We were just about to fire up the grill. You girls want to join us?"

Alex nodded, then looked to Frank, who was staring at the ground.

"Thanks, but I gotta get home. This was the most activity I've had in a week, and it really wore me out." Frank hugged Jordan, then kissed Alex on the cheek. "I'll see you later." She turned and took Bella to her truck.

Alex watched Frank leave, then turned to Jordan. "I'll be right back." Alex ran after Frank and caught her as she opened the door. "Hey, are you okay?"

Frank got Bella into the truck and turned on the air-conditioning before closing the door. "Yeah, I'm just tired."

Alex cupped Frank's cheek. "Are you sure? It seems you shut down when I asked if you had siblings."

Frank's eyes watered and her voice cracked when she spoke. "Can we not talk about this?"

"Oh, honey, of course." Alex wrapped her arms around Frank's neck and pulled her down to her chest. When she felt Frank's arms wrap around her waist, she held her tighter, but was careful of her injury. "If you ever want to talk about it, I'm a really good listener, okay?"

Frank nodded against Alex's shoulder, then gave her a kiss so sweet, it nearly broke Alex's heart. Frank opened the door to her truck and looked back to Alex. "I'll talk to you soon." Frank got behind the wheel and waved to Alex as she drove away.

Oh, baby, what happened to put that pain in your eyes?

Alex went into the house and headed for the kitchen, where she heard Jordan and Kirsten talking. Aiden was on the floor playing with a few of his toys. She opened the fridge and pulled out three beers and handed one each to Jordan and Kirsten.

"What's up with Frank? She seemed a little down before she left."

"I'm not sure. We were having a nice time at the park, getting to know each other, and when I asked about siblings, she sort of checked out. What's the deal?"

Jordan sighed deeply. "Her twin sister died a few years ago of breast cancer. She told about it one night over drinks."

Alex covered her mouth with her hand. "Oh my God." She

couldn't think of anything else to say. She was stunned speechless. The sadness in Frank's eyes made so much sense now. Alex had never lost anyone close to her except for her grandparents, but that was because of old age. She couldn't fathom what it would be like to lose someone so young. The fact that Frank lost her twin made Alex's heart ache even more.

Kirsten embraced Alex when she began crying. Alex felt her tears trickle down her cheeks as Kirsten held her, then felt Jordan wrap her arms around them both. Alex thought about what it would be like if she lost Jordan or Kirsten. These two women were practically her sisters, and just the very thought made Alex sick to her stomach. As much as she wanted to remain safe in this cocoon, she stepped away and took a long pull of her beer. She needed a little space. This information was suffocating her.

Jordan took a drink from her bottle, then went back to helping Kirsten prepare their meal. "So, what's going on with you two anyway? After the pool party, I thought you weren't interested in Frank."

Alex shrugged. "I don't know exactly. I guess we're getting to know each other. We had a date last night. I brought takeout over to her house, but she was so wiped out from her pain, we didn't spend more than a couple of hours together." She picked up Aiden when he toddled into the kitchen and she held him tight against her. "I brought her some soup the day after the injury, we talked a little, and I wanted to get to know her better. I like her, J. There are so many facets to her personality that sometimes I feel like my head is swimming, but she's sexy as hell, and I want to get to spend time with her."

Jordan smiled and looked at Kirsten, then went back to chopping vegetables. "I'm glad to hear that, Al. You won't find anyone more down to earth than Frank. We just started to get to know each other better, but she's a cool chick and has a heart of gold."

Alex put her lips to Aiden's forehead and thought about what Jordan said. She really did want to know Frank better, and she hoped after dinner she could continue on that journey.

Chapter Eight

Frank had been moping around ever since she got home from the park. Her stomach grumbled with hunger, but she really didn't feel like eating. She never knew how to answer when people asked about her family. She did have a sister, but she died, so did she still have a sister? She also didn't want to see the pity in people's eyes if she told them she died. It wasn't her that Frank wanted people to feel sorry for—it was her sister who had to go through chemotherapy and radiation. It was her sister who had lost her hair. It was her sister who withered away while she fought valiantly for her life. It was her sister who didn't live to see her thirtieth birthday.

Frank stepped into her bedroom and picked up the photo on her dresser. She stared at the face that was so similar to her own—the amber colored eyes, the Romanesque nose, the thick, black hair, and olive-toned skin. Their Italian heritage had contributed to their good looks. But whereas Frank considered herself more butch, Antonia was the epitome of femininity. There was a softness to her face that Frank didn't have. When they were younger, they both had long hair, but the more Frank got involved in sports, the shorter her hair became. Frank was the star athlete; Antonia was the head cheerleader. She had never seen her parents in the stands of her basketball games, but Antonia was the constant support—always waving her pom-poms and screaming the loudest when Frank made a good play.

Frank had a ton of basketball scholarship offers, but she didn't want to go to a school if Toni wouldn't be there. Toni had always been academically smarter than Frank, and she was accepted into every school she applied to. They mutually decided they would attend Los

Angeles State. Their basketball team was decent enough, but it had a great criminal justice program for Frank and a wonderful English department for Toni. She loved literature and had aspirations of becoming a high school English teacher.

Frank put the picture back on the dresser and returned to the living room. It was times like this—when she was melancholy, when she was missing Toni more than she ever thought possible—when she really wanted to lose herself in alcohol, to drink so much that it would numb her pain. That was the exact reason she never kept it in the house. She wouldn't succumb to the drink the way her parents did when Toni died. She was okay with having a beer or two when she was at a party or hanging out with friends because it was usually a happy time, but she wouldn't be so weak as to drown her sorrows in a shot glass. Her parents were weak. She was not.

Frank gave in to her hunger and microwaved the leftover Thai food from the night before and prepared Bella's dinner. The sound of kibble dropping into the stainless steel bowl brought Bella trotting into the kitchen. She put Bella's food down and pulled her own food from the microwave as Bella ate. She sat at the table for five minutes pushing her food around on the plate when there was a knock on the door. When she opened it, she saw Alex standing there with an unreadable expression on her face. "Hey, what's going on?"

Alex stepped inside and wrapped Frank in her arms. Not that Frank didn't enjoy being held by Alex, but she was a little confused as to why she was there.

"Jordan told me about your sister."

Frank gasped and tried to pull away, but Alex held her tighter. The tears that had threatened her all afternoon finally broke free.

"Shh, it's okay. Let it all out. I got you," Alex whispered.

Alex rubbed her hands up and down Frank's back in an attempt to comfort and soothe her. When the tears finally subsided, Frank wiped her eyes and turned away, embarrassed at crying in front of Alex. She was usually able to keep her feelings in check, careful of displaying them in front of people she didn't know well, but it wasn't pity she felt from Alex; it was empathy. And if she was going to talk to anybody about this, why wouldn't it be Alex? She let her defenses down with Jordan one night a few months ago after a couple of drinks and told her about Toni, and she was met with the same expression Alex just gave her.

"I just heated up some leftovers from last night. Do you want some?"

"No, thanks. I ate with Jordan and Kirsten." Alex sat at the table with Frank. "I wanted to come by and see if you were okay."

Frank blew out a breath and resumed pushing her food around on her plate. "I'm okay. I'm sorry I bailed on you. It's been three years since my sister died, but sometimes it sneaks up on me and punches me in the gut."

"I can't imagine what you went through, what you're still going through, but I promise to listen if you want to talk to me about it." Alex reached across the table and held Frank's hand.

Frank rubbed her thumb across the top of Alex's hand. "I really appreciate it. I'm just a little raw right now, so could we do it another time?"

"Of course. Would you like me to go?"

"No. I'd really like it if you could stay for a while."

"I'd love to on one condition."

Frank looked at her quizzically.

"You promise to eat your food instead of just moving it."

Frank laughed for the first time since they were at the park earlier. "You drive a hard bargain, but all right." Frank began to eat while Alex went to get them something to drink. Frank thanked her when she put a bottle of juice in front of her. It didn't take Frank long to clean her plate, and they went into the living room.

They sat next to each other on the couch as the sun began to set through the window behind them. Alex snuggled into Frank's side when she lifted her arm and placed it around Alex.

"How are the ribs feeling after throwing the ball for Bella today?"

"Actually, they're feeling better. I think the throwing motion loosened things up. I'm even breathing a little easier."

Alex positioned herself to straddle Frank's lap and placed her hands behind her neck. "Want to give that kissing thing another try, Sarge? I mean, since you're feeling better now and all."

Frank noticed Alex's brown eyes turn almost black and felt her own pulse speed up. She grabbed Alex's hips and pulled her closer.

Alex lowered her head and met Frank's lips with a soft, sweet, gentle kiss. Alex moved her hands to Frank's face and held her there while she deepened the kiss. Like Frank had any thoughts of stopping now. They spent hours, or maybe just minutes, exploring each other's mouths, exploring each other's bodies with their hands. There was nothing Frank would have liked to do more than to carry Alex to her bed and make love to her all night, but although she was feeling better, she knew she wasn't quite up for something so physical. Once again, she cursed Robbins for being such a strong tackler. She needed to slow things down, needed to regain control. But, Christ, it was so easy to lose control with Alex. She broke the kiss, gasping for breath, and placed her forehead against Alex's chest.

Alex cupped the back of Frank's head and held her close to her heart. "You okay?"

Still breathing hard, Frank said, "Yes and no. I'm so incredibly turned on right now that I ache. But I don't think I'm physically recovered enough to make love to you, at least not the way I want to."

"I know what you mean about the aching, but I understand. I don't want to make you feel worse, so you better offer me a rain check, Sarge. You can't be kissing me like that without being able to finish the job."

Frank laughed and kissed her again. This time it wasn't long enough to ignite the embers that were already glowing. "I promise to make it up to you."

Alex climbed off Frank's lap and resumed her place next to her. "Whew." She ran her fingers through her hair and straightened her top. "You sure can kiss."

Frank chuckled. "I'm not the only one. Holy shit, woman!"

Alex kissed Frank's cheek and smiled. "I'm going to get going since it's getting late. You get some rest and hurry up and get better, will you? I'm not sure how much longer I can wait." She gave Bella a quick belly rub. "Take care of your mama for me, sweet girl."

Frank escorted Alex to the door and kissed her once more. "I really appreciate you coming by to check on me. I promise to tell you all about Toni some other time, okay?"

Alex brought her hand up to Frank's cheek and caressed it with her thumb. "I'd really like that. You get some rest and I'll talk to you later."

Frank stood in the doorway until Alex was safely in her car and didn't close her door until she drove away. When she sat back down on the couch, Bella came over and looked at her expectantly. "Okay, come on up."

Bella jumped up on the couch and lay across Frank's lap. Frank methodically rubbed Bella's head and ears, and felt her world start to calm. "You never knew Toni, but when I tell Alex about her, I want you there. I have a feeling I'll need your support when I talk about your auntie."

Chapter Nine

Frank couldn't stand it anymore, so first thing Monday morning, she arrived at the doctor's office in hopes of being released back to work. It wasn't exactly what she was after, but she strode out of the office with a form allowing her to return to desk duty. She'd rather be out on the streets for patrol, but riding a desk was better than sitting at home doing nothing. She spent most of the previous day cleaning house, having to rest after every chore to give her ribs a break. She also spoke for a little while with Alex, who was also getting chores and laundry done. They wanted to get together again soon, but Frank would have to see which schedule her lieutenant would have her work.

A chorus of "Hey, Sarge," "Welcome back, Sarge," and "How ya feeling, Sarge?" came her way with most every officer she passed. God, she missed this place. She loved being a cop and really couldn't imagine what it would be like to do anything else. She turned the corner, and at the end of the hall, the door to her lieutenant's office was open. Frank couldn't imagine having a better supervisor. Lieutenant James was a cop's cop with a reputation for being more than fair and having an open-door policy. Frank knocked on the doorjamb and waited for him to invite her in. She smiled when he stood and offered his hand.

"Greco, how are you?"

"Feeling better, Lieutenant. Doc says I can return to modified duty. He gave me this paper to give to you." She handed the report to Lieutenant James and he slipped his reading glasses on as he sat down.

"Have a seat," he said as he pointed to a chair in front of his desk. It didn't take him long to read the report. He took his glasses off and stared at her, making her feel a little uncomfortable with the scrutiny. "You took a pretty hard hit from Robbins. How are you really feeling?"

"Honestly, Loo, he knocked the crap out of me." He joined her in laughter. "The first few days were difficult, but I'm able to breathe easier and sleep better. I'm bored out of my mind at home, and I want to come back to work."

"Okay, start back tomorrow at thirteen hundred hours. You'll be at watch commander's desk until you're released back to full duty. Take this form over to human resources before you leave."

"Yes, sir. Thank you. I'll see you tomorrow." Frank left her supervisor's office and stopped in at human resources to drop off her release form. She left the building with a little bounce in her step. She wanted to celebrate, but the only one she wanted to celebrate with was a certain ER nurse who was currently on duty. She should just go home and get ready for work tomorrow, but ten minutes later, she pulled her truck into the parking lot of the hospital. It couldn't hurt to see if Alex had a few free minutes to grab a cup of coffee.

Frank waved to the clerk behind the safety glass and smiled at her. "Hey, Marie, I was wondering if Alex Taylor was busy."

Marie shook her head. "You know better than to ask that, Frank. It's an ER, for Christ's sake. There aren't any traumas going on, so let me see if I can find her. You can come on back."

Frank pushed through the door and waited only a few minutes before Marie came back. "She's in with a patient, but she wanted me to tell you to wait for her at the nurses' station."

Frank nodded. "Thanks, Marie." She made small talk with a few of the nurses at the nurses' station until Alex arrived five minutes later. Frank's heart did a little flutter when she saw Alex make her way toward her. She looked so sexy in her scrubs with her chestnut hair pulled back in a ponytail, exposing her slender neck. Frank's mouth watered as she recalled the taste of Alex's skin. Alex looked at her and raised an eyebrow as if she knew what Frank had been thinking.

"Hey, Sarge. What are you doing here?" Alex stood close but didn't touch Frank.

"I just came from the station and wanted to see you. Can you take a break and grab some coffee?"

Alex looked at the intake board, then asked the charge nurse, "You mind if I take a quick break?"

"We're fine here for now. You go ahead. Good to see you again, Frank."

Frank waved and followed Alex to the stairwell. They made it down to the next landing when Frank pinned Alex against the wall and kissed her hard. Alex pulled Frank closer and Frank insinuated her leg between Alex's. Alex opened her mouth, and Frank took full advantage, sliding her tongue in and exploring Alex's hot, sexy mouth. Alex began thrusting her pelvis against Frank's leg, the heat from her center easily felt through Frank's jeans. She reluctantly broke the kiss and wrapped her arms around Alex's waist and nuzzled her neck. "You feel so good. God, you taste so good." She licked the neck that had taunted her earlier. What she really wanted to do was take Alex home and make love to her all night long, but her senses came back to her. "What time do you get off?"

Alex laughed shakily. "I could get off with just one more minute with you." She looked at her watch. "I have another four hours."

"How about you come over after and I'll make you dinner?"

Alex kissed Frank again and Frank felt it all the way to her toes. "Dinner sounds great, but what I'm really looking forward to is dessert."

"I promise, dessert can and will be served tonight."

❖

Alex couldn't remember the last time when four hours felt like four days. After her shift ended, she went home to shower and wash the day off her. She arrived at Frank's two hours later and was greeted at the door by Frank and Bella. It might have been a tie as to who was more excited to see her. Bella whined and wagged her tail as she bathed Alex's hand, making her laugh. She discreetly wiped her hand on her jeans before wrapping her arms around Frank's neck and kissing her hello.

"Mm, you smell good," Alex said as she nuzzled Frank's neck.

"Are you sure that's not the lasagna you smell?"

Alex laughed. "Now that you mention it—" Her words were cut off by Frank's lips pressing against hers. Alex had kissed more than a few women in her life, but none of those kisses elicited the type of thrill she felt when Frank kissed her. She felt Frank's kisses surge through her entire body like an electrical shock. "Maybe we can have dessert first?"

Frank laughed at the hopeful look on Alex's face. "Are you sure you don't want to start with my homemade lasagna? I've been slaving away in the kitchen since I got home."

"Oh, okay. I guess I can be patient a little while longer," Alex teased her.

As they wandered into the kitchen, the smell of the sauce, cheese blends, and garlic made Alex's stomach growl. She noted two glasses of red wine sitting on the dining table and looked at Frank questioningly.

"Tonight is a special occasion and I wanted to celebrate."

Alex wrapped her arms around Frank's waist and looked into her eyes. "What's the special occasion?"

"Well, I was released back to light duty today, and I'm spending the evening with a wonderful woman." Frank kissed the tip of Alex's nose.

"Do you want to tell me the reason why you don't normally keep alcohol in the house? I mean, you don't have to, but I really want to know you better."

Frank rubbed her hands up and down Alex's back. "Tell you what. When we sit down to eat, I'll tell you the reason, and about my sister."

"All right. What can I do to help?"

Frank extracted herself from Alex's arms and took the pan of lasagna out of the oven. "Not a thing. Just take a seat and I'll be there in a minute."

Alex sat at the table and watched Frank plate their food. In addition to the mouthwatering lasagna, there was also Caesar salad. Frank placed the plate in front of Alex and took her seat. She lifted her glass to Alex's. "To getting to know each other." Alex clinked her glass and took a sip of the deep, red wine.

She took a bite of the lasagna and moaned in appreciation. "God, Frank, this is delicious."

Frank smiled. "Thank you. It's Nonna Greco's recipe from the old country. She and Nonno came over to America in the early fifties. My mom wasn't exactly a whiz in the kitchen, so Nonna taught Toni and me how to cook whenever we spent the weekend with her and Nonno."

"Is 'nonna' and 'nonno' Italian for 'grandma' and 'grandpa'?"

"Yep."

"And is Toni your sister?"

"Yes." Frank took a bite of her lasagna and took her time swallowing. Alex thought that was all she would get as an answer until Frank cleared her throat and took a sip of her wine. Alex noticed Frank's hand tremble as she placed the glass down.

"Toni was my twin, fraternal, but we looked almost exactly alike. Even though I was older by four minutes, she acted like she was the big sister. She always acted as my protector even though I was physically stronger than her."

Tears started to well in Frank's eyes, and Alex felt her heart break. She placed her hand over Frank's. "Baby, you don't have to…"

Frank turned her palm up and laced her fingers with Alex's. "I want to tell you about her. I want you to know how amazing she was."

Alex squeezed Frank's hand and nodded for her to continue.

"Our parents never paid much attention to us. The little attention they did shell out went mostly to Toni. I guess they thought more of her since she acted like a girl. You know, dresses, makeup, cheerleader. I think they were ashamed of me because I was a tomboy. I only wore jeans and T-shirts. I never wore makeup. I cut my hair short when I started playing basketball. Anyways, Toni was always my greatest supporter. I think the way our parents treated me angered her more than it did me. She always protected me, and when she got sick, I couldn't protect her."

Dinner was forgotten when tears started falling. Alex stood, grabbed Frank's hand, and led her to the living room. She sat next to Frank and cradled her head to her chest. She would do anything to take away the pain Frank had experienced, to bring her sister back to her, alive and well.

After Frank regained her composure, she continued. "Breast cancer didn't run in our family, so Toni thought she had no reason to be concerned. She occasionally performed self-exams, but wasn't consistent about it. By the time she felt the lump and had it diagnosed, the cancer had spread. She fought hard, had chemotherapy and radiation, but it was too advanced. She was only twenty-nine when she died. She never got married, never had children, and hardly traveled because she was so busy with school then with work. We thought we had time to do all of those things. One of our dreams was to travel to Italy, but she was too sick by the time she was diagnosed." Frank wiped her eyes and took a shuddering breath.

"Anyways, our parents were always drinkers, but after Toni was diagnosed, they hit the bottle harder, probably to numb their pain. The night of Toni's funeral, we were all at my parents' house for the wake and it didn't take them long to get hammered. My mom started freaking out, yelling and screaming. Then she came over to me and started beating her fists against my chest, screaming she'd wished it had been me who died and not Toni. When I tried to protect myself and pushed my mom away, my dad grabbed me by the shirt, shoved me to the floor, and yelled, 'Get out of my house, you dyke! You're not welcome here. It should've been you. You're the one who lived a life of sin!'"

Alex hugged Frank tighter and clinched her fists. The fury that consumed her was something she'd never experienced before. How dared Frank's parents treat their own child like that? She began to rock Frank back and forth, as much to calm herself as to comfort Frank. She sat there and continued to hold Frank, afraid to speak, not knowing what to say. What could she say? That she was sorry her parents were such assholes? The type of person Frank turned out to be despite her parents amazed Alex.

Frank sat up and scrubbed her face with her hands before giving Alex a watery smile. "So, I had to tell you that long story to get to the reason why I don't keep alcohol in the house. I spend a lot of time alone, and in that time, I think of Toni and how I failed to keep her safe."

Alex opened her mouth to speak but quickly closed it when Frank held up her hand.

"I know I didn't make her sick and there was nothing I could really do, but it's that whole survivor's guilt thing my therapist warned me about. Anyways, it would be very easy to numb my feelings with alcohol, to drink myself into a stupor whenever I started feeling sorry for myself, but it's impossible to do that if I don't have alcohol here. Toni would come back to haunt me if I allowed myself to behave like our parents." Frank looked down to her lap. "So, there you have it."

Alex gently grabbed Frank's chin and forced her to look in her eyes. "You are an amazing woman." When Frank tried to look away, Alex held firm. "My regrets are that I never got to meet Toni. I'm sure she and I would have become great friends."

Frank looked at her questioningly. "You said regrets. Plural."

Alex squinted her eyes in her best outraged look. "That I never met your parents just to tell them where they could go."

Frank hugged Alex. "Believe me, they're not worth the breath you'd waste. They're no longer in my life, so it's not an issue anymore."

"What about your grandparents? How did they react?"

"They both passed away when Toni and I were in our early twenties. Nonna died of a heart attack, and Nonno died only a couple of months later, probably from a broken heart. They had been together since they were kids. It gave me a little comfort knowing they were there to welcome Toni to heaven."

"You unloaded a lot tonight, honey. How are you feeling?"

Frank ran her fingers through her hair and expelled a deep breath. "Honestly? Like a ton of weight was lifted off my shoulders. I actually feel pretty good. It's good for me to purge like that every once in a while. Sometimes I keep it in too long and I begin to feel overwhelmed."

Alex cupped Frank's cheek and gently kissed her. "Thank you for telling me."

Frank gave her a sheepish smile. "We didn't finish dinner and now I'm starving. Let's go eat."

Frank placed their uneaten lasagna on a separate plate and warmed it up in the microwave. When they resumed eating, Alex asked, "Can you show me a picture of Toni?"

Frank nodded. "Of course. I'll show you after dinner."

Once they finished their meal and cleaned the kitchen, Frank led Alex to her bedroom and stopped in front of the dresser where many framed photos were displayed. "This was the last picture taken of us before Toni got sick."

Alex held the photo and studied it intently. Toni and Frank did look a lot alike, but there were a few subtle differences Alex noticed. Frank's face was a little thinner, and there was what Alex would describe as a serious innocence in her eyes whereas Toni's eyes held a hint of playful mischief. Toni's arm was slung around Frank's shoulders and she did look like she was protecting Frank as Frank had described. She set the photo down and picked up another of them as babies. There were more pictures of them throughout their childhood and young adulthood. She came to another photo of an older couple. "Are these your grandparents?"

Frank looked at the photo with fondness in her eyes. "Yep. Antonia and Francesco Greco."

"You and Toni were named after them?"

"Yeah. Our dad wanted to honor his parents, so they named us Antonia and Francesca."

Alex noticed the blush that tinted Frank's cheeks when she said her given name. "Francesca?" Alex kissed Frank, a slow, sensuous kiss. "That's sexy." Alex kissed her again and felt Frank's hands on her backside, pulling her closer. Alex pulled Frank's black polo shirt over her head and tossed it on the floor. Alex cupped Frank's small breasts that were covered with a black satin bra. The black against Frank's olive-toned skin looked fabulous. Alex's breathing hitched when she ran her fingers down Frank's muscular abs and felt the muscles quiver under her touch.

Frank slowly unbuttoned Alex's blouse and tossed it next to her own discarded top. Alex felt her body catch fire as Frank's eyes landed on her white lacy bra. Alex felt her nipples harden against the lace and closed her eyes to the sensation.

"Alex, you're so beautiful." Frank stepped closer, and as she unhooked Alex's bra, Alex did the same to Frank. The feel of their breasts and nipples against each other was almost more than Alex could handle.

She'd wanted to have sex with Frank since the day Frank pulled her over. She'd envisioned the harried removal of clothes and frantic pawing of each other, bringing each other off in a series of screaming climaxes, but now that the time was here, after the emotional evening they'd had, Alex wanted a slow exploration of Frank's body. She wanted to worship every glorious inch of Frank. She wanted Frank to methodically learn every erogenous zone over hours of lovemaking. She wanted to make Frank moan with pleasure as she licked her, tasted her, filled her up. And after, she wanted to curl up behind Frank and hold her all night long.

Alex noticed a tattoo that ran down the side of Frank's ribs—four interlocking hearts with the words *Hope*, *Courage*, *Strength*, and *Love* written in cursive, one in each heart. She traced the pattern with her finger, admiring the bold ink that was both powerful and beautiful.

"I got this done in memory of Toni. The strength and courage she showed while trying to fight that horrible disease made me so proud of her. I had always loved her and admired her, but seeing her fight the way she did, well..."

Alex wiped an errant tear from Frank's cheek. "She sounds like a remarkable woman. I'm glad you had each other." Alex unbuttoned her pants and pushed them off along with her underwear before doing the same to Frank. She led her to the bed, pulled back the sheets, and invited Frank to join her. "I just want to hold you tonight and comfort you. Will you allow me to do that?"

Frank nodded and slid into Alex's arms and rested her head on Alex's chest. Alex slowly ran her fingers over Frank's shoulders and arms as she kissed the crown of her head. As Frank's breathing evened out and her body relaxed, Alex replayed the evening in her mind. She had every intention of coming over and having sex all night long, but the way it ended was even more special. Frank had let her in, told her about her sister and her failed relationship with her parents. Alex had a strong feeling Frank didn't let many people see that side of her, that vulnerability. The fact she trusted Alex enough to let her see that side of her made her heart swell. The more time she spent with Frank, the more she began to feel for her.

CHAPTER TEN

Frank woke to the sensation of arms wrapped around her and a warm, soft body pressed up against her backside. She recalled telling Alex about Toni and her estrangement from her parents. She thought the night would end with her and Alex having sex, but Alex surprised her when she said she just wanted to hold Frank and comfort her. Frank had relaxed into Alex's arms and fell asleep feeling safe and cared for. She couldn't remember the last time she'd slept so peacefully. She chuckled to herself when she thought of the last time she'd been naked in bed with a sexy woman and hadn't had sex. Never. That had never happened. But what was going on between her and Alex was turning into more than sexual attraction. She felt Alex begin to stir and noticed the clock on her nightstand said it was just six in the morning. Plenty of time to fool around before she needed to get ready for work.

Frank turned over and looked into the sleepy eyes the color of milk chocolate. "Good morning." Frank kissed Alex on her full, luscious lips.

"Good morning. How are you feeling?"

"Actually, I'm feeling better than I have in a very long time. But I feel like I'm letting you down."

"What do you mean?"

Frank grinned. "I promised you dessert last night and I fell asleep on you."

Alex wrapped her arms around Frank. "I'm ready for a little nibble now if you're ready to serve."

Frank chuckled. "Coming right up." Frank rolled Alex onto her back and hovered over her as she lowered her mouth to Alex's. The kiss was passionate and made the butterflies in Frank's stomach flutter like crazy. She moved her hand to cover Alex's breast and felt her nipple harden against her palm. Frank continued to squeeze Alex's breast, then rolled her nipple between her thumb and index finger. Alex's moans added fuel to Frank's fire as she lowered herself down Alex's body and took the firm nipple in her mouth. Alex's pelvis began to move, and Frank took that as permission to lower her hand to Alex's center. Frank found Alex soaking wet and spread the moisture over her sex with her fingers. She felt Alex's clit grow with each stroke, and more moisture flooded her fingers.

"Go inside me, Frank. Fill me up," Alex gasped.

Frank entered two then three fingers and felt the warm, slick walls clamp around her fingers. Alex was so responsive to Frank's touch, and she didn't think she would ever get enough of Alex. She continued to suck on Alex's nipple as her pelvis moved in time to Frank's thrusting fingers. Alex's fingers clutched the back of Frank's head, forcing more of her breast into Frank's mouth. Frank gently bit down on the nipple, and it made Alex cry out as the walls of her sex clamped down on Frank's fingers. Frank's thumb rubbed Alex's clit as she squeezed out the last of her orgasm.

Alex threw her arm over her head and breathed hard. "Whew! Damn, Sarge, that was definitely worth the wait."

Frank withdrew her fingers and used the moisture to paint Alex's other nipple. "Oh, yeah? You ain't seen nothing yet." She lowered her head and licked Alex's juices, savoring the salty taste. The moans that erupted from Alex encouraged Frank to continue. As Frank continued to suck Alex's breast, she felt Alex's hand slip between her legs and lazily stroke her hardened clit. Frank began to move her hips, silently pleading for a firmer touch. Alex took the hint and stroked Frank's bundle of nerves harder, faster, and had Frank panting and chanting Alex's name. Frank felt the impending explosion travel from her toes to her center and came on Alex's hand. Frank collapsed on Alex as she tried to catch her breath. It'd been way too long since she came that hard. Oh, yeah, definitely worth the wait.

Frank peppered Alex's neck and face with kisses until her lips landed on Alex's. They spent a good amount of time kissing languidly as Frank came down from her powerful orgasm.

"That was amazing." Frank rolled onto her back and smiled.

Alex rolled onto her side and lightly grazed Frank's nipple with her finger. "You had me so worked up. I can't believe I came that fast."

Frank barked out a laugh. "You? Jesus, that was embarrassing how I came so quickly. I guess that's what happens when it's been so long."

Alex looked into Frank's amber eyes. "How long has it been?"

"Over a year. How about you?"

Alex smiled wryly. "Not quite that long. But I promise it won't be another year that you have to go without. I'll take good care of you."

Frank brought Alex's hand to her mouth and kissed her palm. "I look forward to it." She snuck a peek at the clock and groaned. For the first time since her accident, she wished she didn't have to go into work. She would rather spend the day in bed with this sexy woman lying next to her. "How about I make us breakfast?"

Alex looked at the clock and shook her head. "I'd love that, but I have to be at work in a couple of hours. I need to go home and get ready. Can I get a rain check?"

Frank kissed her once more. "Absolutely."

After they got dressed, Frank and Bella escorted Alex to the door. "I'm glad you came over, and I'm glad I told you about Toni. It means a lot to me that you wanted to know about her."

Alex wrapped her arms around Frank's neck. "I'm glad too. Thanks for trusting me." Alex kissed her. "Thanks for an amazing dinner." Alex kissed her again. "And thanks for the scrumptious dessert." Alex kissed her once more before letting go and kneeling to pet Bella. "I'll see you soon, sweet girl."

"Be safe, Alex."

"You too, Sarge."

Frank watched Alex drive away and she couldn't contain her smile. She looked down at Bella and gave her a pat on the head. "Okay, girl, let's go have some breakfast. Mama needs to get ready for work."

CHAPTER ELEVEN

Since Frank was on modified duty, she wasn't allowed to wear her gun or her uniform to work. Thankfully, she had a few suits she could choose from, acquired mostly for the court appearances she sometimes had to attend. As she took her seat at the watch commander's desk, she fielded some teasing from a few of the officers regarding her attire. It was good-natured and made Frank glad to be back at work. Not even the bitter old lady she was speaking to on the phone could dampen her mood.

"Yes, ma'am, I understand you pay your taxes, but the street in front of your house is public property and if the neighbor's son wants to park there, he can." The chuckling behind her made Frank turn her head and smile. She held her finger up to her lips to quiet her best friend, Katie. "I'm sorry, ma'am, but this isn't a police matter. I suggest you speak to your neighbor and ask them nicely to park somewhere else." Frank shook her head and smothered her laughter at Katie's eye rolling. "Good luck, ma'am, and have a nice day." Frank hung up the phone, then stood and gave Katie a hug.

"Hey, Katie. It's good to see you."

"Same here, Frank. How're your ribs?"

"Feeling better every day."

Katie nodded her head toward the phone. "How long do you have this shit duty?"

Frank chuckled and sat down. "Hopefully, not too long. As soon as the doc clears me for full duty, I'll be back on the streets."

"Good, 'cause I'm tired of covering your ass. Don't get me wrong, the overtime is nice, but Michelle is starting to get on my case for never being home."

Katie and Frank were in the same class at the police academy, which was how they met. Back then, they were the only two women in the academy and had to work extra hard just to prove they belonged there. They helped each other with extra training and studying, and they ended up graduating in the top five of their class. All of the shit they had to go through at the academy brought them closer together, and before Frank knew it, she had a best friend. It was luck that they ended up working at the same station, and they continued to grow closer over the years.

"Give Michelle my apologies and tell her I promise to make it up to her."

"Oh, yeah? How do you plan to do that?" Katie teased her.

"Next time we all have a day off, I'd like to take you out to dinner. A double date."

Katie's eyebrows shot up and made Frank laugh. "A double date? You're seeing someone? Why am I just now hearing about this?"

"Well, it's still new, but yeah, I'm kind of seeing someone. I didn't want you to get too excited in case it didn't work out."

"Who? Anyone I know?"

"Maybe. She's an ER nurse and recently transferred to County."

Katie was quiet for a moment, then it appeared she knew who Frank was talking about. "Brown hair and eyes? About five eight? Our age?"

"Yep. Her name is Alex and she's super cool."

"She's super hot too."

That earned Katie a hard glare from Frank. "I'll make sure to let Michelle know you think so."

"You do and I'll kick your ass."

Frank chucked Katie on her arm. "Take your empty threats and get your ass back to work."

Katie hugged Frank before leaving. "Let us know what night works for you."

"Copy that. I'll check with Alex to see when she's off."

Throughout her shift, Frank couldn't help but think about the morning she shared with Alex. The lull between phone calls gave her the opportunity to recall how it felt to have Alex under her, on top of her, responding to every touch, every caress, every kiss. Alex was exactly as Frank imagined with her soft skin and womanly curves. Not for the first time that day, Frank was grateful she was stuck behind a desk instead of being on the streets. Her lack of concentration could be detrimental to the public, her officers, or herself. When she wasn't thinking about their morning, she was wondering how Alex's shift was going. And if she was being honest with herself, she wondered what Alex thought of their morning together, and if Frank had crossed her mind.

Alex had been busy from the time she clocked in, moving from one patient to the next and getting them the appropriate care. She hadn't had time to think of Frank and the time they spent together the previous night and that morning until she finally found some free time to go to the cafeteria and grab some dinner. Once she sat down with her salad, she pulled out her cell phone and sent Frank a text.

Hey there. Just wanted to see how your first day back went.

She placed the phone on the table and began to eat her salad. She was surprised when Frank texted back so quickly.

I'm feeling good, glad to be back at work, but I'm tired of talking on the phone. I'm ready to go back on the streets.

Alex set her fork down and replied. *I'm glad you're feeling better. You'll be back on the streets soon enough.*

I know, but I hate riding the desk.

Alex grinned and her mind went to the gutter. *How would you like to ride something else tonight?*

A few minutes went by without a response. Alex thought she might have been a little crude, and felt a knot form in the pit of her stomach. The responding text changed the knot into butterflies when she read it. *I'm off at twenty hundred. You want to come over after work?*

Alex felt relieved and the tension in her body released. *I'll be there at twenty-one hundred. Be ready.*

Roger that. See you later.

Alex finished her salad and tea and hurried back to the ER with a bounce in her step. She hoped for the rest of her shift to fly by so she could hurry and get to Frank's. As she pushed through the doors to chaos, all thoughts of Frank fled her mind, and she returned her focus to medicine.

Once her shift ended, Alex quickly showered and dressed. She decided against underwear before putting on her jeans, but looked forward to the future lingerie modeling show she would privately give Frank. She and Kirsten shopped frequently at Victoria's Secret after Kirsten shared with her how fun it was to model her purchases for Jordan. Frank appeared to be cut from a similar cloth as Jordan, and Alex wondered if Frank would appreciate the lingerie as much as Kirsten said Jordan did.

Commando would have to do for tonight. She hadn't planned on going over to Frank's after work, otherwise she would have been more prepared. She would have to remember to pack a bag for such future occurrences. She had a feeling that they would have spontaneous sleepovers until they were able to work out their schedules. Alex's body trembled with excitement and anticipation as she drove to Frank's.

Frank answered the door wearing baggy boxer shorts, a white tank top, and no bra. Alex could see Frank's dark areolas through the white shirt and felt a flood of moisture in her jeans. Frank's dark hair was wet and slicked back as if she used her fingers to comb her hair. Alex felt her nipples harden at the sight before her.

When Alex walked in, Frank shut the door, then pinned Alex against it with her body. Alex felt the prominence pressed against her center as Frank kissed her hard. She reached into Frank's boxers and the surprise she found sent her pulse racing. She groaned her pleasure into Frank's mouth as she wrapped her hand around Frank's dildo and began slowly stroking her. Frank's hips began thrusting in time with Alex's stroking, and she broke the kiss, panting for air.

"I thought maybe you would like something to ride tonight too." Frank's deep voice made Alex shiver with need.

Alex bit her bottom lip and nodded. They went straight to Frank's bedroom, and Alex told Frank to sit on the edge of the bed. The dildo jutted out from the unbuttoned flap of Frank's boxers, and Alex had a difficult time taking her eyes off it. She finally peeled her eyes away and looked at Frank, where she saw total desire on her face. She took two steps back, just out of Frank's reach, and began to slowly unbutton her blouse. As each button was released, Frank's breathing quickened. She slid her blouse off her shoulders and let it drop to the floor. When she unbuttoned her jeans and slowly slid the zipper down, Frank's hand began to stroke her own cock.

"No starting without me, Sarge."

Frank's hand stilled and Alex pulled her jeans down, stepped out of them, and stood between Frank's legs. Alex lifted the tank over Frank's head and knelt to remove Frank's boxers. Alex licked her lips before taking the head into her mouth. She gripped the base and moved her hand in time with her mouth up and down the shaft. She could feel wetness dripping down her inner thighs, and her clit throbbed.

"Fuck, Alex, you're gonna make me come."

Alex released Frank from her mouth and straddled her lap. "Not without me, you won't." She moved her hips so the length glided along her sex, and she threw her head back. "I need you in me. Now!"

Alex lifted her hips as Frank grabbed her cock and teased Alex's opening.

"I'm not kidding, Frank."

Frank chuckled as she slowly penetrated Alex's opening. Alex lowered herself and felt the fullness fill her up. She stayed in that position as she began to kiss Frank. When their tongues met, Frank began to play with Alex's nipples, pinching and twisting them just the way Alex liked. Alex started moving her hips back and forth, each thrust bringing her closer to orgasm. When she felt her impending climax, she broke the kiss and watched Frank's cock move in and out of her. "Oh, God, Frank, I want you to come inside me."

Frank grunted as she thrust her hips upward, and Alex felt her shudder, which helped release her own orgasm. Alex had her arms wrapped around Frank's shoulders, and she slumped against her, breathing erratically. She kissed the pulse point in Frank's neck until their breathing returned to normal.

"We are definitely using this again."

"Oh yeah? You liked it?"

"Eh, it was okay."

That earned Alex a pinch on the butt, which made her yelp. "Don't move. I'm going to pull myself off." Alex stood on shaky legs, and she felt the loss immediately. She sat on the bed and watched Frank slip out of her harness and drop it next to the bed. Frank put her boxers and tank back on and Alex eyed her questioningly.

"I need to let Bella out, but I'll be right back." She leaned down and kissed her sweetly. "Get into bed and I'll be right there."

In the time Frank was gone, Alex replayed their encounter in her mind. Frank seemed to instinctually know exactly what Alex needed and how she needed it. If Frank was indeed the real deal, Alex could really see herself falling for her. She felt cautiously optimistic, but she couldn't seem to shake the feeling that something was about to happen that could change her life.

CHAPTER TWELVE

Frank couldn't take much more of riding the desk. For the first couple of days, it was fine because she just wanted to be back to work. But as the days dragged on, she was itching to get back on patrol. The pain in her ribs was gone for the most part unless she bumped up against something, but even then the discomfort was mild. She returned to the medical clinic for a follow-up visit with her doctor. It had been four weeks since the injury, and she would beg the doctor if she had to in order to get released to full duty. Repeat x-rays showed the rib was healed, and the doctor gave her the form releasing her back to work without restrictions. She went to the station to inform her lieutenant, then over to the shooting range to re-qualify and get back her service weapon. There was one more call she had to make before heading home.

"Hey, Jordan, it's Frank."

"Hey, buddy! How are you?"

"I'm great. I just saw the doctor and he said my ribs are healed. Can I still join the team?"

"Absolutely! Our first game is next week. We have practice tomorrow, but if you want to come over tonight, I can go over some stuff with you."

"That'd be good. What time should I come by?"

"Come for dinner and bring that crazy best friend of mine with you. I know she doesn't have any shifts for the next couple of days."

"Copy that. We'll see you in a little bit."

Frank hung up and called Alex.

"Hey, baby. Jordan invited us over for dinner so we can go over some stuff for the team."

"Wait a second. You're not ready to play basketball."

"Why can't I?"

"I don't want you to get hurt again. What about your rib?"

"Don't worry, Alex. I saw the doctor earlier, and x-rays showed I'm all better. He released me back to full duty."

"That's great, honey. I'm so happy for you."

"Thanks. So, are you coming with me tonight?"

"Of course. What time shall I pick you up?"

"You're coming to get me?"

"Well, yeah. I figured I'd spend the night. Was I being presumptuous?"

"No, no. I'd love for you to stay with me tonight. In case I haven't told you, I really appreciate your willingness to sleep at my place. Having Bella prevents me from being able to sleep over at your house."

"It's no problem. I like her kisses in the morning almost as much as I like yours."

The melodious tone in Alex's laughter warmed Frank's heart. So far, things were going well between them. "Jordan said to come over around six."

"Okay. I'll be there soon."

Frank had a surge of energy and needed to work it off. She was greeted at her door by Bella, and somehow she seemed to know her person was back to her old self. Bella followed Frank into the bedroom and began to bark excitedly when she pulled her running shoes out of the closet and changed into her running clothes. "I'm a little out of shape, girl, but let's see how long we can go." After doing a few stretches, she attached Bella's leash and headed out the front door. She started off with a slow jog, but after five minutes, she hit her pace, and Bella kept right up. The runs Julie took Bella on hadn't hindered her stamina one bit. Frank was able to clear her mind of any thoughts fairly quickly and was able to enjoy the sound of her feet hitting the pavement along with the even tempo of her breathing. As good as it felt to run again, she didn't want to push herself too hard. She knew from experience how sore her muscles would be the next day after such a long layoff. Bella didn't seem too happy to have her run cut short when they got back to their house.

Frank rubbed Bella's ears, as if that would appease her. "I'm sorry, girl, but obviously I'm not in as good shape as you. Don't worry. I'll get there." She stripped out of her clothes and turned on the shower. Despite her overheated body, she kept the water as hot as she could tolerate to try to lessen some of her muscle soreness that was sure to arrive. She stood under the hot spray and allowed the strong pulse to penetrate her tired body. She downed a bottle of Gatorade as she got dressed, then went into the kitchen to feed Bella.

Shortly after, the knock on the door signaled Alex's arrival. Her pulse quickened the closer she got to the door, and she smiled when she saw Alex standing there looking sexy as could be. Alex stepped into her arms and gave her a luxurious kiss, one that spoke of promises for later. "Hi, baby."

"Hi, yourself. You look and smell great." Alex began nibbling on her neck.

Frank couldn't help but groan at the exquisite assault on her skin. She was quickly becoming aroused and reluctantly broke away. "Don't get me started 'cause we don't have time to finish."

"You just remember something. When we get back here tonight, all bets are off and you're mine."

She grabbed Alex by her hips and pulled her closer. "Maybe we can skip dinner tonight."

Alex tapped the tip of Frank's nose with her finger. "I don't think so, Sarge. You're going to need nourishment for what I have planned later. Now, go grab your bathing suit so we can go for a swim after dinner, and I'm gonna give Bella some love."

Frank returned a few minutes later with her swimwear and a towel, and after Alex gave Bella a kiss on the head, they left for Jordan and Kirsten's. When they arrived, Jordan opened the door and welcomed them in. Aiden toddled over and held his arms up to Alex. She picked him up, and after she made him laugh with her kisses and tickles, she handed him over to Frank. She gladly accepted him and he threw his little arms around her neck to give her a squeeze.

"Aiden, you are such a cute boy."

He rewarded her with a slobbery kiss on her mouth that made them all laugh. Jordan and Kirsten kissed Alex, then hugged Frank, and led them to the kitchen table. Aiden was still hanging on to Frank when she took a seat. She didn't have much experience with babies, but she couldn't seem to get enough of the soft skin against her own. It seemed to soothe her.

Jordan opened the refrigerator and asked, "Do any of you want a beer? We're having tacos for dinner tonight."

They all said yes and she pulled out four beers. Jordan brought them to the table and took a seat across from Frank. "So, are you sure you're feeling up to playing ball?"

Frank chuckled. "Well, it's been forever since I've played, but it'll be fun. After your team sees me play in practice tomorrow, you might change your mind about asking me to play."

Jordan waved her hand in the air, obviously dismissing Frank's assessment. "It's like riding a bike, Frank. You're a pure shooter, and it'll take no time to get your stroke back."

"We'll see."

"Practice starts at two tomorrow, so I'll meet you about fifteen minutes early to introduce you to the other women. You met some of them at our party, and they're a great bunch to play with."

"I'm looking forward to it."

Alex and Kirsten excused themselves to go finish dinner, which allowed Frank and Jordan to speak privately.

"Hey, I'm sorry about telling Alex about your sister. I hope you weren't upset with me."

"No, but I was surprised when she came over that night. I wasn't in the right space to tell her about Toni that night, but I told Alex about her the next time we saw each other." Frank ran her hand across her forehead and blew out a breath. "It's been only a few years, but I still miss her so much." She tried to hold back the tears that threatened to fall.

Jordan reached across the table for her hand. "I can't imagine what that would be like, but I want you to know that you mean a lot to me, and I can tell you mean a lot to Alex. We're not your family by blood, but we'll be your family by choice."

She squeezed Jordan's hand and just nodded, not trusting herself with words at that moment.

"So, you and Alex, huh?" Jordan asked.

Frank grinned. "Yeah. You okay with that?"

Frank almost laughed at the serious look on Jordan's face, but she refrained, knowing a serious talk about her relationship with Alex was about to occur.

"It depends. What are your intentions?"

She held up her right hand. "Only the best, Jordan. I care about her and we have a great time together. I like that we can have a serious conversation one minute then joke around the next. So far, the only thing I'd change is the time we get to spend together. Her shifts at the hospital can be crazy sometimes, and we might not get to see each other for a few days, but other than that, I think things are going well."

"That's good. And just for the record, I think you're good for her."

Kirsten called out that dinner was ready, saving Frank from having to come up with a response. Jordan took Aiden from Frank and set him up in his high chair while they fixed their plates. Jordan and Frank told stories of each other during their college playing days, playfully insulting each other, which made Alex and Kirsten roll their eyes.

When they were done with dinner, Alex led Frank to the guest room to change into their bathing suits. No sooner had the door closed than Alex grabbed her and kissed her hard, all thoughts of them being in Jordan and Kirsten's home leaving her mind. She pulled Alex's shirt above her head and dropped it on the floor. Alex cupped her ass and pulled her close, gyrating into her pelvis, making her moan in pleasure. Frank pulled her own shirt over her head and dropped it next to Alex's before resuming their kissing. She felt like a teenage boy that was about to have sex for the first time. What was it about Alex that made her lose all control and just want to ravish her? As she was reaching the point of no return, Alex broke the kiss and stepped back. Her breathing was ragged as she took a step closer to Alex, only to have her put her hand on Frank's chest, preventing her from further advancement.

"They'll be waiting for us."

"Who?"

Alex laughed. "Jordan and Kirsten."

"Shit! I forgot about them."

"Come on. We'll get back to that later."

She couldn't keep her eyes off Alex's sexy body as they finished disrobing. She was ready to say good night to Jordan and Kirsten and take Alex home where they could resume what they started. Miraculously, common sense reintegrated its way into her brain, and she was able to control her lust-filled body. They walked out to the pool, where Jordan was carrying Aiden through the water and making motor boat sounds. Kirsten was sitting in the hot tub, looking blissful amongst the bubbling water. She watched Alex descend the steps into the pool and decided to join Kirsten. The hot water and jet stream would feel great against her body after her earlier run.

She sat next to Kirsten and was startled when she felt a hand on her shoulder.

"I'm really glad you and Jordan got to know each other and that you've come into our lives."

A lump formed in Frank's throat. "Thank you. That means a lot to me. You have a very lovely family." She looked across the pool to watch Jordan and Alex play with Aiden. "Your son is adorable."

"We think so too, but I guess we're a little biased."

"Are you planning on having more?" Frank cringed. "God, I'm sorry. That's none of my business."

Kirsten smiled and made Frank more at ease. "That's okay. We're thinking about it. We'd love to give Aiden a little sister or brother, but we'll have to see if it's in the cards."

"Well, I bet he would make a great big brother. It seems Jordan was made to be a parent."

"Yes, I think she was. She's a great mom. I'm not sure what I did in this life to deserve them, but I'm grateful every moment of the day for being this blessed."

"You both are very lucky."

"You know," Kirsten had an amused look in her eyes, "Alex would be a wonderful mom too."

Frank chuckled. "I know she would. She loves Aiden like he was hers. But we just started seeing each other, so we'll have to see where this goes."

"And where do you see this going?"

"I like her very much, and as I told Jordan before dinner, I have only honorable intentions. But we've only been dating for a few weeks. I don't think either one of us is ready to rent a U-Haul just yet." Frank's heart began to pound as she thought of a future with Alex.

"I don't expect you two to get married next week, but you won't find anyone kinder than Alex. That woman," she discreetly pointed at Alex, "is as good as they come."

Frank looked at Alex playing with Aiden. She turned and locked her eyes with Frank, and Frank saw the soft smile meant only for her. "I already know that," she said, unable to tear her gaze away from Alex.

CHAPTER THIRTEEN

Alex pulled back the curtain from cubicle two to see Frank standing at the nurses' station. She stopped to observe Frank looking so gorgeous and commanding in her uniform. Since Frank had resumed patrol, she'd seen her a few times in the ER. The difference in Frank's officer personality and lover personality aroused Alex, but for different reasons. When Frank was working, she exuded confidence and control, especially when she was dealing with a suspect. Her "take no shit" attitude was something Alex absolutely loved. As her lover, Frank also held a commanding presence, but was flexible enough to let Alex lead when she wanted to. Frank was attentive, inventive, and unselfish in bed.

As talented as Frank was when it came to their bedroom activities, the moments that followed were what really got to Alex. Cuddling, gently caressing, and intimate conversations were the norm, but occasionally one of them would make a sarcastic comment that would lead to a bout of tickling that would lead to another bout of lovemaking before they'd collapse for the night in each other's arms. In Frank's case, she was hot in the streets and even hotter in the sheets. Alex could feel the flush overcome her face as Frank turned to her and caught her staring. The look on Frank's face told her she wasn't there to see her; she was all business.

She approached her, and as much as she wanted to reach out and pull her into a heartfelt hug, she kept a respectable distance. "What's going on?"

"We brought a baby in. Unconscious. Shaken by her mother's asshole boyfriend."

"Oh, Frank, I'm so sorry. Have you heard anything?"

Frank shook her head. "I'm waiting for someone to come out and give me an update."

This time Alex did reach out and take Frank's hand to hold for a moment. "Let me go see if I can find out anything."

Alex noticed on the board that the baby was in trauma two, and she quickly headed that way. When she approached, she saw a distraught woman looking through the glass window in the door. She went a little farther down the hall to the second door and entered to see various medical personnel surrounding the unmoving child. The constant shrilling tone on the monitor told her all she needed to know, but the quiet voice from the doctor confirmed it.

"Time of death, eighteen forty-six."

A nurse rushed past Alex with tears in her eyes, and she felt her own well up. It didn't matter how long you were at this job, seeing a child die was the most difficult to endure. If that didn't affect you, it was time to get out. She left and went to find Frank, and saw her standing at the end of the hall waiting. Her face fell when Alex got closer and shook her head. The scream behind her made her turn as the woman collapsed in the doctor's arms. Frank turned and quickly vanished behind the door to the stairwell where Alex followed. She grabbed Frank from behind before she could pound the cement wall with her fist again.

"Baby, I'm so sorry."

Frank turned around and threw her arms around Alex and cried into her shoulder. Alex cried too—for the loss of a child, for the hurt Frank was going through, for the mother who would never again tuck her child into bed at night. This was one of the reasons it made it so difficult to date someone who didn't know what they went through on a daily basis. But they knew, and they would help each other, comfort each other through the nightmares they were sure to have from this senseless act.

Frank stepped back and wiped her eyes. "I need to get back. I have to take a statement from the mother ,then go to the station to arrest that motherfucker for murder." She put her hands over her face and screamed, "Goddamn it!"

Alex held Frank in her arms again. "Call me when you get home and I'll come over."

"You don't have to."

"I know I don't, but I want to. Please, baby, let us help each other tonight."

Frank nodded her head once and kissed her on the cheek. "Okay. I'll talk to you later."

Alex could only stand and watch Frank's retreating form, her heart breaking a little more with every step Frank took away from her.

❖

Frank sat on the couch nursing a beer while Bella lay across her lap. When the doorbell rang, she slid out from under her and went to the door to let Alex in. She held up the bottle. "Do you want one?"

"Where'd you get that? I thought you didn't keep alcohol in the house."

"I don't, but I figured I'd make an exception after the clusterfuck day we've had. Do you want one?"

"Sure. Let me drop off my bag in your room and I'll meet you on the couch."

Frank downed the rest of her beer on her way to the kitchen and took two bottles out of the fridge. She walked back to the living room to see Bella lying next to Alex with her head in her lap and Alex running Bella's soft, floppy ear through her fingers. She handed the beer to Alex, then sat on the other end of the couch.

They didn't speak a word for a few minutes. Frank sat silently looking into space, desperately wishing she could start that day over, that she didn't have to catch that call. Of all the things she had to deal with on a daily basis, an attack on a poor, defenseless child was the worst. Frank reflected back to when she had returned to the station after leaving the hospital. She normally had a calm demeanor, but she honestly wouldn't lose a wink of sleep for killing that bastard, to beat the living shit out of him the way he did that baby. That was exactly her intention as she pushed through the doors of the station house. The determined strides she took on her way to the holding cell were stopped abruptly by Katie. Her body shook with fury as Katie led them into the women's locker room and locked the door behind them.

Frank stalked the floor like a caged animal, ready to let loose on anyone who tried to stand in her way. But it was the fury on Katie's face, the fire in her eyes that stopped Frank from throwing away her career on that scum. They sat on the bench together and released tears of anger and frustration at having to deal with reckless violence day in and day out. It sometimes felt like an uphill battle that they would never overcome. Katie said to her before she left the locker room, "Frank, for every piece of shit that commits a crime like this, there're another one or two that we put away before they can. We have to continue to fight for the victims. If we don't, who will?"

She contained her anger as she drove the suspect to the county jail to have him booked. She wanted the satisfaction of seeing him humiliated by the officers before being locked behind bars. It was of little consolation to her. At least he had the good sense to keep his mouth shut during the ride over. On the way home, she stopped for a six-pack, knowing Alex would want a beer or two to help wind down from her day. She had every intention of waiting for her, but found herself popping the top off a bottle before she put the other five in the refrigerator.

"Tell me what happened when you spoke to the mother."

Frank took a drink from her beer and let out a deep sigh. "She said the babysitter called her last night to say she had the flu and didn't want to get the baby sick. Jasmine, that's the name of the baby. The mother had just started a new job last week and didn't want to call in sick. Her boyfriend of two months finally agreed to watch Jasmine after she pleaded with him. The bastard doesn't work, so Mom thought he could earn his keep by taking care of her daughter. He called nine-one-one at around three, saying Jasmine fell off the bed and stopped breathing. We arrived at the residence to find the baby unresponsive with marks on her arms that looked like he grabbed them and held too tight."

Frank took another drink of her beer and realized tears were falling down her cheeks. "Two of the officers arrested him while I drove the baby to the ER with another officer. I had her in the backseat with me, performing CPR on her until we got to the hospital and the doctors and nurses took over. The mom came home right after we left and another officer brought her to the hospital. She was going to have her first birthday in two weeks."

Frank wiped the tears from her face as Alex got up and sat in her lap. Alex placed her head on Frank's shoulder and cried with her as Frank soaked up the comfort like a sponge. She whispered, "I had every intention of going back to the station to beat the shit out of the boyfriend, but Katie talked me off the ledge."

Alex had met Katie and her partner a couple of weeks earlier when the four of them had had dinner together. Alex told Frank later that night that she really liked them and wanted to hang out again.

"I'm glad she was able to do that for you, but if I can be honest, I wouldn't have minded one bit to see you beat him if you could get away with it without losing your job or who you are. There should be a special place in hell for animals like that."

"I agree."

They sat there a little while longer, holding each other until the tears ceased. Frank hadn't eaten dinner, not with the turmoil tumbling through her body, but she asked Alex if she wanted something to eat.

"You know what I want? I want to take you to bed and hold you all night long. Can I do that for you? For us?"

Frank felt a lump form in her throat that prevented her from speaking, so she nodded.

Alex stood, grabbed her hand, and led her to the bedroom, where Frank curled up in Alex's arms and savored the compassion Alex showed her.

❖

Alex had a difficult time falling asleep as she held Frank in her arms. Every once in a while, Frank would twitch, and Alex imagined Frank was dreaming of pulling the trigger on that fucker. She thought of Aiden, who was about the same age as Jasmine, and she knew without a shadow of a doubt that she would have no problem killing anyone who tried to hurt him. She was finally able to sleep knowing he was safe in his crib and protected by people who loved him, and that Frank was safe in her arms.

CHAPTER FOURTEEN

After a few more days and a few more tears, Frank was feeling like her old self. She and Alex had the upcoming weekend off from work and they planned to spend their downtime together. Frank wanted to take her away for the weekend, but she had a basketball game on Saturday evening and didn't want to miss it. Alex had to work last Saturday and missed Frank's first game, but Frank was relieved. She had a lot of kinks to work out in her play. Missed shots, missed passes, missed plays plagued her game that night, but she was able to go to the park a couple of times that week to try to regain the shooting rhythm she'd had when she was younger.

On Saturday, she spent a great deal of time visualizing the game, the way her teammates would cut to the basket, the passes she'd deliver, her shots hitting nothing but net. She took Bella out for a run early in the morning. Her body felt great, and her mind was clear. When Alex arrived, she put her bag in Frank's bedroom and they headed off to the gym.

Jordan and Kirsten were sitting in the bleachers with Aiden sitting on the lap of a woman Frank didn't know. When they approached, Kirsten introduced her to her friend Brenda, who managed to shake Frank's hand while holding on to Aiden, who was squirming in her arms. She held her hand up to Aiden, who gave her a clumsy high five. She was inordinately pleased to see Aiden remembered what she taught him a couple of weeks ago. Alex took Jordan's seat when she and Frank climbed down the bleachers to get ready for their game.

They stretched in a corner of the gym with the rest of their teammates and went over the game plan. Since Frank was new to the team, and because of her dismal play the week before, she started the game on the bench but didn't stay there long. At the first timeout, she subbed in for Jill, their shooting guard, and heard Alex and Kirsten scream their approval. She smiled at Jordan and shook her head at the ruckus as she jogged on to the floor. Frank got the pass on the wing from their point guard and saw an open lane. She drove to the basket, and when Jordan's defender came over to help, she dished off the pass to Jordan, who scored an easy lay-up.

The next time down the floor, her defender gave her plenty of room, so she took a dribble, stepped behind the three-point line, and the only sound she heard was the swish of the ball falling through the net. By the end of the game, Jordan and Frank were responsible for forty-two of the team's sixty points. Frank felt like she was floating on clouds. She still had it after all this time, and she wanted to celebrate. Alex, Kirsten, Brenda, and Aiden made their way down the stands to congratulate the team. Frank nearly lost her footing when Alex jumped into her arms.

"You were great, baby!"

Frank laughed at Alex's enthusiasm and gently lowered her to the floor so she could kiss her. "Man, that was fun!"

Jordan and Kirsten greeted each other similarly while Brenda held Aiden.

"You guys feel like going to Lucy's?"

"Absolutely! I'm buying the first round," Frank replied.

Brenda graciously offered to babysit Aiden so Kirsten and Jordan could go and enjoy a night out together.

They went back to their respective houses to shower and dress, and they met up at the local neighborhood lesbian bar that sponsored their basketball team. Frank and Jordan went to order the drinks while Alex and Kirsten grabbed a table. They sat together for a while rehashing the game.

"You guys played so great." Alex slid her arm around Frank's waist and scooted closer to whisper in her ear. "You looked so hot out there."

Frank felt the wetness flood her boxers and shifted in her seat to relieve the pressure of her jeans from her swollen tissues. Alex's hot breath in her ear sent chills throughout her body. She wanted to hold Alex in her arms, and when a slow song began, she led Alex to the dance floor, followed by Jordan and Kirsten. Alex stepped into her arms, and they moved their bodies to the slow, sensual beat. This was the first time they'd danced together, but they moved as one, like they'd been partners all their lives. One slow song led to another, and Frank wanted nothing more than to take Alex home and make love to her all night. They hadn't been dating long, and she wasn't ready to say those three little words that were anything but little. Frank cared for Alex and loved spending time with her. She made her laugh, she was thoughtful, and sex with Alex was the best she'd ever had. She definitely saw a future with Alex and hoped she felt the same. They hadn't discussed what came next, but they were monogamous and committed to enjoying each other's company.

After a couple of hours of laughing, talking, drinking, and dancing, they decided it was time to leave. They hugged each other good-bye, then Frank and Alex drove back to Frank's. Bella excitedly greeted them at the door.

"You take care of Bella and I'll meet you in the bedroom."

Alex's sultry voice and look of desire made Frank's pulse race and mouth dry. She nodded and watched Alex sashay down the hall and disappear through the door.

"C'mon, sweet girl, let's hurry this up." She stood in the backyard as Bella took her time smelling the grass, chasing crickets, and finally doing her business. *It's about time. Alex better still be awake.* She grabbed two biscuits and placed them on Bella's bed. "You're sleeping out here tonight. No interrupting, got it? Even if you hear moaning or screaming." Bella quietly lay down on her bed and went to eating her treats as Frank hurried to her bedroom. She was pleasantly surprised to see some lit candles that added a romantic ambiance to the space. She knocked on the bathroom door to check on Alex.

"I'll be out in a minute. Go sit on the bed and don't move."

Frank did as she was told and wondered what was in store. The door to the bathroom opened, and her breath hitched when she saw the vision of loveliness emerge. Alex stood in the doorway of the bathroom with one hand high on the frame and the other on her hip, and Frank couldn't remember ever seeing anything so fucking sexy in her life. Her eyes glazed over as she watched Alex walk toward her in a navy blue lace teddy, garters holding up black silk stockings, and black pumps with an impossibly high heel. She felt the moisture leave her mouth and accumulate in her boxers.

Alex moved slowly toward her with a practiced sway of her hips and stepped between her spread legs. "You're a little overdressed, baby."

Frank took her time letting her eyes roam every glorious inch of Alex's incredible body. "You told me not to move." Frank knew she sounded stupid, but at that point, she didn't care.

Alex laughed lustily. "I'm glad you obeyed my orders. That deserves a reward. If you keep being a good girl, I'll keep rewarding you. Are you a good girl, Frank?"

She absently nodded her head, and Alex smirked.

Alex had placed the tip of her finger on Frank's cheek and trailed the newly manicured nail down the side of her neck, down her chest to the top button of Frank's blouse. "Unbutton your shirt."

Her hands flew to the first button, but before she was able to release it, Alex said, "Slowly."

Frank finally understood the game Alex wanted to play, and she was more than willing—as long as it didn't take too long. She wasn't sure how long she could hold out as her clit began to throb. She slowly undid every button and waited for Alex's next order.

"I want you to stand and unbuckle your belt."

Being the good girl she was, Frank followed Alex's orders. When Alex gave her next instruction, she unbuttoned her pants and slowly slid her zipper down. Her pants fell and pooled around her ankles, but she waited for Alex to speak.

"Sit back down, baby. You're obeying very well tonight." Alex squatted before her and removed her shoes, socks, and pants. She stood back up and spread Frank's thighs so she could move closer. Alex slid Frank's shirt off her shoulders and down her arms, and added it to the already discarded clothing.

"You were a good girl, Frank. You may now undress me."

Molten blood rushed through her veins as she placed her shaking hands on Alex's lower legs. Rather than hurrying though, she decided to give Alex a taste of her own medicine. She ran her hands achingly slowly up the sides of Alex's legs until they reached the lace bands at the top of her stockings.

She leaned forward and licked at the edge of the lace. When she heard Alex gasp, she smiled inwardly. *Oh yes, Alex, we'll see just how good a girl you want me to be.* With a flick of her thumbs, she unfastened the garter clips, lifted Alex's leg, and gently lowered one stocking with her teeth, then the other. She looked up at Alex and saw desire darkening those gorgeous brown eyes.

She continued to move her hands up Alex's smooth thighs and around her backside until they were cupping her shapely ass. She pulled Alex closer until her sex was right in front of her face. She didn't move closer but kept massaging Alex's ass while she inhaled the musky smell of her arousal. She decided she wasn't going to do anything else until Alex instructed her—begged her—for release.

Alex's hands moved to Frank's head and alternated between running her fingers through her hair and squeezing her head. Breathing hard, Alex demanded, "Fuck me, Frank. Fuck me right now!"

She stood, lifted Alex, and placed her on the bed. She ripped off Alex's matching panties and thrust two fingers into her as she latched aggressively on to her nipple. She withdrew, then added a third finger. She slid in and out of Alex's slick sex, and it didn't take long for her walls to spasm around Frank's fingers as Alex cried out her release. Frank released Alex's nipple and delicately kissed her breast, working her way up her neck before finding her lips. They kissed languidly as Alex's breathing slowed.

"You can come out of me now."

"I kind of like it here." Frank wiggled her fingers and laughed when Alex grasped her wrist.

"I'm spent, Sarge. You wore me out."

Frank slowly withdrew her fingers and licked them clean. "You taste so sweet."

Alex drew her back to her lips and they continued to kiss as she climbed on top of Frank. She kissed her way down Frank's chest where she lingered for a while, tasting, licking, and nibbling her dark nipples until she could feel Frank's hips start to move beneath her. She continued downward, dropping soft kisses on Frank's stomach until she settled between her legs. She used her fingers to spread Frank's inner folds and wrapped her mouth around the bundle of nerves that was swollen and red. She sucked tenderly until Frank started moaning, and didn't let up until she screamed Alex's name. Physically sated, they fell asleep in each other's arms.

CHAPTER FIFTEEN

Alex woke the next morning and stretched her arms above her head. She smiled at the slight soreness in her muscles and the smell of sex that still permeated the room. She roamed her hands down her chest and quietly gasped at the tenderness in her breasts and nipples, recalling how Frank nearly sucked them raw while fucking her hard the night before.

Of the many lovers Alex had enjoyed over the years, Frank seemed to be the most attuned to her body, her likes and dislikes. She really cared about Frank and was more than happy with the direction their relationship was heading. Relationship? Was that what this was? Their schedules didn't allow them to spend a whole lot of time together, but when they were able, they always had a good time. Right now they were keeping things light, but she had no desire to look elsewhere for companionship. Frank fulfilled Alex in many different ways. She was attentive, but not in a clingy sort of way. She appreciated that Frank opened the door for her, that she pulled out the chair for Alex to sit, that she made sure Alex was comfortable or if she needed anything. Frank was a true gentlewoman, a trait that was old-fashioned, but desperately needed to make a comeback in this seemingly self-absorbed society. Frank would be a perfect protagonist in the romance novels Jordan and Kirsten read incessantly before Aiden was born.

She turned her head to discover Frank looking at her with those unique amber eyes. "Good morning."

"Yes, it is. What were you thinking about? You had this faraway look in your eyes, but a grin on your beautiful lips."

"I was just thinking you would make a perfect character in a romance novel."

Frank laughed. "Seriously? Why do you think so?"

Alex turned to face Frank and cupped her cheek. "I was recalling how you open the door for me, pull out my chair. You know, those sorts of things. You're polite and have excellent manners, which is sorely lacking in today's world."

Frank turned her head and kissed Alex's palm. "You deserve to be treated with respect."

She smiled and her heart fluttered at Frank's declaration. "You see? That's what I mean. You know how to properly treat a woman. You're also the hottest woman I've ever seen, and this woman is going to make you breakfast in bed."

Alex started to get up when Frank pulled her back. "Hang on a minute. I want to say good morning properly."

They kissed passionately, but when Frank squeezed Alex's breast, she gasped and pulled away.

Frank looked alarmed. "What's wrong?"

"They're just tender from all of the attention you gave them last night."

"I'm sorry. I didn't realize I was so rough."

Alex leaned in and kissed her again. "It's okay, baby. Rough is exactly the way I wanted it last night, and you were perfect. You'll just have to take it easy on them today. Now, I'm going to make you a nice breakfast, then we'll take Bella to the park and let her chase the ball."

She went to the bathroom to clean up and wrapped herself in Frank's robe. She blew a kiss as she left the room and greeted Bella. "You go potty while I make you and your mama some breakfast." She left the sliding glass door open as she went about preparing the food. She placed the plates and some juice on a tray and returned to find Frank sitting up in bed, freshly showered, and looking all kinds of sexy sitting there naked, the sheet pooled at her waist and her wet black hair slicked back.

"Stop looking at me like that."

Frank leered. "Like what?"

"Like you want me for breakfast instead of the eggs and toast I slaved away on. Be a good girl and eat your food, then I'll see what I can do about dessert."

Frank held up her hands in mock surrender and took the tray from Alex to allow her to get back into bed. They made quick work of their breakfast so they could tend to more pressing matters. After they made love, they took a quick shower together and gathered Bella's supplies.

As the three of them strolled to a nearby park, Alex realized it had been a while since they'd gone to the park to play and she mentioned it to Frank. "The last time we went was the day I found out about Toni. Did you two play at the park often when you were kids?"

"Yes, there was a small park down the street from our house that had swings, slides, and a teeter-totter. One of the great things about being a twin was that we were the same size, which makes all the difference on the teeter-totter. I'm not sure if you were aware of that or not."

Alex smiled at Frank's childlike observation. "No, as a matter of fact, I wasn't aware of that. Who took you to the park?" From what Frank had told her about her parents, Alex couldn't imagine they were the ones to take Frank and Toni.

"Nobody. We went by ourselves. You have to remember it was a different time back then. It was safer. Besides, we lived in a safe neighborhood and you could see the park from our house."

Alex took Frank's hand and intertwined their fingers. She noticed the look of pain was absent from Frank's face this time when they talked about Toni. Maybe Frank needed to talk more about the good times they had so that could be her focus, and not her illness. Alex made a mental note to try to continue talking to Frank about her happy childhood memories. Those would probably have more to do with Frank's grandparents rather than her parents, but it might continue to ease Frank's hurt.

They arrived at the park and Alex sat in the shade as Frank threw Bella the ball. Alex pictured Frank and Toni swinging on the swings, competing to see who could go higher, chasing each other on grass, playing tag. She could feel her eyes moisten at the innocence of it all, the simpler times of two children playing before illness, abuse, and death set in.

"Toni, I feel like I'm getting to know you better with the stories Frank shares with me. I hope you're looking down and can see what an amazing woman your sister is. I really like her and care about her, and I promise to try to keep her safe if you'll do the same. I know she's really good at her job, but it can be so dangerous and I want to keep her around for a long time." Calm and warmth enveloped her, and she knew in her heart that Toni had heard her prayer.

Soon after, Frank and Bella returned to the shade and drank their water. The three of them lay down on the blanket and remained silent as they listened to the birds chirping and the leaves rustling from the breeze. Alex had never known such peace and contentment as she did right then.

CHAPTER SIXTEEN

Alex was back to work two days later after spending most of her free time with Frank. They'd had Jordan, Kirsten, and Aiden over for a barbecue once they'd returned from the park. Frank had a lovely backyard with lots of grass, and while they sat at the table talking, Aiden played with Bella. They laughed when Aiden tried to throw a tennis ball for Bella, accidentally hit her in the face, then patted her head and said something that sounded like "boo boo."

She was coming around a corner in the hospital when one of the other nurses going in the opposite direction ran into her left side. "Ouch!" Alex grabbed her left breast and winced in pain.

"Oh, Alex, I'm so sorry. Are you all right?"

"Yeah, I'm okay. What about you?"

"I'm fine. I'm so sorry. I was in a hurry and wasn't paying attention."

She felt bad and tried to lighten things up. "If you put my tits out of commission, Frank may come and arrest you."

The nurse laughed. "I don't play for your team, but if Frank wanted to use her handcuffs with me, I wouldn't object."

"Hey!" They burst out in laughter.

"So, things are going good for you two?"

"Yeah, they are. I'm so glad I got to know her and that we're seeing each other."

Nancy leaned in close and lowered her voice. "Is she as hot in the sack as she looks like she'd be?"

Alex looked around, leaned back in, and said, "Hotter."

The silent "oh" that formed on Nancy's mouth made Alex giggle. "Gotta go, Nance."

She continued down the hall on her way to the lab. She couldn't believe how tender her breast was still. It was weird that her right one felt fine. She tried to remember if the left breast got rougher or longer attention the other night, but she couldn't recall. It was possible that she was starting her period soon, but she would have to check her calendar later. That's probably what it was. At least her and Frank's work schedules conflicted for a few days and they wouldn't see each other again until Saturday. Frank loved to play with her breasts, and Alex loved it too. They were what she loved most about her body. They hadn't shown any effects of gravity; her areolas were light pink, and her nipples were small. She loved them kissed, nibbled, licked, and bit. She had come more than once with a skillful lover during breast play. In Alex's mind, her breasts were her womanhood.

She returned to the nurses' station with the lab reports and gave them to the doctor. She was about to accompany him to the patient's cubicle to give him the results when Frank walked through the door. Her body tingled at the sight of Frank in uniform striding toward her with her confident and commanding gait. She waved, then held up her finger to tell her she'd be back in a minute.

After the doctor gave the patient his results, Alex handed him a bag with his belongings and told him he was free to go. She ached to go see Frank, but when she got back to the nurses' station, she was gone.

"Hey, Nancy, did Frank leave?"

"No, she went to the cafeteria. I told her I'd send you down when you were done with that last patient."

"Great. I'll be back in about fifteen minutes."

"Take your time. I'll page you if anything urgent comes up."

Alex took the stairs as fast as she could, but the jarring of each step hurt her breast. She nearly forgot about the pain when she saw Frank sitting at a table with two cups of coffee. Frank sat facing the entrance because it was a cop thing to do. Frank had told her once when they were out to dinner that she preferred to be able to see the entrance, to see who was coming and going so she could be ready if anything was hinky. Their smiles were nearly simultaneous. She sat next to Frank and took her hand.

"Hi. What are you doing here?"

"I just stopped by to say hi."

"Just to say hi? There's no injured suspect or officer that you're checking on?"

"Nope. I missed you and wanted to see you."

"Frank." Alex shook her head and stood. It was times like this, when Frank said these things, that made her feel warm and fuzzy inside. "Come with me."

Frank tossed the coffees into the trash and followed Alex to the end of the hall and into an empty room.

When the door shut, Alex pinned Frank up against it and kissed her like their lives depended on it. Damn the Kevlar vest and duty belt. She wanted to feel her body pressed up against Frank's. She finally broke the kiss and they panted heavily.

"You are such a sweetheart."

"I'm not sweet. I'm a cop." The grin that tugged at the corner of Frank's mouth made Alex's body heat up.

"You're my sweet cop." She went back to work on Frank's mouth, loving the taste of peppermint on her breath. Frank reached up and squeezed Alex's left breast, making her break the kiss and inhale sharply.

"What?"

"Still sore."

"What? I wasn't that rough on Saturday night."

"I ran into one of the nurses coming around a corner a little while ago and her elbow hit it."

There was skepticism written all over Frank's face.

"And I think I'm about to start my period. They always get tender a few days before." She wrapped her arms around Frank's neck and kissed her again. "Really, baby, everything's fine."

Frank put her hands on Alex's waist and pulled her closer. "Okay, but be careful. They aren't my favorite thing about you, but they're high on the list."

"Roger that, Sarge." She checked her watch and frowned. "I gotta get back to work."

"Same here. I have bad guys to arrest."

"Be safe and watch your six."

"You do the same," Frank said as she swatted Alex's butt. "Talk to you later."

They headed off in different directions as they continued with their workdays. Alex again reminded herself to check her calendar when she got home.

CHAPTER SEVENTEEN

Alex ended up having to work the day shift on Saturday, so she packed an overnight bag that morning and drove directly to the basketball game after work. She hadn't had a chance to see Frank for most of the week and found herself missing her more as each day passed. They were only able to text each other, as they kept playing phone tag. She was really looking forward to getting reacquainted with Frank this weekend. Her left breast was still tender, but as long as Frank stayed away from it, there wasn't any reason they couldn't have a sex-filled marathon.

The game had already started by the time she arrived at the gym, but she quickly spotted Kirsten and Aiden in the stands. She sat next to Kirsten and greedily accepted Aiden into her arms. She nearly melted when Aiden threw his tiny arms around her neck and gave her a sloppy kiss. God, there was no such thing as a bad day when she got to see this kid.

"Hey, big boy. I missed you."

"Awa."

Stunned, Alex looked at Kirsten and asked, "Did he just say Alex?"

Kirsten smiled and nodded. "We've been telling him all day that he would get to see Auntie Alex tonight and he kept repeating it over and over. It would have driven me nuts if he didn't sound so adorable."

"Awa."

Alex felt the sting of tears form in her eyes and hugged Aiden closer, but when she felt the tenderness in her breast, she moved him off to the right side of her body. The discomfort was quickly forgotten when Aiden tried to say her name again. "You'll be talking up a storm in no time, huh, monkey? But don't you worry. When your moms start to get sick of it, you can come stay with me. I'll never tire of you saying my name."

Aiden pointed to the gym floor. "Mama."

"That's right. Your mama is playing basketball." She turned him around in her lap so they could watch the game. They cheered loudly when Frank hit a shot from the outside. The next time down the court, Frank drove to the basket and passed the ball to Jordan, who scored an easy lay-up.

"Damn, they play well together." Alex couldn't keep her eyes off Frank. It seemed everything about Frank fascinated her.

"That they do. I wish I could have seen them play against each other in college."

"Yeah, if I had met Frank back then, who knows what might have happened."

Kirsten patted Alex's knee. "So, things are going well then?"

She felt all warm inside and she smiled at the thought of their time together. "Very well. There are so many things about her that I admire and find sexy. I never thought I'd say this, but the day she pulled me over was one of the best days of my life."

"You didn't think so at the time. I couldn't believe the colorful language that came out of your mouth when you got to our house that day. I think I actually saw steam coming out of your ears."

Alex turned and winked at Kirsten. "Yeah, well, now my body's on fire for an entirely different reason."

Kirsten laughed. "Watch what you say." She pointed to Aiden. "He's really starting to jabber and seems to hear *everything*."

"Ha! Got it! Anyway, remember what I bought on our last shopping trip? Best. Purchase. Ever."

"Uh-huh. She was pleased with the lingerie?"

"Oh, yes. But she really turned the tables on me. I came out of the bathroom thinking I was going to tease her a little, but before I knew it, I was begging for her to—"

"Ahem."

She felt the warmth flood her face when Kirsten nodded in Aiden's direction. "Right. So, anyway, that had to be the hottest encounter I've ever had."

"Have you told her you love her yet?"

She turned to Kirsten in horror. "What? No. We're not there yet."

Kirsten rolled her eyes, which Alex decided to let go.

"Really? In the three-ish years I've known you, I've never seen you this excited over a woman. Jordan was saying the same thing the other day, and she's known you for almost fifteen years."

Alex turned her head to watch the game. After a minute, she turned back to Kirsten. "She said that?"

"Yep."

"Shit." Her hand flew to her mouth, and she shot Kirsten an apologetic look. "I really like her and care about her. We're having a great time, but honestly I don't think either one of us is there yet. I do think there's a legitimate shot at this turning into a long-term deal, though."

The buzzer sounded, indicating the end of the first half, which delayed any further talk about their relationship. She turned her focus to Frank, who looked so incredibly sexy with her soaking wet hair and rivulets of sweat running down her face, her chest, her arms. Damn, Alex never thought of sweat as an aphrodisiac, but she was realizing all kinds of crazy new things lately. She blew Frank a kiss when she looked her way that caused Frank to laugh and shake her head. Frank tried to act cool, especially around her teammates, but Alex knew she was treated to something different when they were alone. Oh, Frank was always cool, but when it was just the two of them, all bravado disappeared and she was just so sweet and attentive toward Alex. Yes, they most definitely had a good chance at making this a long-term relationship.

❖

Frank was on fire, not only with her play, but her body was set aflame when she saw Alex in the stands. As much as she loved playing basketball, she loved playing with Alex even more, and she wished the game would end quickly so they could go back to her place. She loved her job and playing ball, but she also loved spending time with Alex. Some days felt like torture when they couldn't see or talk with each other. They had lucked out that at least they had a couple of days off together, which she knew wouldn't always happen.

When the game finally ended, all she could think about was getting Alex home. The girls suggested going out for drinks later, but Frank really wasn't in the mood. She politely declined, then went to go greet Alex. Once Alex reached the last bleacher, she jumped into Frank's arms, nearly knocking her off her feet.

"You were great tonight."

"Thanks. Alex, I'm going to get you all wet with my sweaty clothes."

"Too late," Alex growled in her ear, eliciting a delicious shiver throughout her entire body. "I'm already wet just from watching you."

Frank lowered Alex to the ground but kept her arms around her waist. "The girls wanted to go out for drinks, but I told them we couldn't. Is that okay or do you want to go?"

Alex shook her head. "I'm actually tired from working today. I just want to go back to your place and lie in your arms."

"I was hoping you'd say that." She kissed the tip of Alex's nose. "I missed you."

Alex leaned back and looked deep into her eyes. She felt something pass between them, something that spoke to the depth of her soul. "I missed you too. Now go get your sweats on so we can go home."

Frank smiled. Home. She liked the sound of that. She quickly donned her sweats, said good night to Jordan and Kirsten, and then gave Aiden a high five before they left the gym.

They were once again greeted by a very excited, wiggly dog. Once the kisses and head pats ended, Frank said, "I'm going to go take a shower. I'll be right back."

"You go on and I'll take care of wiggle-butt here."

Frank laughed when Bella started to get excited again. "Okay. See you in a few."

Frank stripped off her soaked clothes as the water heated up. She stepped under the hot spray and let out a soft moan when she felt her body start to relax. She squirted the white citrus shower gel Alex seemed to love on a cloth and began to wash her body. She imagined Alex licking her, nibbling her, unable to get enough of Frank's taste. She didn't want to get too excited while in the shower. No, she wanted Alex to do that for her in bed. She turned off the water, toweled herself dry, and walked into the bedroom to find Alex under the sheets—naked.

The soft glow of the bedside lamp was the only light in the room, and it made Alex look like an angel.

Frank got into bed and scooted close to Alex when she turned on her side. She wrapped an arm around Alex's waist and pulled her closer until their bodies were flush. "Hi."

"Hi, yourself."

They brought their lips together in a gentle kiss, not in a rush to move things too quickly. As much as she loved sex with Alex, it was the quiet, intimate moments like this, the slow build, that led her to believe they were in it for the long haul, that their relationship was becoming more serious. The softness of Alex's lips invited her in for more kisses, each one more fevered than the last. She rolled Alex onto her back and covered Alex's body with her own. She caressed Alex's hip, slowly ascending until her hand reached the pliable flesh of Alex's breast, only to cause Alex to gasp and wince.

"Are you all right?" Frank kept her hand still, but it continued to cover Alex's breast.

"Still tender, baby, but the right one could use some attention."

Frank's eyebrows furrowed as she gently palpated Alex's left breast, sucking in a deep breath as she felt a bump on the outer part of the breast. She felt her entire body tremble as she looked into Alex's eyes. "I feel a lump." Her bottom lip trembled as she searched Alex's face for something, anything that could reassure her that this couldn't be what she thought it was.

She removed her hand as Alex brought hers to feel it. She pressed her fingers into the tissue, then stopped. "I feel it."

Tears stung Frank's eyes as she pulled Alex into a fierce hug and started pleading. "Please, God, no. Not now. Not her. Please."

"Hey, it's okay. Shh. Don't cry. I'm sure it's not what you're thinking. It's probably just a hematoma from when Nancy ran into me the other day." Alex took Frank's face in her hands and pulled her away far enough to look at her. "Really, honey, it's okay."

"I can't lose you."

"You're not going to lose me. I'm fine." Alex ran her fingers through Frank's hair, which normally relaxed her, but her hammering heart failed to slow. "I'll call my doctor on Monday and make an appointment to see her."

She took in a deep breath and nodded. She rolled off Alex and reached for a tissue to wipe her eyes and nose. She remained on her back and looked blankly at the ceiling. Alex slid closer and wrapped her arm around Frank's waist and kissed her cheek.

"Well, that was a buzzkill."

"That's not funny, Alex."

"It wasn't meant to be. I missed you this week and I was really looking forward to spending a nice, relaxing weekend with you, but then this happened." Alex pointed to her breast. "I'm not trying to downplay this, but let's look at a couple of things here. One, there's no history of breast cancer, hell, any cancer in my family. Two, I did get elbowed there earlier this week, and it would be a reasonable explanation to have a hematoma. But out of respect for you and Toni, I'm going to have it checked to ease your mind." Alex grabbed Frank's chin and made her look at Alex. "Okay?"

Frank nodded.

"Good. Now wrap your arms around me and act like you think I'm the sexiest woman you've ever seen."

Frank grinned and kissed Alex. "I don't have to act. You *are* the sexiest woman I've ever seen." She buried her face in Alex's neck and breathed in her scent. "I'm sorry I freaked out on you."

"Don't worry, baby. I understand. But like I said, I'm sure it's nothing. Now kiss me good night and close your eyes."

Frank let her lips linger on Alex's, hoping to convey the depth of her affection. She held Alex in her arms all night long, but sleep eluded her as she thought of all the possible scenarios, including worst-case. She offered up a silent prayer to God, to Toni, to her grandparents and anyone else that would listen for Alex to be healthy and live a long, happy life. And if Frank happened to be a part of it, all that much better.

❖

Alex woke to sunlight streaming through the blinds and Frank staring at her. She looked so sad, so worried that it nearly broke Alex's heart. She wished she could come up with something to say to ease the crease between Frank's eyebrows, but she knew the only way to bring peace to Frank was to have a healthy exam. She would have to try her best to take Frank's mind off her discovery until she could get in to see her doctor. She used her thumb to trace the dark circles under Frank's eyes. "Did you get any sleep last night?"

Frank shrugged and looked away. "Yes. No. Not much."

"Please try to not worry. I'm sure everything is fine."

"You can't ask me not to worry, Alex. I care about you and I don't want you to go through what my sister did."

"I appreciate that, but you're getting ahead of yourself. There's nothing we can do about it until I can see my doctor, so let's try and enjoy today. How about we take Bella to the dog beach? We can throw the ball for her, watch the surfers, and enjoy the sunshine."

"Are you sure? Don't you want to go see Jordan?"

"Why would you ask that?"

"Well, uh, I thought maybe you'd want to tell her."

Alex shook her head. "Why would I tell her before I knew anything? Look, I don't want to say anything to anyone, and I'd appreciate it if you didn't either." Alex turned away from Frank and started to get out of bed before Frank grabbed her arm to stop her.

"Wait. I promise not to say anything. Please don't go."

"I'm going to the bathroom. Just give me a minute."

Frank let her go and she locked the door behind her. She turned on the faucet and splashed warm water on her face. She wasn't quite sure if she felt bad for Frank or annoyed. She understood Frank's fear, with losing her sister to breast cancer. But it was like Frank had diagnosed her and given her a grim prognosis. She wasn't stupid. She knew she could possibly have the disease, but it was likely it was something less serious. Even if it was cancer, she was young and healthy and would fight hard to beat it.

She looked at her reflection in the mirror and stared until the fear in her eyes turned into determination. She opened the door to find Frank and Bella sitting on the bed looking in her direction.

"Bella said going to the beach was a great idea and she's all for it. Do you still want to go?"

Alex kissed each one on the top of her head. "I'd love to. Let me get dressed."

"We'll go get her stuff and meet you at the car."

The drive to the beach was relatively quiet until they were just a few blocks away, then Bella whined and wagged her tail in anticipation. Once they reached the sand, Frank released the leash and threw a ball down the shore, sending Bella in a full-out sprint to retrieve it. The smell of the salt water and sound of the waves crashing to shore eased the tightness in Alex's chest that she'd felt since the previous night. She grabbed Frank's hand and interlocked their fingers. The gentle squeeze Frank gave her released a little more tension from her tight muscles, and she began to relax. Their stroll along the shore was intermittently delayed when Bella would drop her ball at Frank's feet and wait for the next throw.

After they went about a mile down the beach, they agreed to take a rest and spread out a towel to sit on. Frank guided her arm around Alex's shoulders and pulled her closer. "I'm sorry about this morning."

Alex snuggled in and rested her head on Frank's shoulder. "It's okay. I just don't want to worry Jordan and Kirsten unnecessarily. If, and that's a big if, there's something wrong, I'll tell them. But everything is going to be fine, so let's just enjoy the day, all right?"

"You're the boss."

Alex laughed and slapped Frank's stomach. "That's right and don't you forget it." She sifted the flour-like sand through her fingers repeatedly, loving the softness against her skin. "Do you know what I'd love to do?"

"Tell me."

"Go back home, get into bed, and cuddle. Can we do that?"

Frank kissed the side of her head. "There's nothing that I'd rather do more."

They stood and brushed the sand off their shorts, headed back to Frank's truck, and spent the rest of the day wrapped in each other's arms.

CHAPTER EIGHTEEN

A lex tried to stay positive, but as each day passed, she felt the worry set in. She was finally able to get in to see her primary doctor on Thursday afternoon. She was led to an exam room and a nurse took her vitals, all of which were normal. She had been seeing Dr. Cummings since her early twenties, and in the age of treat-and-street appointments that lasted no more than five minutes, Alex appreciated the time her doctor took with her. She was always unhurried and very thorough with her exams.

"We don't usually see you more than once or twice a year, Alex, and since you just had a physical a few months ago, what brings you here today?"

Alex took a deep breath, trying to calm the fluttering in her stomach. "I found a lump in my left breast and wanted to get it checked out. I'm sure it's nothing, but I'd rather be safe than sorry."

The nurse took her hand and squeezed. "I'm sure it's nothing too, sweetie. Put this lovely paper gown on with it open in the front and Dr. Cummings will be in in just a few minutes."

The nurse quietly closed the door, and Alex continued to take deep breaths. She fiddled with the flimsy paper gown while she sat on the edge of the exam table. Finally, there was a knock on the door and the doctor entered and pulled up a stool. The glasses perched on her nose always reminded Alex more of a librarian than a family physician.

"Hi, Alex. Dori told me you felt a lump in your breast. Are you having any other symptoms?"

"Hi, Dr. Cummings. It's tender to the touch. A couple of weeks ago, a coworker accidentally bumped into me, and I think she elbowed me in that location. The lump or tenderness hasn't gone away."

"When did you notice the lump?"

"A few days after that. My lover felt it last Saturday night while we were making love."

Dr. Cummings looked up from her tablet and winced. "I bet that killed the mood."

Alex laughed, pleased that she had such a great relationship with her doctor. "You have no idea."

The doctor tapped the screen a few times. "It says in your file that there's no history of breast cancer in your family."

"That's right."

"Lie back and let me take a look." Dr. Cummings palpated around the breast and areola and pinched the nipple during the exam. The doctor's fingers stopped when they found the lump, then resumed the movement. "Well, you're only thirty-two with no history of breast cancer, so I'm sure it's nothing. Just keep an eye on it and if it gets bigger, come back and see me." The doctor started to stand, but sat back down when Alex raised her hand.

"I want you to refer me for a mammogram."

"Alex, I don't think—"

"Dr. Cummings, you know I'm a nurse and know all about the odds of this being cancer. But my lover lost her twin sister to breast cancer when they were just twenty-nine years old. She's very worried and I'd like to get the mammogram to ease her mind. Please."

Dr. Cummings nodded. "All right. I'll have Dori call down to the breast center on the first floor and see if they have any openings. You can put your shirt back on, but wait here until Dori comes back, okay?"

"Thank you."

Alex had just finished buttoning her blouse when the nurse knocked and entered. "Hey, sweetie. The breast center had a cancelation and has an opening in an hour. There's a coffee stand outside if you want to grab something before your appointment."

"Thanks, Dori, I appreciate it."

The nurse handed Alex the referral slip. "Try not to worry, okay? I'll keep positive thoughts for you."

She nodded and followed her down the hall to the door. She stepped outside into the warm sunshine and ordered a bottle of water from the coffee vendor. What she really wanted was a drink to calm her frayed nerves. She took her water and sat on a nearby bench. She looked to the sky and let the sun beat down on her face. She pulled her phone out of her purse and texted Frank that she was getting a mammogram in an hour, but that her doctor didn't think it was anything serious.

A text came back immediately. *I'll be right there.*

No, don't leave work. They're just doing the test, but I won't get the results right away.

Are you sure? I want to be there for you.

I'm sure. I'll be done before your shift ends so I'll just meet you at your place.

Copy that. See you tonight.

Alex turned off her phone and went for a short walk. She tried to clear her mind of any negative thoughts, and after about fifteen minutes, all she thought about was the white noise of traffic on a nearby street and the birds chirping in the trees. She kept the negative thoughts at bay until she entered the breast center. The wave of trepidation stopped her in her tracks. She took another deep breath and squared her shoulders before making her way to the registration desk. An elderly woman looked up and smiled.

"May I help you?"

"Yes, my name is Alex Taylor and Dr. Cummings called down for my appointment a little while ago."

"Of course. I'll need an ID and your insurance card." She handed her a clipboard with a stack of papers. "I'll need you to fill these out, please."

Alex took the papers and sat in the only free chair between an older man and middle-aged woman. She set about the mundane task of completing her paperwork, then returned them to the woman at the desk. She collected her insurance and ID cards and returned to her seat. She looked at every woman in the waiting room, ranging between forty and eighty years old. She wondered if any of them had felt a lump in their breasts or if they were there for a routine exam. She picked up a magazine and idly flipped through the pages, not being able to focus on any one article. After what felt like a lifetime, she was called back and led to another waiting room that had changing stalls, lockers, and chairs.

"Take off your shirt and bra and place them in this locker." The woman handed her a key and a wipe. "You can use this to clean the deodorant off your skin, then put this gown on so it can open in the front. When you're done, you can have a seat and someone will be with you shortly."

Alex thanked her and closed the door to the stall. She unbuttoned her blouse, unhooked her bra, and hung them from the hook in her locker. She was tempted to feel her breast, search for the lump that brought her to this place, but she resisted. She put on the gown and tied it at her side before she went to sit and wait some more. She didn't wait long before another woman dressed in pink scrubs came in.

"Are you Alex?"

She nodded and stood.

"I'm Jill and I'll be doing your mammogram. Is this your first?"

"Yes," Alex squeaked out.

"Since your doctor detected a lump, we're going to do a diagnostic mammogram and ultrasound. Once that's done, the tests will be read and a doctor will come in to give you the results."

"Today?"

"Yes. If they don't find anything then you won't need another exam for a while."

"And if they do find something?"

"The doctor will discuss further plans."

Alex's legs trembled and she staggered down the hall.

Jill stopped when Alex did. "Are you all right? Do you need to sit down?"

Alex shook her head slightly. "No, I'm just nervous."

"Just take some deep breaths for me."

She barked out a laugh devoid of humor. "I've been taking so many deep breaths today, I may hyperventilate." She took another deep breath and let it out slowly. "Okay, let's get this over with."

She followed Jill into a room that had a strange-looking machine in the far corner.

"Let me just enter some information into the computer and we'll get started. I want to warn you that this will be more uncomfortable than if we were doing a screening mammo. We'll have to compress the tissues more with the diagnostic test."

"Great." This was not what she wanted to hear.

Jill stepped out from the protective barrier and approached Alex. "Go ahead and untie your gown while I get the machine set up."

She untied the strings, and her gown fell open, causing her to wrap her arms around her chest. She had never been a modest woman, but she had never in her life felt so exposed.

"Step closer. I'm going to place your left breast on this tray and move the top tray down to compress it."

Jill took her left breast in her cold hands and delicately placed it on the bottom tray. Before it was even smashed, Alex could feel a tear leak out of the corner of her eye. She knew she shouldn't be, but she felt incredibly humiliated. She didn't know she would get the results today, and now she fervently wished Frank was here to hold her hand, to wipe away the tears that she knew would continue to fall. Instead, there was some woman named Jill who was wearing scrubs the color of Pepto-Bismol, handing her a tissue.

"I'm sorry, Alex. I promise this will all be over soon. I want you to take a deep breath and hold it while I take the picture."

She did as she was told. Jill had promised her this would be over soon, but she didn't promise her a negative study, that she would go home tonight with a clean bill of health. After a few more images from different angles, Alex shoved the troublesome breast back into the gown and followed Jill to another room with an exam table and ultrasound machine.

"Diane will be with you in a few minutes to do your ultrasound." Jill led her to the table and held her hand as she sat down, holding her steady. "Why don't you lie down and close your eyes? Try to think good thoughts."

Alex lay down on the table and closed her eyes as Jill suggested. Frank, Jordan, Kirsten, and Aiden flooded her mind. She envisioned all of them at a park on a blanket, talking and laughing while Aiden chased Bella. The sky was deep blue with a few clouds that looked like cotton balls. The canopy of leaves from a tree they were sitting under offered them protection from the blistering sun. Her daydream was interrupted by yet another woman in the drab pink scrubs.

"Hi, Alex, I'm Diane and I'll be doing your ultrasound." Diane keyed in some information on her computer and powered up the machine before bringing it to her left side. "I'm going to open your gown and squeeze some gel onto your breast, then I'm going to move this transducer over the area."

An image popped up on a screen, but Alex didn't know what to look for. She'd never dealt with this type of imaging on a breast in the ER, and she felt inept. Shouldn't she know what she was seeing? It all just looked like blobs on the screen, and she thought of images psychiatrists would show their patients. God, she wished Frank was here with her.

Before she knew it, Diane was wiping the gel off her breast and telling her the doctor would be in soon to go over the results. She wanted to text Frank, even Jordan. She needed reassurance. She needed to be told that she would be okay. But her phone was in the fucking locker. She pounded her fists on the padded table and felt the tears fill her eyes. She swiped at them, but they continued to fall. She sat up to look for some tissue when there was another knock at the door. A different woman in a white lab coat came in and handed her some tissues from a box on the ultrasound tray.

"Ms. Taylor, I'm Dr. Nguyen."

Alex shook the hand that was offered her. The doctor pulled up a stool, sat, and crossed her legs. She was wearing a skirt that hiked up her thigh when she crossed her legs, and Alex would have normally found that sort of thing sexy, but there was absolutely nothing sexy about this entire day. She had come across a few different women who had touched and handled her breast. Frank should be the only one touching her breasts. Frank would lovingly fondle and worship her breasts as only a lover should. She now felt violated and wondered if she would ever enjoy having her breasts touched again.

"I reviewed your tests and a mass was detected. It doesn't mean that the mass is cancer, but I want you to get a biopsy so we can be certain. I want you to have a core needle biopsy because it takes a larger piece of tissue."

Alex held up her hands and shook her head. "No. No. I can't take anymore. This can't be happening. I'm only thirty-two years old."

The doctor handed her some more tissues and placed her hand on Alex's knee. "Ms. Taylor, the sooner we know what we're dealing with, the sooner we can start to treat it. We can do the biopsy right here and now."

Her entire body went numb, and she swallowed the bile that was quickly ascending her throat. She didn't know what to do. She didn't have anyone there with her. This was supposed to be just a simple exam to put Frank's mind at ease. Frank. Jesus. How was she going to tell her? She already went through so much with her sister. Now she was going to have to deal with this. Would Frank be able to handle her being sick? Fuck. She didn't know what to do.

"Ms. Taylor. Alex. I really think you need to have this done. We can call someone to come be with you."

Alex thought about it, but her people, Frank, Jordan, and Kirsten, were all at work, and it would take too long for them to get there. She just wanted it over with so she could go home, crawl into bed, and pull the covers over her head. "Do I need a ride home after the procedure?"

"No. We'll use a local anesthetic to numb the area. We can do it right here and get it sent to the pathology lab. Since it's Thursday afternoon, you'll probably get the results on Monday."

"Monday? I have to wait all weekend, pretend to go on with my life as usual? Like everything's fine?" Alex's voice rose and her body shook. How could she wait three fucking days to get the results?

"I know, and I really wish we could know something today, but we have to send it to an outside lab. I'll put a rush on it, but Monday will be the earliest."

Alex waved her hand in the air and blew out a forced breath. "Fine. Just do it now." She just wanted to go home.

"Lie down and I'll be back in a few minutes."

She covered her face with her hands and squeezed her eyes shut. She would do anything to make this day go away.

Dr. Nguyen returned with Diane and some needles. She injected Alex's breast with lidocaine and got set up as they waited for the area to numb. The doctor inserted the needle into the lump, but all Alex felt was pressure. Because the lump was palpable, Diane didn't need to use the ultrasound to guide the needle. Alex flinched when she heard a click.

"That's the needle and sampling instrument getting the tissue. We'll do this six times to make sure we get a sufficient sample."

Alex stared blankly at the ceiling as the doctor continued to take the tissue—her tissue. She tried to remove herself from the room and return to her happy place at the park, but within a few minutes, the doctor and Diane were helping her sit up. The doctor placed a small, round, flesh-colored Band-Aid at the site of the intrusion.

"Okay, Alex, we're all done for today. Are you sure there's nobody we can call for you?"

Alex shook her head and continued to stare into space.

Dr. Nguyen placed her hand on Alex's shoulder. "We'll call you when we get the results."

Diane led her back to the room that held her clothes and purse. She was in a daze as she slowly dressed and left the office. She managed to find her way back to her car and was relieved no one was around when she vomited into the bushes. Beads of sweat broke out on her face from the exertion and she tried to wipe them away. She waited until she was sure nothing more would come up, then she took a swig of her water, swished it around her mouth, and spat it out. Her hands shook when she tried to unlock her car. It took a couple of attempts, but she was finally able to get in. She pounded her fists against the steering wheel, then gripped it tightly as she let out a wracking sob. She wasn't sure how long it took for the tears to stop and her body to stop shaking, but she finally felt she had a little more control. As if on autopilot, she was finally able to drive herself home.

Frank arrived home after shift and was surprised Alex's car wasn't in the driveway. She said she'd meet her there after work, didn't she? She scrolled through the last text she had from Alex and it did say she would meet Frank at her house. She sent off a quick text to Alex letting her know she was home. She went inside and played with Bella for a little while before starting dinner. She realized she'd been home for thirty minutes and hadn't heard back from Alex. She called Alex and it went straight to voice mail. That was odd. Could she still be at her appointment? Maybe she got called in to work, but she was sure Alex would've at least texted her to let her know. She left a message for Alex to call her. She thought about calling Jordan to see if she'd heard from Alex, but decided against it.

By the time dinner was ready, she still hadn't heard from Alex.

It wasn't like her to be so quiet, and Frank felt dread in the pit of her stomach. She made another call, this time to her friend Julie, who would look after Bella sometimes. "Hey, it's me. Would you mind taking Bella for the night? I was expecting Alex over an hour ago and I haven't heard from her. I have a feeling something's wrong and I need to go look for her."

"Of course. I'll be over in half an hour. Let me know what you find out."

"I will, Jules. Thanks."

She grabbed her keys and wallet, said good-bye to Bella, and hastily left her house. She sat in her truck for a moment to organize a game plan. She closed her eyes and rubbed her forehead, trying to focus on what should be her first move. She decided to go by Alex's house first, then, if she wasn't there, swing by Jordan's.

Frank hadn't been to Alex's all that often since she had Bella at home, but she'd gone over for dinner a few times or swung by to pick her up for a date. Alex lived in a two-story townhome about twenty minutes from where she lived. Driving through the city had never taken so long. At least it seemed like an eternity for Frank. She drove these streets repeatedly while on shift and knew them like the back of her hand. Even though she was taking a shortcut, it seemed interminable.

She was relieved and worried when she pulled up and saw Alex's car in her parking space. She wondered how long Alex had been home and why she didn't answer. Her heart thudded through her chest as she thought Alex might be in some sort of danger. She unlocked her glove box, removed her gun, and took off in a full sprint to Alex's door. She was thankful they had enough sense to give each other a key to their respective homes "in case of an emergency." Frank keyed the lock quietly and entered Alex's home with her gun at her side. The house was dark, and it took a moment for Frank's eyes to adjust. She stealthily made her way up the stairs and down the hall toward Alex's bedroom, where she found the door wide open and Alex lying in a fetal position on her bed. She flicked the safety lever on her gun and placed it on the dresser before she slowly approached her. Her heart continued to race, and she found it difficult to catch her breath.

"Alex? Baby?"

"Go away," Alex mumbled.

Frank stopped. "What's going on?"

"Please, Frank, just go."

Frank took another step closer and stopped again when Alex turned over, away from her. "Honey, you're scaring me. Please tell me what's wrong. What happened?"

Alex began crying, ragged breaths echoing through the silent room, and Frank closed the gap between them in two long strides. She sat on the edge of the bed and rubbed her hand along Alex's back.

"They did a diagnostic mammogram and ultrasound. The doctor said I had a mass and did a biopsy."

Frank had a hard time understanding what Alex said. The words were halting between gasps of breath while she sobbed. She stopped moving her hand and her eyes filled with tears. "Is it cancer?"

Alex cried harder but didn't answer Frank's question. Frank lay down behind her and wrapped her arms around Alex. She didn't let go even when Alex's body stiffened from the contact. This wasn't the time to lose her shit. She needed to be strong for Alex, needed—no, wanted—to comfort her, soothe her, take care of her. "I'm here, baby. I'm here. Everything's going to be all right."

Alex pulled out of Frank's arms and started pacing. "How can you say that? You don't know that I'll be all right."

Frank stood and approached Alex. "I do know. I can't lose you. I love—"

"Don't! Don't say it, Frank," Alex pleaded as she held up her hand and took a step back.

Frank held up her hands in surrender but took a step, then another toward Alex. "Okay, I won't say it. Not yet anyway. But please don't push me away. Let me help you. I want to be here for you."

Alex's legs gave out, and Frank lunged and caught Alex, preventing her from falling to the floor. She picked her up and carried her to bed. When Alex crawled under the covers, Frank kicked out of her shoes and took off her pants, opting to remain in her shirt. She got into bed, lifted her arm, and was relieved when Alex moved closer and snuggled up against her side. She peppered kisses all around her head and held her tight. "I promise to take care of you, Alex. I'll do anything you need."

The deep, even breathing coming from Alex told her she wouldn't be receiving an answer. Silently, she pleaded, "Please, Toni, keep an eye out for Alex. She's very special to me and I can't lose her. Losing you nearly killed me, and I don't think I have it in me to go through it twice. I love her and I'll do everything in my power to keep her safe." Frank fell asleep with the feeling that another set of arms was wrapped around her like a security blanket.

❖

"Frank, try not to worry about Alex."

Frank saw Toni sitting next to her on the bed and felt her hand in her sister's hand. "Toni?"

"Hey, sis. I want you to know that she's going to be okay. She'll have a fight ahead of her, but you two are going to live a long, happy life. Just make sure you're there for her. Let her vent her frustrations, let her yell, let her cry, and make her laugh."

"I tried to do that for you, Toni, but it didn't help. You left me."

"I know, honey, but it wasn't because of anything you did or didn't do. I was too afraid to go see the doctor when I first felt the lump. I foolishly thought that if I ignored it, it wasn't really there. But Alex caught it."

"I'm afraid, Toni. I don't want to lose her."

"I promise you won't. Not to say you two won't have your ups and downs, but you'll have a full life together. By the way, nice job. She's perfect for you."

"I think so too. And I'm so glad you're able to watch over us."

"I'm watching, sis. But I have to go now. I'm doing important things up here. Nonna and Nonno wanted me to tell you to behave yourself. We love you and we're always here with you."

Frank opened her eyes, and they felt like grit from sandpaper. She was exhausted from the emotional night before.

She wanted more time with her sister, even if it was just through dreams. When Toni came to her deep in the night, she was beautiful and healthy, like she was before the cancer had ravaged her body. In the end, Frank had barely recognized the one woman she had spent her whole life with, but the woman who came to her at night was the face she recognized when she looked in the mirror.

She felt Alex start to stir, and it brought her back to the present.

Alex looked at her with red, puffy eyes and put her head back on Frank's chest.

"I got snot all over your shirt last night."

Frank squeezed her tight. "I don't mind. I like everything about you—even your snot."

"We should probably talk about what happens next."

Frank cupped her chin to get Alex to look at her. "We wait for the biopsy results, then we go from there. That's what happens next."

"But what if it's cancer?"

"What if it's not?"

"Frank, I don't want you to have to go through this again. We haven't been together very long, and if you want to call it quits, I'll understand. No hard feelings."

Frank was speechless. Even though she believed Alex's words were sincere, they cut her to the core. She got out of bed and roughly pulled on her pants. She began pacing around the room, running her fingers through her hair in disbelief, stopping occasionally to look at Alex, who was watching her.

"What kind of asshole do you think I am? Do you think so little of me, that I would look for a way out?" Frank said.

"I didn't mean—"

"Stop, Alex. I haven't been with you for the past few months just so we could have sex. If you were just some woman I liked to have in my bed, I wouldn't have come looking for you last night. I was attracted to you the first moment I laid eyes on you, but you've come to mean a lot to me. I"—*love you*—"care about you, and I thought you cared about me."

Alex crawled to the edge of the bed and knelt on her knees. "I do care about you, Frank, but I also know what you went through with Toni, and I was trying to spare you more pain…because I care about you."

She stepped closer and placed her hands on Alex's shoulders. "Then show me. Let me be here for you." The pressure in her chest eased slightly when Alex hugged her.

"I'd really like that."

"Good."

"I think I want to tell Jordan and Kirsten today. I could use all the positive vibes and emotional support I can get."

"Okay. Would you like me to go with you?"

The sad look on Alex's face when she nodded made Frank want to cry, but she held her tears in check. She leaned down and kissed Alex. "Good. Let me call Julie and let her know our plans. She came and got Bella last night, and I want to let her know I found you."

Alex hugged her. "I'm sorry I worried you. I just wanted to be alone, but I'm glad you came to be with me last night."

"I was worried, but I was relieved you were safe."

"I'm going to take a shower. Call Julie and start the coffee, will you? I need all the caffeine I can get this morning."

"On it. Take your time."

After she finished her call and brewed the coffee, she began making breakfast. She wasn't that hungry and wasn't sure if Alex felt like eating, but they needed to get something in their stomachs. She had their coffee and food on the table by the time Alex emerged from her bedroom. The sight of her made Frank's stomach clench. Alex looked so small and fragile and young dressed in her oversized T-shirt and pajama bottoms with her wet hair combed back. She pulled the chair out for Alex to sit. "I made us some breakfast."

Alex gave her a sad smile. "I'm not hungry."

"I'm not either, but we have to try and eat. Just take a few bites of the toast at least. We can put the eggs in a storage container and you can eat them some other time."

Alex took a small bite of her toast, as did Frank. They each managed to make it through one slice as they sipped their coffee.

"I sent Jordan a text asking if we could come over. She said they'd be home all day, but I told her we'd be there within the hour if that's okay. I want to get this over with."

"Sure. Let's swing by my house so I can take a quick shower and change into some clean clothes. You go get dressed and I'll clean up the kitchen."

Frank got the dishes washed and dried, then retreated to Alex's room. She found her standing in front of her mirror, naked, touching her breast as a tear fell down her cheek. She quickly crossed the room and stood behind Alex, wrapping her arms around her waist. Their eyes met in the mirror. "We'll get through this."

Alex nodded and stepped out of Frank's embrace. She went over to her chest of drawers and removed the clothes she'd wear. She pointed to Frank's gun, which she had placed there the night before. "What's with that?"

"I didn't know what I'd be walking into last night, if you were in trouble, so I brought it in as backup."

"I'm sorry."

"Don't be. I'm just glad you were safe. Come on, get dressed."

They left the house ten minutes later, and it only took another ten for Frank to shower and dress before driving over to Jordan and Kirsten's.

Jordan answered the door and looked at them both before asking, "What's wrong?"

Alex hugged her, then Frank. "Geez, that's some way to greet your best friend. Where's your better half?"

"She's putting Aiden down for a nap."

Alex looked at her watch. "Isn't it a little early for one?"

"Normally, but he was up all night with chest congestion, which means we were up too. I'm glad we have Fridays off so we can take a nap later. Now, what's wrong?"

"I'd rather wait to tell you when Kirsten is here."

Alex ducked into the kitchen, and when Jordan looked at Frank, she just shrugged, not wanting to give anything away. Alex returned with four bottles of water as Kirsten sat next to Jordan on the couch. Alex took a seat next to Frank on the love seat across from them and reached for Frank's hand.

The anxious eyes on her made Alex's pulse race, and she decided to dive right in and not stop until she finished her story. "I found a lump in my left breast last weekend. Yesterday, I saw my doctor, who didn't think it was anything to worry about, but I asked her for a mammogram anyway. The breast center was able to fit me in an hour later, and with the mammo and ultrasound, the doctor saw a mass and biopsied it. I'll get the results on Monday." The words came out so quickly, she had to remember to breathe. The silence that filled the room was deafening, and Jordan and Kirsten stared at her with their mouths open, speechless.

Jordan blinked, then cleared her throat and shook her head. "Um, what?"

Kirsten grabbed Jordan's hand and placed her other hand over her mouth, apparently still not knowing what to say. This was why Alex didn't want to tell them right away, at least not until she got the results.

But she needed her friends, especially today. She had her meltdown last night and a little more this morning, but now was the time to put on her brave face and help Jordan and Kirsten through this shocking news.

"I know this isn't what you expected me to say, and I didn't want to tell you until I had a diagnosis, but I really need some positive juju from you guys."

Jordan moved over to her, extended her hand, and helped Alex stand. She embraced her tightly. "Anything you need, we'll give you. I love you and we'll deal with anything that comes along."

"I love you too, Jordan." She looked over to Kirsten, who was now crying, and held out her hand to invite Kirsten into the hug. Alex felt immensely better, even stronger, with the unconditional support she'd received from these three women.

They returned to their seats and they all wiped their eyes and laughed.

"Christ, Al, you sure know how to be a Debbie Downer."

That made Alex laugh harder. They said laughter is the best medicine, and with Jordan and Kirsten, she might overdose. "This is nothing. Frank found the lump last Saturday night while she was—"

Jordan and Kirsten nearly burst when Frank slapped her hand over Alex's mouth. "Um, honey, TMI."

Kirsten giggled. "Oh, Frank, if you're going to hang around us, you're gonna have to lighten up. There are no secrets between us."

Alex took pity on Frank when she turned a deep shade of red. She cupped her cheek and gave her a chaste kiss. "Okay, ladies, she's still a work in progress, but she'll eventually get there. For now, we'll try to keep the embarrassment to a minimum."

"I'd appreciate it."

They spent the rest of the day making each other cry from laughter rather than sadness, offering up the emotional support Alex would need to get through this journey. She wasn't looking forward to telling her family, but decided to wait until she got the results. She didn't feel the need to worry them so soon. Until then, she had her family of choice to help her through.

Chapter Nineteen

Alex went to work Monday morning as if it were going to be a regular day. She hadn't slept well all weekend, but in her restless nights, she was somewhat comforted by being held in Frank's arms. They were both quiet as they dressed for work that morning, and Bella stuck by Alex's side as if she knew what was wrong. Alex kissed Frank good-bye and said she'd call her later. During a break in her day, Alex went to her locker to check her phone. She had texts from Frank and Jordan, and a voice mail from the breast center. Her hand shook and her heart raced as she stared at the phone number that taunted her. She took a deep breath as she lifted the phone to her ear to listen to the message.

"Hi, Ms. Taylor. This is Barbara from the breast center. Dr. Nguyen asked me to call you and schedule an appointment to discuss your biopsy results. Please give us a call at your earliest convenience."

Alex sat in a chair and lowered the phone to her lap. She felt her body go numb and her vision blur with the tears that filled her eyes. If the biopsy had been negative, they would have told her over the phone instead of asking her to come in to speak to the doctor. She had cancer. She just knew it. She dropped her head and allowed the tears to fall. She had to call Frank. No, she had to call the breast center to make an appointment.

Frank would probably want to go with her. God, how was Frank going to take the news? She had been a rock for Alex over the weekend, but Alex was worried if Frank would be strong enough to go through this again. Alex cared deeply for Frank and wanted to spare her the pain of reliving what she went through with Toni. What was she going to tell her parents? Alex thought of Aiden. She wanted to be there with him as he achieved every milestone.

She wiped the tears from her face and took a few deep breaths before dialing the number for the breast center.

"Thank you for calling the breast center. This is Barbara. How may I help you?"

Alex cleared her throat. "This is Alex Taylor returning your call."

"Oh, yes, Ms. Taylor. Thank you for calling back."

Like I had a choice.

"Dr. Nguyen would like you to come in and discuss your biopsy results. She has an opening tomorrow morning at ten thirty if you can make it."

Alex appreciated the calm, businesslike tone of Barbara's voice. This couldn't be an easy part of her job, calling people to basically tell them they had cancer without actually telling them. "Yes, ten thirty is fine. Um, would it be okay if I brought my girlfriend?"

"Of course. We'll see you tomorrow."

Alex hung up and was about to text Frank when the charge nurse came in the lounge.

"Alex, are you all right?"

"No, Val, I'm not. I need to talk to you."

Valerie sat next to Alex with concern in her eyes. "What is it?"

"I found a lump in my breast and had it biopsied on Thursday. I just got a call that the doctor wants to see me tomorrow. That can only mean one thing."

"Oh, Alex, I'm so sorry."

"Thanks. I'll need tomorrow off from work."

"Of course. Don't worry about it. I'll take care of getting your shift covered. Why don't you take the rest of today off? I can call in a float nurse."

"I appreciate that. I don't think I'd be much good today, but I'll be back on Wednesday."

Valerie gave Alex a warm, comforting hug, and Alex allowed herself to lean into Valerie's body.

"Take the time you need. We're family here, Alex. We'll have your back and help you fight this."

Alex had difficulty finding her voice and instead just nodded. Once she regained her composure and Val left her alone, she texted Frank to tell her about the appointment and that she was taking the rest of the day off. She told her she would come over later that night. She gathered her things from her locker and slipped out of the ER unnoticed. She liked her coworkers but wasn't ready to talk to them or let them know what was happening just yet. She trusted Valerie to keep her secret for now. She'd learned Val was the queen of discretion, which wasn't all that common in the hospital.

Alex drove home wondering what she would do for the rest of the day. She decided it was time to go tell her parents but wasn't sure what exactly she would say. Alex was an only child, and they had always been close. Not a day went by that Alex didn't feel loved and protected by her parents, and she knew she wouldn't feel any less protected when she told them her news.

Alex took a shower when she got home and stood under the hot spray in an effort to get her tight muscles to loosen up. After she got dressed, she packed an overnight bag and called her mom.

"Hi, Mom. I was wondering if you and Dad were free."

"Hi, honey. We're just finishing up some yard work. What's going on?"

"I need to tell you and Dad some news, so I wanted to make sure you're free. Can I come over?"

"Of course. Are you all right, honey?"

Alex could feel the tears well in her eyes and a lump form in her throat. "No, Mom, I'm not, but I will be. I'll be right over."

"Okay, Alex. You be careful. I love you."

"Love you too, Mom. See you soon."

Alex's entire body trembled as she drove to her childhood home. Her parents bought their home almost forty years ago when they were first married. She spent her first twenty-three years of life in that home until she was making enough money to move out and get a place of her own.

Alex pulled into her parents' driveway, and as she made her way to the front door, her parents stood there with a look of fright on their faces. Alex burst into tears when she saw them and ran the last ten feet into their waiting arms. They stood in the doorway huddled together, and Alex felt herself gathering strength from the two strongest people she'd ever known, her real-life heroes.

Her dad's deep, soothing voice broke up the emotional scene. "Let's go sit down and you can tell us what's going on."

They went into the living room, and Alex sat between her mom and dad, holding their hands, gathering the courage to tell her parents she was sick.

"Mom, Dad, I have a lump in my breast." Neither of her parents spoke, allowing Alex to continue. "I had a biopsy on Thursday afternoon and the doctor called me today to say she wanted me to come in tomorrow."

Her mother spoke up. "What are you saying, honey?"

"Come on, Mom. You're a retired nurse. You know if it wasn't serious, they would have told me over the phone. I'm pretty sure when I go see the doctor tomorrow, she's going to tell me I have breast cancer."

"Maybe," her father cleared his throat when his voice broke, "maybe it's not cancer."

Alex squeezed his hand. She knew he wasn't that naïve, having been married to a nurse for almost forty years. He probably just couldn't bear to have his little girl sick. "Dad, I'll know for sure tomorrow, but I'm pretty sure that's the diagnosis."

"Honey, what time is your appointment? Would you like for us to go with you?"

"It's at ten thirty, and Frank is going with me. I promise to call you after the appointment."

"Are you sure?"

"Yeah, but I appreciate it."

"How are things going between you and Frank? And why haven't we met her yet?"

"Honestly, I wasn't sure how serious we were getting until the other night. I was supposed to meet her at her house Thursday night, but after my appointment at the breast center, I just wanted to be alone, so I went home. She got worried when I didn't answer her call or text, so she came and found me curled up on my bed crying my eyes out."

"Oh, baby." Her mother put her arm around Alex's shoulders and pulled her closer.

"She was so strong, trying to comfort me. The next morning, I told her if she didn't want to go through this again, we could call it quits with no hard feelings."

"Why would you say something like that?" her father asked.

"Her twin sister died from breast cancer a few years ago. Frank took care of her until she died. I just didn't want her to have to face this again."

"What did she say?"

Alex shrugged. "She put me in my place. Told me how much she cares about me, and if I cared about her too, then to let her be there for me."

Her father nodded. "She sounds like good people."

"She really is, Dad. She's kind, compassionate, and honorable. When she's in uniform, she has an air of authority about her, like she's in control of the situation and everything will be fine."

"Are you ready for her to meet us?"

"I am now. After this weekend, I realized that I have strong feelings for her and that we may have a future together."

"Why don't you two come for dinner on Saturday? I'd like to have a talk and find out her intentions toward you."

"Dad, I'm thirty-two and quite capable of choosing my own mate."

Her father pulled Alex into a warm embrace. "You may be thirty-two, young lady, but you're still my little girl. As your dad, it's my responsibility to protect you, no matter how old you are."

Alex laughed and squeezed her dad. "She's a police sergeant and carries a gun, Dad. She's quite capable of protecting me."

"Stop arguing with your father and just bring her to dinner."

"I promise. I'll ask her if she's free on Saturday." Alex looked at her watch and couldn't believe how late it was. Frank should be home. Alex hugged her parents. "I've gotta go and meet my girl now. I love you both so much."

"We love you too, honey. Call us after your appointment tomorrow."

"I promise."

Alex got in her car and texted Frank that she was on her way over. Maybe they could order dinner to be delivered. She was exhausted and just wanted to fall asleep in Frank's arms.

❖

Frank had hardly slept. When she got home from work the night before, she found Alex and Bella curled up on the couch together, seemingly in a different world. Alex was staring at the wall, running her hand over Bella's coat with Bella's head in Alex's lap. Frank blinked back her tears before she sat on the other end of the couch. They didn't speak much, just discussed the specifics of Alex's doctor's appointment. They went to bed, and Frank held Alex in her arms all night long. Frank wasn't sure if it was anxiety or not wanting to miss a moment of holding Alex that kept her awake. Maybe a little of both. She finally nodded off right before dawn.

When they both woke around seven thirty, they spent some intimate time kissing and cuddling. Frank sincerely hoped that Alex knew how she felt about her since Alex wouldn't let Frank actually say those three words. It seemed that Alex instinctually knew the words were about to come out of Frank's mouth, and she would shut them down with just a look. She supposed saying the words really didn't matter since she made sure to show Alex how she felt about her.

Unfortunately, this wasn't Frank's first time dealing with this illness. She was with her sister when she was given her diagnosis, through every imaginable treatment, and when Toni took her last breath in Frank's arms. Frank's greatest fear at that moment was that she would lose Alex too. She honestly didn't know if she would be able to go through that again. The treatment and disease didn't just affect the patient. As Toni's caregiver throughout the disease, it took its toll on Frank too, having to watch her sister suffer and not being able to do a damned thing about it. She had never felt so helpless in all her life, and she wasn't sure if she was strong enough to watch Alex suffer—to stand by and see the disease eat her away. Frank was going to find a way to make sure Alex came out of this alive and well. She had been waiting all her life for a woman like Alex to come along—a woman with a great sense of humor, who was aware of what Frank's job entailed, a woman who was every bit her equal, a woman she could spend the rest of her days loving. Frank barely survived when she lost Toni but didn't think she had it in her to survive losing Alex too.

They took their time getting ready, as if the longer they took, the longer they could delay the diagnosis. Frank could feel Alex trying to shut down, trying to pull away, but Frank wasn't going to allow her to do it. If she had to be strong for the both of them, then goddamn it, she would do it. The drive to the breast center was a long and quiet one. Although Alex seemed to be in her own world, Frank did her best to stay connected by reaching for Alex's hand and holding it in her lap. After they pulled into the parking lot, Frank turned off her truck and turned to Alex, cupping Alex's cheek in her hand.

"No matter what happens in there, you're strong and you have a lot of people who love you and will help you fight." Frank leaned closer and kissed Alex. When she pulled back, Alex nodded and opened the door.

CHAPTER TWENTY

Alex and Frank sat down in the waiting room and Frank resumed holding her hand. It was odd that even though her entire body and brain felt numb, her heart threatened to explode through her chest. Her saving grace at that moment was the quiet strength of Frank's hand holding hers. Where Alex felt her anxiety heighten, Frank was giving off a confident energy. The calmness Frank exuded was starting to make its way into Alex. She wondered how Frank could be so quiescent at a time like this. Having to go through this again, how could Frank just calmly sit there and be the strength Alex needed?

Alex couldn't believe this was actually happening to her—to Frank. She lived a fairly healthy life. She was a moderate drinker, she didn't smoke, she worked out, and she didn't have any type of cancer in her family. Why her? She knew cancer wasn't discriminatory, but she still couldn't believe this was happening to her. The sound of a woman's voice calling her name pulled Alex out of her thoughts. She was calling Alex back to the doctor's office. She didn't want to move, didn't think she could move.

"Come on, baby."

Frank stood and helped Alex to her feet, never letting go of her hand. They followed the nurse down a series of halls until they reached the doctor's private office. They sat in the two brown leather chairs that were in front of a mahogany desk and waited a few more minutes for the doctor to come in.

Dr. Nguyen came in, said hello to Alex, and extended her hand to Frank, introducing herself.

"I'm Francesca Greco, Alex's girlfriend."

Alex looked at Frank, shocked that she had introduced herself as Alex's girlfriend. They hadn't discussed labels. They were certainly more than friends, way more than sex partners. She cared for Frank a lot, and before the lump appeared, she might even have been falling in love with Frank. But now her life was uncertain. She couldn't allow herself to fall in love with Frank, could she? Could Frank be strong enough to go through this again? Alex was pretty sure Frank loved her. In fact, Frank almost told her a few nights ago until Alex stopped her.

She looked over at Frank with her jaw set in determination and decided to let the word "girlfriend" roll around on her tongue. It didn't take long for Alex to decide she liked the taste of it, but at the same time it scared the shit out of her.

There was a knock on the door and Dr. Nguyen invited the woman in. "Alex, Francesca, this is Sophia Douglas. She's what we call a nurse navigator, and she's going to help you through this journey." Dr. Nguyen folded her hands on her desk and looked at Alex and Frank. "I'm sorry to tell you this, Alex, but you have breast cancer."

Alex had been expecting to hear those very words ever since the day of her biopsy, but it still didn't prepare her for actually *hearing* she had cancer. The whooshing sound in her head prevented her from hearing the doctor. Suddenly, there was silence in her head, and she felt at peace when she felt a hand on her shoulder and a voice in her head say that she would be fine, that she would beat the cancer. Her entire body warmed, and she felt the tension in her muscles start to loosen. She squeezed Frank's hand and spoke to the doctor and nurse. "Okay, what's the game plan? What happens next?"

"Your pathology report indicates you have invasive ductal carcinoma. I want to schedule you for an MRI to determine the size of the tumor and to see if the cancer has spread."

"When will this happen?"

"We'll get it set up in the next couple of days. I'm also going to refer you to Dr. Angela Moreno. She's an oncologist that specializes in breast cancer. Sophia will set up your appointment with Dr. Moreno and arrange for your MRI results to go directly to her."

Sophia handed her card to Alex and Frank. "I'm here for both of you and I'll do everything I can to get you through this journey. Any questions or concerns, you can contact me anytime. Even if you think it's a silly question, I want you to call me. I'll call radiology after our meeting and I'll call you with your appointment time."

"Thank you. What do you think the best treatment options would be?"

Dr. Nguyen folded her hands on the desk. "We can't answer that just yet. Once we get the MRI and other tests, we'll be able to come up with a plan."

"What should I do in the meantime?"

"There's nothing to do, Alex. Go back to your regular routine until we get the test results back."

Alex barked out a humorless laugh. "My regular routine? You tell me I have breast cancer and I should go back to my regular routine? Nothing about my life will ever be routine again."

"I'm sorry if I sounded insensitive. What I meant was there's nothing you can do until we get the results."

Sophia knelt next to Alex and placed her hand on Alex's forearm. "I know this was probably the last thing you were expecting, but try not to worry too much too soon. There isn't anything we can do until we get the results back. But when we do, we'll go at it full force and kick its ass."

The determination in Sophia's voice made Alex feel stronger. And she liked the fact that Sophia said "we," that she wouldn't be fighting this alone. She had Frank, Jordan, Kirsten, and her parents, but Sophia knew exactly what to expect and what needed to happen. Alex was relieved that Sophia was on her team.

"I'll call you with your appointment, Alex."

"Thank you, Sophia. Thank you, Dr. Nguyen. I'm sorry for getting upset earlier."

"No need to apologize. I'm sorry I don't have better news for you, but Sophia is the best nurse navigator we have, so don't be afraid to utilize her. Good luck to you."

Alex and Frank exited the office through the waiting room, and once again, she wondered if anyone there was going to get the same news she just got. God, she hoped not. Once they got in Frank's truck, Alex turned to face Frank. "Do you know what I want to do right now? Let's go get Bella and take her to the park. You can throw the ball for her and I can lie on a blanket and enjoy the fresh air."

"Are you sure? You don't want to go to your parents' or to see Jordan and Kirsten?"

"No, I just need some time to process the news we just got, but I don't want to be alone. Is that okay?"

Frank leaned across the seat and gave Alex a sweet, lingering kiss. "It's more than okay."

❖

After two hours at the park, they returned to Frank's for lunch and to relax. Frank went to the kitchen to prepare a salad and sandwiches, and to give Alex some privacy when she called her parents. When she heard a loud sob coming from the living room, she ran in to find Alex sitting on the couch with her knees to her chest. Bella was dutifully sitting in front of Alex whining. Frank sat next to Alex and cradled her in her arms. Frank had remained strong emotionally throughout the doctor's appointment and at the park, but seeing Alex like that broke her resolve. Tears fell as she held Alex close to her.

This had been the reaction she expected from Alex when they were told Alex had breast cancer. Other than a brief outburst, Alex had remained surprisingly stoic, and then it seemed she was ready to go to battle against this horrific disease. But she had finally broken down, and it ripped Frank's heart into pieces to see her that way.

"It's okay, baby. It'll all be okay."

Alex looked at Frank with red, swollen eyes. "You don't know that. Everything is so uncertain. I have so many decisions to make that can't even be made until all of the tests are done. Will I lose my breast? Both of them? Will I have reconstruction? Will I need radiation? Chemo? Hormone therapy? I can't answer any of these fucking questions or come up with a fucking game plan until we get the results from these fucking tests. I just want this fucking cancer out of my fucking body," Alex screamed.

Frank remained quiet as she continued to cry. Of course, Alex was right. They didn't know for sure if Alex would be all right. They could only hope. She hated that Alex had to go through this, that *she* had to go through this—again. It so wasn't fair. Alex was so young—Toni was so young. It nearly killed Frank when Toni died, and if she lost Alex too…well…she couldn't let her thoughts go there. She had to try to stay positive, not only for Alex, but for her own sanity. She had to keep her head clear, her thoughts positive and pure. She had to believe they would both come out on the other side intact.

Alex's weak voice brought Frank back to the present. "I'm sorry I yelled."

Frank pulled Alex into her lap and held her tighter. "No, don't be sorry. I remember when Toni and I found out she had cancer, and you have every right to be upset."

Alex snuggled closer into Frank. "Are you sure you want to go through this again?"

"I definitely do not want to go through this again. I don't want you go to through this either. But if you're asking if I want to leave, the answer is a resounding no. I'm going to be with you every step of the way. I'll do and give anything you need from me."

Alex kissed her. "I need you to make love to me. I need you to make me feel alive."

Frank kissed her tenderly. "You are alive, and there's nothing more I'd rather do." Frank stood with Alex cradled in her arms and took her to bed.

Chapter Twenty-one

Frank had decided to set up an appointment with her former psychologist to talk about her feelings regarding Alex's diagnosis. She felt fortunate that she was able to get in to see her that week.

"Thanks for seeing me right away, Dr. Cook."

"Of course, Frank. I'm glad to see you, but I have to admit I was surprised to hear from you. How have you been?"

"I've actually been feeling quite good. I met a woman and we started seeing each other a few months ago."

Dr. Cook smiled. "That's wonderful. Tell me about her."

Frank started seeing Dr. Cook shortly after Toni died. She was an older woman whose once dark brown hair was now mostly gray and she wore nondescript wire-framed glasses perched on her nose. They had worked extensively together for over a year after Toni died. They talked about the cancer, Toni's death, her estrangement with her parents, and her job. Frank owed her life to Dr. Cook and to Katie for helping her survive the loss of her sister—hell, the loss of her family. Now she again needed Dr. Cook's help to come to terms with Alex's diagnosis.

"Her name is Alex and she's one of the most amazing women I've ever met. She was also just diagnosed with breast cancer." Frank felt the sting in her eyes and knew the tears weren't far behind. She pressed the heel of her hands into her eyes to stanch the flow of her tears.

"Oh, Frank, how awful for you both."

"Yeah. She needs to go through some tests to know what she's dealing with exactly and how to properly treat it. She'll meet with the medical oncologist once all the tests have been completed."

"I see. How is she handling all of this?"

"I'm not sure exactly. One minute she's understandably scared. She'll cry and yell and withdraw. The next minute she's determined to fight and beat this."

Dr. Cook steepled her fingers and rested her chin on the tips. "I can only imagine how shocked she must be at this diagnosis, so it doesn't surprise me her emotions are all over the place. How are you handling all of this?"

Frank laughed mirthlessly. "Pretty much the same. I freaked out on her when I found the lump. I practically demanded she get it checked out. And look where that got her."

"Yes, look where that got her. Maybe she caught it early enough."

Frank threw her hands in the air. "And maybe she didn't. What if she found it too late and she dies too?"

"That's also a possibility, but why do you want to jump to that conclusion?"

Frank was silent, trying to gather her thoughts. Finally, she said, "I don't know if I can do this again. I don't know if I can watch someone else I care about go through this and possibly lose them. I don't think I'm strong enough."

"Have you talked to Alex about this?"

"Not really. I mean, she actually brought it up the morning after her initial exam when they did a biopsy. She's a nurse and figured if the exam warranted a biopsy then it probably wouldn't be good news. She told me that since we were pretty new into the relationship, that we could end it and just go back to being friends. She said she didn't want me to go through this again."

"That was a pretty selfless act."

Frank nodded. "Yeah, that's the kind of person she is. One of the many reasons I care about her so much."

"How did you react to that offer?"

"I told her I wasn't going to desert her when she needed me most, that I cared about her too much."

"But now it seems as if you're having second thoughts. Why is that?"

"I guess I was caught off guard with her offer, and it was a gut reaction answer because I don't want to be a jerk."

"I understand that, but what's going to make you look like a bigger jerk—your word, not mine? Breaking up with her now or later because you realized you really couldn't handle it? Do you think that's fair to Alex? That you give her a false sense of security then you pull the rug out from under her when she needs you most?"

"No," Frank mumbled.

"I'm not trying to make you feel bad, Frank. But you really need to figure out if this is something you can do again. Not only for Alex but for yourself. I saw what losing your sister did to you, and I worry about you. You grew a lot stronger during our sessions, and I felt very confident in releasing you from my care. Whatever you decide, I'll help you through it. But I want you to think about it. You don't have to make your decision now, but it should be soon, before you and Alex get too far into treatment."

"I understand."

"Good. I want to see you again next week. If you haven't decided by then, that's all right. We can talk about anything you want."

Frank stood and shook Dr. Cook's hand. "Thanks again and I'll see you next week."

Frank got in her truck and called Katie. "Hey, can you meet up for a drink? There's something I need to talk to you about."

"Sure, Frank. I'll meet you at the Joint in twenty."

"Great. See you then, Katie."

The Joint was the nickname of a local cop hangout. Some of the officers would go grab a beer after their shift to decompress or celebrate a promotion. It was a dive bar with dark lighting, music playing from a jukebox, and the smell of stale cigarette smoke permeating the walls. Stools lined the bar, and tables and chairs were scattered throughout the room. There was one pool table and one dartboard in the back of the bar.

Frank entered and stood off to the side waiting for her eyes to adjust. She finally saw a hand wave and she walked in that direction. It wasn't crowded, only a couple of guys sitting at the bar, and it was easy to spot Katie and the two mugs of beer on the table. Frank gave Katie a hug and sat next to her.

"Thanks for the beer."

"Anytime. So, what's up?"

Frank took a deep breath and let it out slowly while wiping away the condensation from her mug. "Alex was diagnosed with breast cancer yesterday."

"Jesus Christ."

"Yep, that pretty much says it all." Frank took a long pull from her beer.

"How is she doing?" Katie placed her hand over Frank's. "How are you doing?"

"I'm not exactly sure. I just came from seeing Dr. Cook. She said I need to decide if I can go through this again."

Frank knew Katie would understand since she was with Frank and Toni during Toni's fight. Katie was there for Frank after the storm too. She knew about everything Frank went through, including her own recovery from losing her family.

"I know it won't be easy for you to go through this again, but I think the main question is, can you walk out of Alex's life and be okay? I'm your best friend and I know you better than anyone. You're in love with her, and you belong together."

"How do you know that? You've met her and hung out once."

"I just told you I know you better than anyone. I saw how you looked at her, how you hung on her every word, how you couldn't get close enough to her."

Frank tried to hide her tears by taking another drink from her mug.

"Buddy, I know you're in love with her. Fight this with her. I'll help you. Dr. Cook will help you. We'll be strong for you so you can be strong for her."

Frank looked down and shook her head. "I can't believe I'm going through this again with someone I love."

"I was going to be a smartass and ask what you did to piss off the universe."

Frank glared at Katie, which made her hold up her hand.

"But you know I'm a big believer in things happening for a reason. There's obviously a reason why you're going through this, why Alex came into your life when she did. We may never know the reason, but I think this journey can be a positive one for you both."

Frank's eyebrows shot up. "You think cancer can be a good thing?"

"I said the *journey* can be positive. But you'll have to stick around to find that out."

Frank shook her head again. "Motherfucker."

"Indeed," Katie said before taking a drink of her beer. "You can do this, Frank. I believe in you and I'll be there for you."

Frank finished up her beer and put her mug on the table. "I hope you're right, Katie, because I don't think I'd survive if I lost Alex too."

Frank ordered another round at the bar. When she returned to the table, she told Katie about finding Alex a few nights ago and the conversation they had the following morning.

"She actually gave you an out?"

"Yeah. That's the type of person she is. She doesn't want me to get hurt again."

"I knew there was a reason why I liked her so much."

"She's pretty fantastic."

"Are you going to take her up on her offer?"

Frank took a few more gulps from her beer and strummed her fingers, pinkie to index, on the table.

"No, I'm not leaving her. I love her and I'm going to help her fight this."

Katie hugged her and said, "You won't regret this."

"I know this won't be easy for any of us, but we need to help each other through this."

When they finished their beers, Katie asked Frank if she wanted to join her and Michelle for dinner.

"No, I'm going to call Dr. Cook and let her know my decision, and then I'm going to go spend time with my girl. Thanks for everything, Katie."

"No thanks needed, Frank. I love you and I'll help you girls through this."

"Love you too. Talk to you soon."

Frank drove to Alex's without the inner turmoil in her gut she'd had earlier that day. She felt at peace with her decision. She wasn't delusional enough to think she wouldn't have any negative feelings or doubts, but she would continue her sessions with Dr. Cook, and Katie was an excellent listener. She was certain she'd be able to be there for Alex as long as she had her own support system in place.

CHAPTER TWENTY-TWO

Two weeks had gone by since Alex had her MRI and blood tests, and now she, Frank, and Sophia were sitting in the private office of Dr. Angela Moreno awaiting the results. The time it took for Dr. Moreno to join them gave Alex the opportunity to view Dr. Moreno's framed diplomas and certificates on the wall. As someone who worked in the medical field, Alex was very aware of the exemplary reputations of the universities where Dr. Moreno got her education. The numerous certificates indicated that the doctor took her continuing education and advancements very seriously. When Dr. Moreno finally came into the office, Alex detected a confident demeanor without the arrogance she saw in so many surgeons. Dr. Moreno hadn't said one word, but already Alex liked her.

"Hello, everyone, I'm Dr. Moreno. It's nice to see you again, Sophia. Why don't you introduce me?"

"Doctor, this is Alex Taylor and her girlfriend, Francesca Greco."

Dr. Moreno shook their hands and smiled warmly. Alex noticed Dr. Moreno's handshake was firm and unrushed, and her positive assessment of her doctor continued.

"I'm sorry we have to meet under these circumstances, but please be assured that I and the rest of your medical team will do everything we can for you. I'll start off by giving you your MRI and pathology results, then I'll be happy to answer any questions you have. Then I'd like to take you into a private room, Alex, where I can do a physical exam. Once the exam is over, we'll come back here and discuss with Francesca and Sophia what the plan of care will be."

Alex was pleased that Dr. Moreno didn't appear to be rushed and was willing to discuss and answer questions with all of them.

"First off, according to your MRI, your cancer is infiltrating ductal carcinoma, and the tumor appears to be a little less than four centimeters. It doesn't appear that the cancer has spread beyond the breast or into your chest muscles. It also looks like the lymph nodes are clear, but we may want to do a sentinel node biopsy just to be sure. Those are the nodes in the armpit closest to the tumor. If the sentinel nodes are clear, then we won't need to take more.

"According to the pathology report, you tested positive for hormone receptor, more specifically, estrogen receptor positive and progesterone receptor negative. What that means is that it can trigger cancer cell growth. You also tested positive for HER2, which indicates your breast cancer cells are producing a protein that can cause the cancer cells to grow and divide more quickly. There are therapies we can give you to treat the HER2 and hormone receptors. You did test negative for the BRCA one and two genes, which is good. Women who carry those genes have an increased risk of developing breast and ovarian cancer."

Alex's head was swimming with all of the information she was being given. Out of the corner of her eye, she could see Frank writing down the information, while on her other side, Sophia was sitting calmly with her hands in her lap, nodding as Dr. Moreno spoke. As a nurse, Alex knew better than to ask "why me?" She knew bad things happened to good people every day. But seriously, why her? Why now? Life was going her way; everything was falling into place. She loved her job. Her relationship with Frank was looking promising. She had Aiden to watch grow up. Why her?

She always believed people came into one's life, and things happened, for a reason. Was this why Frank came into her life? Because she went through it with Toni? That she would have some idea of what to expect and would be able to help Alex with her journey?

"Do you have any questions?"

Alex shook her head. "I'm sorry. What?"

"I know I've given you a lot of information," Dr. Moreno said, "but do you have any questions so far?"

"Am I going to lose my breast?"

Dr. Moreno smiled that warm smile again. "How about I do your exam first, then we can talk about how to proceed?"

"All right." Alex stood and followed Dr. Moreno to an exam room.

"You can go ahead and remove your shirt and bra, then put this gown on with it open in the front. I'll be back in a few minutes."

Alex watched the door close behind Dr. Moreno, and she felt the tears pool in her eyes as she began to slowly unbutton her blouse and remove her bra. This had to be some sort of mistake, Alex thought as she put on the cloth gown. She vacillated between wanting to curl up in a ball and cry, and wanting to fight and kick cancer's ass, depending on the moment. Hearing the results of the tests only increased her disbelief.

Dr. Moreno returned and handed Alex some tissue. "I know you must be feeling overwhelmed right now, Alex, but I want you to know we'll do everything we can for you. This is treatable. You need to know that."

Alex nodded and wiped her eyes.

"I'm going to do a general exam now. I have your primary physician's report, but I like to see for myself what's going on."

After taking Alex's blood pressure and temperature, Dr. Moreno asked her to lie back and then proceeded with a breast exam. The offending area on her left breast wasn't as tender, and as much as Alex wanted to believe this was all a big misunderstanding, she knew her MRI and pathology reports indicated she had cancer. The entire exam lasted only ten minutes, and she returned with Dr. Moreno to her private office. Alex took her seat between Frank and Sophia and resumed holding Frank's hand, needing the comfort that Frank was able to give her.

"Okay, Alex, we have a coupld of options on how to proceed. We could start you with a course of chemotherapy to try to reduce the size of the tumor. We may then be able to preserve your breast by performing a lumpectomy and radiation. My concern would be that because you're estrogen receptor positive and HER2 positive, there could be recurrence of the cancer. Another option is to have a mastectomy of your left breast with or without reconstruction. We would follow up the surgery with chemotherapy to kill off any possible remaining cancer cells. We could also give you hormonal therapy for the hormone receptor and targeted therapy for HER2."

Alex sat there staring at Dr. Moreno. She heard her options but couldn't think. How could she be expected to make a decision like this? Save her breast or lose it? Kill the cancer or risk recurrence?

Frank squeezed her hand and asked, "Could we have some time to make a decision?"

"Of course. I can also refer you to my colleague for a second opinion. But I want to be honest with you. I don't need your decision by tomorrow, but I also don't want you to take a month to decide either. Because your cancer cells could grow and divide quickly, time is of the essence. The sooner we get started, the better."

Frank nodded. "We understand. Baby, do you have any questions?"

Alex shook her head.

"Alex, like I told you earlier, this is very treatable. This is by no means a death sentence."

"You don't know that, Dr. Moreno." Alex finally spoke. "Frank's twin sister died from breast cancer three years ago. She was only twenty-nine years old."

"Baby, Toni didn't get checked out until it was too late and the cancer had spread. We caught this early and we can treat it, right, Dr. Moreno?"

"Absolutely. Alex, there have been a lot of discoveries and advancements made just in the past few years. It's terrible that Francesca's sister didn't survive, but that doesn't mean you won't. I need you to try to stay positive."

"I'll try. I'm sure I'll have questions later. Is it okay to call you?"

"Of course. I'm on your side, Alex, and I'll do everything I can for you."

"I appreciate that. I'll call you when I make my decision."

Alex, Frank, and Sophia left the office after getting the phone number of Dr. Moreno's colleague for a second opinion.

"Sophia, I want to discuss this with my parents and best friends. Would it be possible for you to join us? I don't have a lot of experience with oncology, and I thought you might be able to answer some questions."

"Yes, I'd be happy to. Just let me know when and where."

"I think I'll get the second opinion first and set up a time for all of us to meet."

"Sounds good. I'll talk to you soon."

Alex and Frank walked to Frank's truck in silence. Alex felt she had so many decisions to make and didn't know where to start. She needed the advice and support of those she loved most. She couldn't make this decision alone.

CHAPTER TWENTY-THREE

Alex, Frank, Jordan, Kirsten, and Sophia sat in the living room of Alex's parents' house. Alex, Frank, and Sophia had met with Dr. Moreno's colleague on Friday afternoon. He had agreed with Dr. Moreno's assessment and suggestions. Alex did get a good vibe from Dr. Moreno despite her being the bearer of the bad news. It was now Sunday afternoon and she had to make a decision regarding her care. She couldn't put this off much longer. She had to get started and get the cancer out of her body.

"Thanks for being here for me, everyone. I have to make a decision in regard to my treatment, and I need your help. Sophia is my nurse navigator and can answer any questions I can't. I've been diagnosed with infiltrating ductal carcinoma. Dr. Moreno says it's stage two and doesn't look like it's gotten into the lymph nodes. I'm also estrogen receptor positive and HER2 positive, which means the cancer cells can divide and grow quickly.

"She's given me a couple of options. One would be to have chemo first and try and reduce the size of the tumor and kill the cancer cells, then I would have a lumpectomy and radiation. The second option would be to have the mastectomy first, then follow up with chemo and other systemic therapy to treat the estrogen receptor and HER2." Alex looked at her parents and friends as they paid rapt attention. She saw the shock on all of their faces, but she also saw how strong they were trying to be for her. Frank sat next to Alex and held her hand, giving her silent support.

Her father asked Sophia, "What do you know about Alex's doctor? Is she good?"

"Yes, she's the best doctor I've worked with when it comes to dealing with breast cancer. Dr. Moreno is very aggressive and progressive with her treatment regimens, and every woman I've worked with that has had her as their doctor has done very well. If I was diagnosed with breast cancer, Dr. Moreno is the one I would want to treat me."

Her parents nodded, and Alex saw some of the worry leave their faces.

Jordan cleared her throat. "What's the prognosis?"

"We won't know for sure until after the treatment, whichever Alex decides to do," Sophia answered. "But the fact that it appears to be stage two without lymph node involvement is pretty positive."

"How soon will you start the treatment?" her mother asked.

"As soon as possible, Mom. I don't want to give it a chance to spread."

"Honey," Kirsten said, "speaking for myself, I want you to get whatever treatment will make you healthy and live a long life." Kirsten began crying, which set off the tears in everyone else. "We need you. Aiden needs you. We want you with us when he starts school, when he goes off to college, when he gets married, and when he makes us grandmothers. You do whatever you have to to make that happen."

Alex took in a deep breath and let it out slowly. She had been leaning toward a lumpectomy to save her breast, to limit the size of the scar, but after researching and hearing the opinions of those she loved most in the world, she made her decision.

After Sophia answered the rest of their questions, Frank and Alex returned to Frank's. Alex had been silent on the ride home, for which Frank was grateful. Frank hadn't spoken much, and she had felt a little like an outsider at Alex's parents' home. She didn't want to interfere in Alex's decision, didn't want to interfere in her family's opinions. She saw the love they had for and shared with Alex. Frank loved Alex too. She couldn't imagine living her life without Alex in it. There had been so many times these past few weeks when she wanted to tell Alex, but the fear of rejection made her swallow her words.

As they were lying in bed, Alex finally spoke. "What do you think about all of this?"

Frank turned on her side to face Alex. "What do you mean?"

"I mean, you've been awfully quiet tonight. I want to know what's going on in your head."

"I think you made the right decision."

"That's it? That's all you have to say?"

"What do you want me to say, Alex? I mean, shit, haven't I been supportive?"

"Forget it." Alex turned away from Frank and faced the wall.

Way to go, asshole. Why don't you try to be a little more supportive?

"I'm sorry, baby. I didn't mean to raise my voice."

Alex sniffled, which made Frank feel like a bigger jerk. She scooted closer and wrapped her arm around Alex's waist, pulling her closer. "I think we have the right information, you were able to make an informed decision, and now we can go back to Dr. Moreno and we can come up with a game plan."

"Do you think I made the right decision?"

"Yes, baby, I do."

"What if you don't find me attractive anymore?"

Alex's voice sounded so small, so insecure, Frank wished she could do *something* to make Alex feel safe. "You are the most beautiful woman I've ever known. Whether you have two breasts, one breast, or no breasts won't change my opinion of you. There are so many things that attract me to you, but the biggest attraction for me is what sits behind your left breast—your heart. I love you, Alex. I love everything about you, and I just want you healthy and here with me."

"Frank, I told you not to say that."

"Whether I say it or not, it's true, and you already knew how I felt. Just like I know how you feel about me. You can say it or don't say it, but I know you care about me, and that's enough for me."

"Oh, Frank, I do care about you so much. I worry what this will do to you."

"Don't. I want you to put all of your energy into fighting this and making a full recovery. Your parents, Jordan, Kirsten, and I will be just fine, and we're here to support you."

"I'm scared."

"I know. I am too. But we have Sophia to help. And I really like

Dr. Moreno. I wish I knew about her when Toni got sick. She seems invested in your recovery, and I know she'll put together the best team to give you the best outcome."

"Do you really think so?"

"I do. Now let's try and get some sleep. We have a lot to take care of at work before your surgery."

CHAPTER TWENTY-FOUR

In the ensuing two weeks it took to get the medical team prepped and scheduled, Alex got her affairs in order. She discussed her diagnosis with her closest friends at work. Valerie was especially supportive and helped Alex with all the necessary paperwork for her time off work and disability pay. She met with her attorney and had a will drawn up, leaving her life insurance policy in Aiden's name. It wasn't a lot of money, but in case she didn't survive, she wanted to make sure he had money to go to college, or maybe travel a bit when he was an adult. Alex had always wanted to travel, but she never found the time. She vowed that if she survived, she'd visit the places she'd always wanted to see.

Alex was charting at the nurses' station when she saw Frank striding toward her. Her heart fluttered as she watched Frank's cocky swagger. She didn't think she'd ever get tired of seeing Frank display the confidence she did when she wore her uniform. Frank leaned in and gave Alex a kiss on her cheek.

"Well, this is a nice surprise, Sarge. What are you doing here?"

"I'm here for the party."

Alex tilted her head. "What party?"

Nancy shot Frank an evil eye. "The party that was supposed to be a surprise."

Frank had the decency to blush. "Oops."

Alex looked to Frank then Nancy. "Still not getting it, guys."

"We wanted to throw you a party since today is your last day of work for a while," Nancy said. "We all wanted you to know that we're here for you and if you need anything, just let us know."

Alex could feel the tears form in her eyes, and she quickly wiped them away. "You guys didn't have to do that."

"What? And give up an excuse to have cake?"

Alex laughed and slipped her arm around Frank's waist. "So, when is this party?"

"Now. Come down to the lounge."

Frank and Alex followed Nancy down the hall and entered the lounge to a chorus of "surprise" from some of the staff. There was a sheet cake decorated with a pink ribbon and the words "fight like a girl" written in pink frosting that sat on the counter along with some bottles of soda and lemonade. People made their way to Alex to give her hugs and offer their support. Alex felt grateful that she worked with such a wonderful bunch of people. She could feel the love in each of their hugs.

Frank brought Alex a piece of cake and a cup of lemonade.

"Thanks, baby. I can't believe you kept this a secret from me."

Frank laughed. "I can keep a secret when I need to, but it was hard. Hey, I talked to my lieutenant yesterday, and he approved my time off so I can take care of you after surgery."

"Oh, Frank, you didn't have to do that. My parents can take care of me."

"I want to take care of you, Alex. I love you and I'll do anything for you. I already have it arranged. I figured you could stay at my place so Bella can help take care of you too. Of course, Bruce and Kathleen are welcome to come over and spend time with you. I know how much it will mean to your parents to help with your care. Please let me do this for you."

Alex placed her cake down on the counter and wrapped her arms around Frank. "Okay, baby. Thank you." Alex pulled Frank down and gave her a sweet, lingering kiss.

"Great. Okay, I have to get back to work. Julie is taking Bella for a few days so I can be at the hospital with you and your parents. I'll come over to your place tonight, and I'll drive you tomorrow morning."

Alex watched Frank leave and thought about the three words Frank declared that made Alex feel so good and warm inside. Frank had professed her love two weeks ago and although Alex had yet to say it back, she did love Frank. She had been so strong throughout this ordeal, so positive, doing and saying all the right things. Even if Frank hadn't told Alex she loved her, Alex knew. She hoped when all of her treatment was done that Frank would be there in her life. Alex loved Frank so much that she wished she could spare Frank the turmoil of going through this again. She offered Frank an out and she turned it down. She hoped Frank was all in because she was in for the fight of her life and needed everyone's help if she was going to survive.

❖

Alex and Frank woke at five a.m., showered, and drove to the hospital. They went to admitting, signed all the forms, and made their way to the waiting area where they were greeted by Jordan, Kirsten, and her parents. Alex's eyes stung with tears as the group enveloped her in a heartwarming hug.

"We'll be right here, honey. You'll do great."

"Thanks, Mom."

Jordan reached for Alex's hand and pulled her away from the group into a private corner, away from prying ears and eyes. "Remember when we met our freshman year and I declared my love to you?"

Alex smiled. "Vaguely."

Jordan chuckled. "Even though Kirsten is my wife and I love her with all that I am, you're still one of the most important people in my life…a life I can't live without you. Do you understand?"

The tears returned and mirrored Jordan's. Alex nodded.

"I love you, Alex. Not only are you my best friend, you're Aiden's godmother, my sister from another mister, and I need you with me—with us. Do you understand?"

Alex laughed through her tears. "Yes, I understand."

Jordan wrapped her in a hug. "Good. You got this, Al. We'll see you in a few hours."

They returned to the group and Alex sat next to Frank. Frank put her arm around Alex's shoulder and kissed her temple.

"How are you feeling, baby?"

"I'm nervous, but I'm glad everyone is here. I'm glad you're here. Lying in your arms last night after making love made me feel safe, that the surgery was going to be successful." Alex turned to Frank and cupped her cheek. "Do you have any idea how much you mean to me?"

Frank leaned in and kissed Alex. "I have a pretty good idea, and the feeling is entirely mutual. You're going to do great, baby, and Dr. Moreno is going to take good care of you. We'll be right next to you when you wake up." Frank wiped away Alex's tears and kissed her again when Alex was called back to get prepped for surgery.

She changed into a gown, put that lame-looking surgical cap on her head, and climbed onto the gurney. Medical personnel entered and left, asking her the same questions over and over. Dr. Moreno came in and initialed Alex's left breast, the one she would wake up without. The anesthesiologist injected a sedative into her IV, and before she knew it, she was being wheeled into the operating room. The flurry of medical personnel made Alex's head swim—or was that the drugs the anesthesiologist gave her? She was so cold, her body was shaking. A nurse arrived with a blanket fresh out of the warmer and laid it across her body. Dr. Moreno stood above her now, along with the plastic surgeon that would implant the spacer once her traitorous breast was removed. He was the doctor in charge of reconstructing her breast.

"Alex, we're just about ready. Do you have any questions?"

"No, just get this cancer out of me."

Alex could see the smile behind Dr. Moreno's mask.

"You heard her, people. Let's get started."

The anesthesiologist appeared into Alex's sight line and placed a mask over her nose and mouth. "I want you to count backward from one hundred and take deep breaths."

"One hundred, ninety-nine, ninety-eight..." Alex felt her world go black.

❖

Alex's world began to reappear. She felt as if she was trying to emerge from deep below a watery surface; the rays of sunlight began to come into view. The muffled sounds around her were starting to clear. She opened her eyes to see Frank, Jordan, Kirsten, and her parents surrounding her. Her mind was groggy; she had difficulty forming words, even coherent thoughts. Someone squeezed her hand.

"Everything went as planned, sweetheart. Dr. Moreno said they got the cancer and the lymph nodes were clear."

That was all Alex remembered before falling back under the effects of the anesthesia. She awoke a couple of hours later with generic sounds coming from outside her room. She opened her eyes to see she was alone in her room with the lights dimmed. She closed her eyes once again and ran her hand down her chest. Tears leaked out of the corners of her eyes as she realized her left breast was no more. In its place were bandages and an expander. She recalled the plastic surgeon saying he would place an expander under her skin once the breast tissue was removed. The plan was to return to his office every two weeks to have it filled with saline until her skin had stretched out to accommodate her C cup implant. Her hand was pulled away from her chest and kissed by soft lips.

"Your breast is gone, but more importantly, so is the cancer."

Alex opened her eyes to find Frank sitting in a chair beside her bed. She turned away, not wanting to see the pity in Frank's eyes. "Where are my parents?"

"They went to grab a quick bite. They'll be back in a little while. Jordan and Kirsten went home, but they wanted you to know they'll be back later."

"No. I don't want anyone to see me this way. I want you to leave too."

"I'm sorry, but I'm not going anywhere."

"I don't want you here, Frank."

"Listen to me, Alex. I'm not going anywhere. I love you and I'm going to be here for you."

"Why? I'm deformed now. I must look hideous."

"Stop!"

The stern tone in Frank's voice made Alex turn back to her.

"You are not hideous. You are alive and cancer-free. You'll be out of the hospital in a few days, and in three months, you'll have reconstruction and look like your old self."

"But the scars—"

"They're just battle wounds, baby. When all of this is over, you'll have won the war. The only thing that matters is you're cancer-free. You're going to be fine."

Frank wished she could have said those words to her sister. By the time Toni had been diagnosed, the cancer had metastasized throughout her upper body. She fought, but the cancer had invaded too much to get rid of. Why couldn't Alex realize how lucky she was that she found it early? That she had a chance to survive and live a long life? Something

Toni wasn't able to do? Frank understood that this was still probably shocking to Alex, but she wouldn't allow Alex to kick her out of her hospital room—out of her life. Alex meant too much to Frank.

"We're not going to let you go through this alone, Alex."

"Frank's right, honey. Your mom and I are here, as well as Jordan and Kirsten. We're family and we take care of each other."

"Daddy." Alex began sobbing as Bruce and Kathleen went to Alex's side. Frank stepped out of the way and let Alex and her parents have their time together. She sat in the chair that was in the corner, covered her face with her hands, and began to cry herself. She cried for the loss Alex was experiencing. Cried for the loss of her sister. Cried for the loss of a family she would never have—the kind of family Alex had.

Frank felt a hand on her shoulder and looked up to see Kathleen's sympathetic gaze. Frank stood and embraced Alex's mom. She'd never had this compassion from a motherly figure besides her nonna. Kathleen guided Frank's head to her shoulder and held her as she let loose the tears she'd been trying to hold back.

"My daughter needs you, Frank. She needs all of us to get her through this fight. It will get a lot worse when the chemo starts."

Frank nodded against Kathleen's shoulder. "I remember."

"Oh, sweetheart, of course you do."

The hands moving up and down her back in an act of comfort, of motherly love, soothed Frank's frayed nerves.

"Come on, my daughter needs us—all of us."

They stood at Alex's bedside and Frank cupped Alex's cheek, looked her square in the eyes, and said, "I'm here for you. Whatever you want, whatever you need." Frank pressed her forehead against Alex's and felt her nod in agreement.

Later that day, Dr. Moreno came into Alex's hospital room and greeted Frank and Alex's parents.

"Hi, Alex. How are you feeling?"

"I'm a little nauseous, but I'm not having any real pain, just some discomfort."

"That's probably from the anesthesia. If it doesn't go away soon, I'll prescribe something for the nausea. So, we removed your left breast and did a biopsy of the lymph nodes, which came back clear. The next step is to get you started on chemotherapy and hormone therapy. The chemo will kill off any cancer cells that may be in the body and reduce the risk of the cancer returning. The hormone therapy will also kill the tumor cells. The cells that tested positive for HER2 have large amounts of protein, and the drugs we'll give you for that will prevent those cells from spreading or coming back."

Alex, her parents, and Frank nodded their understanding.

"How soon will I start the chemo and other therapies?"

"You'll start chemo within a couple of weeks. During that time, you'll also go to the plastic surgeon to have saline injected into the expander to help the skin stretch. The plastic surgeon can give you more information regarding your reconstruction. You'll start the hormone therapy once chemo is completed."

"Okay." Alex knew the common side effects of chemo and was not looking forward to this part of the treatment. Hell, who was she kidding? She wasn't looking forward to any of this. She looked at her parents, who were standing there looking so brave. But inside, she knew this was killing them. They went through so much to have her, and now she might be taken away from them.

"As long as you continue to improve and there aren't any setbacks, we'll let you go home in two or three days. We placed two drains in your left breast, and I'll take one out either tomorrow or the next day. I'll leave the other one in and take it out when the wound is no longer draining."

"How long will that take?"

"Usually one to two weeks. I placed absorbable sutures, so there shouldn't be a need to remove them."

"Okay."

"A physical therapist will come in tomorrow morning to teach you some simple arm stretches, but I don't want you doing any strengthening exercises until the wound heals. You'll be able to go back to normal activity in two to three weeks as long as you're feeling okay. I don't want you to work while you get chemo because it will lower your immune system. Since you work in the ER, you'd have an increased chance of contracting a disease."

Alex nodded then asked, "What do you think my prognosis is, Doctor?"

"Well, since we did a mastectomy and there was no lymph node involvement, with the chemo and hormone therapies, I think it will be good. I'm not making any promises, but we'll do everything we can to prevent recurrence."

As a nurse, Alex knew nothing was certain, and Dr. Moreno gave her the best response she could, not promising anything, but remaining positive nonetheless. She saw the relief wash over the faces of her parents and Frank. She also saw a calm confidence in Dr. Moreno. For the first time in a long while, she felt hope instead of despair. She knew she had a long road ahead of her, but she finally felt like she had a fighting chance.

Alex reached for Frank's hand. "You need to go home and get some sleep."

"No, I don't want to leave you."

"Frank, your eyes are bloodshot, you have dark circles under your eyes, and I know you didn't sleep last night."

Alex's parents stood and started to leave. "We'll be right outside."

Frank turned back to Alex. "How do you know I didn't sleep?"

"I heard you crying. I know you're having a hard time with this too, that it's bringing up memories of Toni. Please go home and get some rest. You can come back tomorrow. I'm feeling tired myself and I'll be able to sleep better without all of you in here watching me."

"Are you sure?"

Alex almost changed her mind seeing Frank so worried, but she needed some time alone and she wanted Frank to try and get some rest. "I'm sure. I'll see you tomorrow."

Frank kissed Alex good-bye and once Frank walked out the door, Alex felt her tears fall.

Chapter Twenty-five

Frank woke early to clean her house, shop for groceries, and take Bella for a long run. Alex was being discharged from the hospital later that morning, and they had agreed before surgery that Alex would come back and stay at Frank's for a few days since Frank took a week off from work. Her lieutenant had been extremely understanding, having seen what she went through with her sister. Her brothers and sisters in blue had been nothing less than supportive and wished Alex well.

Nerves were in abundance, and the only thing that would settle them would be to go for a run with Bella. During that time, she let everything go from her mind and let her body take over. Her stomach had been in a constant knot since Alex was diagnosed, and the knot seemed to tighten with every doctor's appointment. The stranglehold loosened a little once she had talked with Dr. Moreno after the surgery. To know they got all the cancer and the lymph nodes were clear was a small relief, but she knew the fight was far from over. Alex still had chemo and hormone therapy to go through, as well as breast reconstruction. Not only did Alex lose her breast, but she was likely to lose her hair with the chemo. Frank knew from her experience with Toni's chemo that Alex's energy level would be drained, but she would do everything she could so that Alex could rest and prepare for each upcoming battle.

She arrived at the hospital to find Bruce, Kathleen, and Jordan in Alex's room. She greeted everyone with hugs, then went over and kissed Alex on her forehead. "Hey, baby, how're you feeling today?"

"I'm okay."

"You about ready to get out of here?" Frank noticed Bruce and Kathleen look down and wondered what was going on.

"I decided to stay with my mom and dad. That way you don't have to miss work. Since Mom is retired, it just makes more sense that she takes me to my appointments."

"But, Alex, I have the time to take off. It really isn't any problem."

"I appreciate it, but I think I'd be more comfortable at my parents'."

Frank didn't want to sound like a petulant child, especially in front of Jordan and Alex's parents, so she reluctantly agreed. "Okay, if that's what you want."

"Frank, you're welcome over anytime, and I could use your help," Alex's mother said.

Frank knew Kathleen was trying to make her feel better by saying that, but the knot in her stomach tightened again, and she couldn't help but feel Alex was trying to pull away from her.

"Sure, okay. Whatever you need, Kathleen." Frank turned to Alex. "Do you want me to go?"

"No, of course not. Not unless you have other things to do today."

Frank didn't know where all of this was coming from. Why was Alex treating her like an acquaintance instead of her lover? Alex's statement did nothing to ease the fear building inside Frank, and she felt her body begin to tremble.

"Frank, why don't you drive Alex to our house and stay for dinner? We have plenty of food, and Jordan, Kirsten, and Aiden will be there."

"Thanks, Bruce."

Dr. Moreno entered the room and said hello. "We have your discharge papers complete, Alex, so you can get dressed. Someone will be in shortly with a wheelchair."

"Thanks, Dr. Moreno," Alex said. "I'll see you soon. Mom, can you help me get dressed?"

Frank's heart dropped at Alex's request. She thought she would be the one to take care of Alex, to help her bathe and get dressed, to prepare her meals, to take her to her appointments. It seemed that she was being cast aside, and it hurt like hell.

Jordan slid her arm around Frank's shoulders. "Come on. Let's go get your truck and pull it up for Alex."

They headed toward the elevators, Jordan's arm still around Frank. "I know you must be hurt by the way Alex is behaving, but try and give her a little time. Alex isn't taking this well. Her life is no longer the life she thought she'd have. She's always been carefree and happy. At thirty-two, her mortality was shown to her, and she's understandably upset."

"But she'll eventually be fine. Dr. Moreno said she got all the cancer."

"Yes, she did, but that's not what Alex is focused on right now. She lost her breast, she thinks her body is now deformed, and she'll lose her hair. In Alex's eyes, she's lost her femininity."

"Not in my eyes, she hasn't."

"Nor in mine," Jordan said as she squeezed Frank's shoulder and they entered the elevator. "And we have to keep reassuring her that she'll continue to be beautiful, especially to those that love her. But it's her body, her feelings, and her mind. She'll probably have to go to counseling, maybe to a survivor's group and hear other stories before she accepts the new Alex."

"Yeah, I guess you're right. I'm just so grateful she'll live that I don't care about the rest, but it's also not me who's going through all of this."

"You are going through this, just in a different way. Continue to be strong, not only for Alex, but for yourself. And remember, I'm always here for you, buddy, anytime you need to talk." They arrived at Frank's truck, and Jordan pulled Frank into a powerful hug. "It won't be easy, and Alex might not want anyone around at times, but just continue to let her know you're not going anywhere."

Frank blushed when Jordan kissed her chastely on the lips. "Thanks, J. I really appreciate your understanding."

"Anytime, my friend. I'm going to pick up Kirsten and Aiden, then we'll meet you at Bruce and Kathleen's. Tell your girl we'll see her soon."

"Copy that. See ya."

Frank drove her truck to the front entrance of the hospital where Alex was sitting in a wheelchair with her parents on either side of her. Alex did not look happy to be going home. In fact, her face was devoid of emotion. Frank took a deep breath and let it out slowly as she exited her truck. She could only imagine how the ride back to Bruce and Kathleen's would go. She offered a hand to help Alex out of her wheelchair, but the offer was ignored, and Frank could only stand there and watch Alex step past her, open the door, and get into Frank's truck. She turned to Bruce and Kathleen, not knowing exactly what to say.

Kathleen hugged her. "Just give her some time, honey. She'll be okay. You both will. We'll see you back at the house."

Frank watched them go toward the parking garage before finally getting into the truck. Alex had already buckled her seat belt, but held it away from her chest, looking annoyed.

"Alex, what's going on with you today?" Frank asked as she drove away from the hospital.

"Nothing."

"Something is going on. You're treating me like a total stranger, and I don't get it."

Alex looked out the side window as tears fell. She was acting like a jerk to Frank and she didn't mean to. She just wasn't sure of anything anymore. Her whole life had been in upheaval since the diagnosis. Now she had only one breast and what she imagined to be a huge-ass scar across her chest. She hadn't seen the scar yet because of her bandages, and she really didn't want to. And to put the cherry on top, she was going to start chemo in a couple of weeks, which would lead to puking her guts out and going bald. How could she expect Frank to stay with her when she looked hideous? Frank had told her that it only mattered to her that Alex would live, but how could she be with someone who wasn't whole? Someone who was disfigured?

The truck came to a stop at a red light, and Frank's voice brought her back.

"Alex, please look at me."

Alex turned and saw the worried look on Frank's face. How could she treat Frank that way? After everything she'd done, Alex should treat Frank with more respect, show Frank that she meant so much to her. "I'm afraid you'll leave. I'm afraid if I let you see my body, you'll be disgusted and want to leave."

When the light turned green, Frank pulled into a parking lot and turned off the ignition. "Baby, I already told you I wasn't going anywhere. All that matters to me is that you'll be okay. We still have a long road ahead of us, but I'm going to be there every step of the way, loving you the best as I can."

Alex still had her reservations. She knew Frank meant it, but things happened, feelings changed, and Alex wasn't ready to tell Frank yet that she loved her too. She was too vulnerable, and this was the only way she felt she could protect herself. But that didn't mean she had to behave so badly toward her. "I'm sorry, Frank. I know what you said, and I'll try to be better."

Frank reached across the center console to kiss Alex. Alex had to turn her body to accept the kiss and winced as she felt her bandages pull. She turned back into her seat and refastened her seat belt. "We better get to my parents' house. They'll be wondering where we are."

Frank started her truck and pulled back into traffic. The remainder of the drive was spent in silence, but Alex offered up an olive branch when she reached across the console and intertwined her fingers with Frank's. They arrived and parked behind Jordan's car as they were exiting. Kirsten had Aiden in her arms, and when he saw Alex, he shrieked and reached for her.

"Awex."

Alex wanted to take Aiden in her arms and hold him close, but she couldn't do any heavy lifting. Kirsten held on to him as Alex took his little hand and kissed it. "Let's go inside so you can sit on my lap, monkey."

"Remember, Aiden, Auntie has an owie and you have to be still."

This sucked. Aiden didn't know any better and just wanted Alex to hold him. As soon as they got inside, Kirsten sat next to Alex on the couch. Alex was anxious to have him in her lap, his tiny arms around her neck. Life didn't get any better than when she was around Aiden, giving and receiving love from her little angel. Once he was in Alex's lap, he looked up at her with his questioning blue-green eyes.

"Owie?"

"Yes, baby, I have an owie, but if you give me a kiss, I'll feel better."

Aiden placed his hands on Alex's cheeks and gave her a sloppy kiss. Alex did start to feel better after that kiss. No matter what happened, she would always have this bond with Aiden. She snuggled him into the right side of her chest and repeatedly kissed him on his head, breathing deeply to memorize his smell.

Jordan and Frank went into the kitchen to help with dinner, and Alex turned to Kirsten. "I've been an asshole to Frank."

Kirsten grinned. "I heard."

"What? Oh, Jordan must have told you how I spoke to Frank at the hospital today."

"All she said was that Frank seemed hurt when you told her you'd rather stay at your parents' than with her. Why did you change your mind?"

"I don't want her to see me naked."

"Honey, she's seen you naked before."

"Not like this. She saw the old Alex naked. Old Alex was sexy with great tits. New Alex has one tit and one large scar. Hell, I don't even want to see myself naked." Alex had a different relationship with Kirsten than she did with Jordan. Jordan was like her sister, and there were very few things they didn't talk about. But Kirsten was more like a girlfriend she could talk to about things she didn't feel comfortable talking to Jordan about.

"You're afraid she'll freak out? That she'll run out screaming?"

"Something like that."

"Al, she must have seen Toni's scar. She knows what to expect."

"It's different though. Toni was her sister. I'm her lover. She'd look at it differently. I'm the one she has sex with. How could she get turned on while looking at my scar?"

"Honestly? She'll probably hardly notice it. If it were Jordan, I wouldn't care. All that would matter was that she was still alive and that we could make love."

"I understand, but you two are married with a kid. Frank and I are just dating. There's no real commitment there. I mean, we're dating exclusively, but we haven't really discussed any long-term plans, like moving in together or anything. How do I know she'll stay?"

"You don't, but you have to at least give her a chance. Stop trying to push her away and allow her to care for you."

Alex knew Kirsten was right, but she still wasn't ready for Frank to see her naked. Maybe one day, but not yet.

❖

They all sat around the table at dinnertime, but Frank noticed Alex was pushing her food around her plate more than she was actually eating. Frank suspected Alex's appetite could be diminished from the aftereffects of the surgery, but she didn't think so. Alex wasn't really engaging in any of the conversations, and she had yet to look at Frank, seemingly avoiding any sort of eye contact. After what they'd gone through together, the intimate moments they shared, it hurt Frank tremendously that Alex was ignoring her. Well, that wasn't exactly true. Alex wasn't talking to anyone unless it was to answer a question. The normally outgoing, funny, caring woman Frank had fallen in love with was nowhere to be seen. She fervently hoped Alex would once again be able to smile and laugh as this journey moved forward.

Once dinner was finished and the dishes were cleaned, Jordan and Kirsten hugged everyone good-bye and carried their sleeping son out to their car. Frank was conflicted. Part of her wanted to stay, to curl up on the couch with Alex, and just be with her. The other part felt like Alex wouldn't welcome that idea and that she just wanted to be left alone. The decision was made for her when Alex said she was tired and ready for bed. Frank hugged Bruce and Kathleen then asked Alex to walk her to the door.

Before she opened it, she turned to face her and held Alex's hands in hers. "I know things are going to be different for a while and you'll have a lot going on, but I love you and I want to help you in any way you need."

"I know, but right now I just need some time alone to think about things."

"What things, sweetheart?"

"Everything. I'm so overwhelmed with all that's happening—the surgery, the aftercare—everything I've gone through and everything that's coming up."

"You don't have to do this alone," Frank said as she cupped Alex's cheek. "I'll give you the time you need, but I'll be here for you when you're ready. I love you."

"Thanks." Alex kissed Frank's cheek, opened the door for Frank to leave, and then closed it softly behind her. It wasn't lost on Frank that Alex didn't acknowledge that she would call her or keep in touch. Frank decided on the drive home that she wouldn't pester Alex. As much as it would kill her, she'd let Alex have the time she needed and hope that Alex would decide she needed Frank.

She was greeted at the door by an excited Bella. She got on the floor and allowed Bella to lick her face and climb all over her to express how much she missed her. When Bella finally calmed down, Frank went into the kitchen and grabbed a beer that was left over from some barbecue party a few weeks back. She popped off the top and went to sit on the couch. Bella jumped up next to her and laid her head in Frank's lap. As she repeatedly ran her hand over Bella's back, her tears fell.

Chapter Twenty-six

Alex spent her first full day at her parents' house crying and wallowing in pity. After what she'd gone through so far, she felt she deserved to have her own pity party. Toward the late evening, her mother brought Alex's dinner to her room, just as she had done with breakfast and lunch. Alex had told her mom that she wanted to be left alone, and her mother had respected her wishes for the most part, except for the meal delivery. Alex didn't even look at her mom as she placed the tray of food on the dresser. Even though Alex had moved out of that house years ago, her parents never changed a thing, telling her it would always be her room.

Alex was lying in bed facing the wall when she felt her mom climb into bed behind her. Her mother began to rub Alex's back, and even though she said she wanted to be alone, she soaked up the affection her mom was showing her. After a few minutes, her mother finally spoke.

"It's time to buck up, buttercup."

Alex flinched and turned her head to see her mom. "Excuse me?"

"I said it's time to buck up. I've allowed you this day to cry, think, feel sorry for yourself, and whatever else you needed to do, but it ends tonight."

Alex's eyes widened and her mouth flew open. "I can't believe you're treating me this way."

"Honey, I can't believe I *have* to treat you this way. But your dad and I refuse to let you go down this rabbit hole."

Alex sat up and pulled the covers to her chest. "I just had my breast removed because of cancer, Mom. I have every right to feel this way."

"I know this has been difficult for you. It's been difficult for all of us. But you need to realize a few things. One, Dr. Moreno got the cancer and feels very optimistic for your recovery. Two, the way you've been treating Frank has been awful. You need to start behaving nicer to her."

Alex began to speak when her mother silenced her by holding up her hand. "And three, don't forget there is always someone worse off than you. There are women out there who lost both breasts. There are women out there that are terminal. Yes, you still have a long road ahead of you, but you will survive this, and one day you will be healthy again. I allowed you this one day, but I won't allow you another one." Her mother wiped Alex's tears off her cheeks, then kissed her forehead. "Tomorrow you will get dressed and have breakfast with your dad and me. Maybe we can go for a short walk around the neighborhood and get some fresh air. But you won't lie in bed all day long and shut out the rest of the world."

Alex could only stare at her mother's back as she marched out of Alex's room. To say she was shocked at her mother's rant was an understatement, but it flicked the on switch in Alex's brain, which she figured was her mother's intent.

She walked over to her dresser and started to eat her dinner. Tomorrow, Alex decided, would be the first day of the rest of her new life. One of the first things she'd do was call Frank and ask her to come over and spend some time together. Her mom was right. She did behave badly to Frank and she really needed to apologize.

Alex thought back to when she first met Frank and the course their relationship had taken. Alex thought at first that Frank would be just another woman to have fun with. She never expected her feelings to grow so deeply. Sure, she was attracted to her initially, despite the traffic ticket she received, but the more she got to know Frank, the harder she fell. Perhaps that was why she was pushing Frank away. It would be easier to get over her if Alex pushed her away. Who was she kidding? She already felt too much and it would hurt like hell if they ever broke up. They'd already shared so much with each other, and gone through too much, more than any couple should.

Alex made a pact with herself to stop pushing Frank away, start allowing her to help, and stop being such an asshole toward her.

❖

Frank had called her lieutenant when Alex had basically told her she didn't need her around. She knew Alex's parents would take great care of her, but it didn't ease the ache in her heart any less. If Alex didn't want her help, her community did, so she went back to work. The last thing she wanted to do was mope around her house feeling sorry for herself. Being back at work was good for her—it kept her mind off Alex for the most part and allowed her to stay busy. Her shift had definitely been busy, making traffic stops, supervising vehicle searches, and completing the paperwork that went with the job.

She was about to head into briefing when her phone buzzed. She pulled it out of her pocket to see Alex's beautiful smiling face on the screen. She swiped across the screen as her pulse sped up.

"Alex? Are you okay?"

"Hi, Frank. Yes, I'm doing okay. I just called because I missed you and wanted to see if you wanted to hang out today."

Frank's heart rate began to slow when she realized Alex was okay. Her voice sounded a little brighter, which relieved Frank. "I wish I could, but I'm at work about to begin briefing."

"Oh, I thought you took some time off."

Frank didn't miss the disappointment in Alex's voice and wasn't quite sure how she felt about that. "Yeah, well, when you told me you didn't need my help, I decided to go back to work. I didn't want to sit around my house all day wondering if you were going to call."

"I understand. I had a tough couple of days feeling sorry for myself, but my mom pretty much tore me a new asshole and told me how badly I behaved toward you."

Frank heard Alex sniff, and she wanted nothing more than to race over and wrap Alex in her arms, to wipe away her tears despite the irritation she felt. She shouldn't feel bad about going back to work. She wanted Alex to respect her feelings and her time. "I'm sorry I can't be there right now, but I can come over later if you want. I should be done here by sixteen thirty."

"If you wouldn't mind, I'd love to see you. I want to apologize in person."

"You don't need—"

"Yes, I do. I've been a real jerk, but I promise to be better."

"In that case, I'll see you later."

"Be careful out there, Sarge."

"Copy that." Frank ended the call and felt significantly lighter as she took her place behind the podium to address her officers.

Frank showered quickly after her shift and arrived at the Taylors' a little after five. She had called Julie earlier to see if she could feed Bella and take her for some exercise, which she agreed to. Frank's heart hammered in her chest as she headed to the front door. She felt like a teenager arriving for a first date, but that was crazy. She definitely wasn't a teenager and this certainly wasn't a first date, but she was uncertain of the reception she'd receive from Alex. Sure, she had invited Frank over, but her moods were understandably all over the place, and she wasn't sure which Alex would answer the door. Only one way to find out.

She knocked on the door and was greeted by Alex. God, she looked beautiful. Until then, Frank didn't realize just how much she missed seeing Alex's smile, especially when she was smiling at Frank. "Hi."

"Hi."

Frank was rooted in place, her feet stuck to the ground as she couldn't take her eyes off Alex.

"Are you just going to stand there, Sarge, or are you going to kiss me?"

"Are you sure it's all right?"

That simple question nearly broke Alex's heart. That Frank felt she had to ask it made Alex certain that she had to be honest with her about why she tried to back away. Tears filled her eyes as she spoke. "Oh, baby, of course it's all right. You have to hold me gently since I'm so sore, but I really want you to kiss me."

Frank took a tentative step forward and lightly grasped Alex's hips before leaning in to give Alex the most tender kiss she'd ever had. Alex wanted nothing more than to cleave herself to Frank's muscular body and hold on for the rest of her life, but the discomfort in her chest prevented that. She looked into Frank's eyes and could see the love shining through. "You have no idea how badly I want to hold you in my arms right now."

Frank grinned. "I think I might."

Alex stepped away and took Frank's hand. "Come on, there are some older people who want to see you."

They walked hand in hand through the house and met her parents in the kitchen. Alex couldn't describe the feeling it gave her to see her parents embrace Frank like she was a part of their family. They had seen how much Frank cared for her and welcomed her with open arms. The ease with which Frank spoke with her parents made Alex hopeful for the future she hoped to share with Frank. Alex, Frank, and her father sat at the kitchen table while her mother made dinner. Once they finished eating, Alex stood. "I need to talk with Frank privately. We'll see you in a little bit."

Frank followed Alex to her room. Alex shut the door behind them and led Frank to her bed, where they sat on the edge. Alex took Frank's hand in hers and brought it to her lips.

"I want to apologize for being such a jerk to you."

"Alex, I already told you it was okay."

"No, it wasn't. I want to tell you what I've been feeling and what's been going through my head." Alex took a deep breath then another. She had what she wanted to say all planned out in her head, but seeing the look of empathy in Frank's eyes made her momentarily forget what she wanted to say. She closed her eyes so she could refocus, then opened them again and spoke. "I tried to push you away because I didn't want you to have to go through this again like you did with Toni. But you wouldn't leave, and I can't tell you how grateful I am for that. Then another thought came into my head while I was in the hospital. If I stayed at your house during my recuperation then you would have to help me with everything, including dressing and undressing me. The thought of you seeing me naked with only one breast and a nasty scar made me want to throw up. I'm not ready for you to see me like that—like this—and I'm not sure if I ever will be ready."

"But, Alex—"

"Wait. Let me finish. I'm not sure what or how I'm going to feel when all of this is over, and I don't want you waiting around for something that might not be anything."

"It's already something, Alex. I told you before that I love you and

I'm going to be here for you. We'll figure this out together, and if you need some time alone, just tell me. I'll give it to you. But please stop trying to push me away because you think that's what's best for me. It's not. You're what's best for me."

Alex's tears fell down her cheeks as Frank gently wiped them away.

"I get why you didn't want to stay with me, and I respect that. If and when you're ready, I will be too. But we have more than just a sexual relationship. I care about you and I know you care about me. All I ask is that you talk to me, tell me how you're feeling. I felt like you shut me out at one of the most important times in your life and it felt really crappy."

Alex cupped Frank's cheek and looked into her eyes. "I'm so sorry, baby. I promise to be more open and honest about how I feel and what I need."

"Okay then. That's all I ask."

"Are we okay?"

"We're better than okay. We'll get through this together and we'll come out on top."

They kissed to seal the deal. A soft, slow kiss—a kiss of promises made and promises to come.

CHAPTER TWENTY-SEVEN

Frank went with Alex to her doctor's appointment when she had her bandages removed but respectfully remained in the waiting room with Bruce and Kathleen. Frank attempted to look through a magazine, but all she could think about was Alex. Alex had been quiet during the drive to the doctor's office. They sat in the backseat of Kathleen's sedan and Frank asked Alex if she was all right.

"I'm nervous to see the scar, to see my chest."

"I don't understand, Alex. Haven't you seen it when you did the dressing changes?"

"No. I let my mom change the bandage and I would close my eyes. I haven't seen it."

"Oh, baby. Do you want me to go into the exam room with you? I'll hold your hand if you'd like."

Alex shook her head. "I'm not ready for you to see it. I need to be comfortable with it before I want you to see it. I hope you understand."

Frank nodded. "Of course, baby. I'll stay in the waiting room with your folks."

Frank continued to switch between flipping through the magazine and looking at the clock on the wall. When Alex emerged with her eyes red and swollen, they took her home and gave her the time she needed to grieve. She had barely eaten her lunch, more or less just pushing her food around her plate. Alex had remained quiet and subdued, and Frank just remained close by, allowing Alex to explore her feelings. She knew Alex would have a difficult time coming to terms with losing her breast, but she fervently hoped that she would come to accept her new body and be grateful she was alive.

Alex stood from the table. "I'm going to my room. I'm tired and want to lie down."

Frank looked at her hopefully. "Do you want company?"

"I don't really feel like talking, honey."

"You don't have to talk. I can just be with you and hold your hand."

Alex seemed to think for a moment, then gave a slight smile. "Sure. I'd like that."

Frank stood and looked at Bruce and Kathleen, almost silently asking their permission to accompany their daughter to her bedroom. They gave a slight nod, and Frank felt some of the tension drain from her shoulders. She followed Alex to her room and shut the door. Frank stood by the bed as Alex lay down, unsure if she should join her or sit in a chair. Her question was answered when Alex asked her to lie next to her. Frank kicked off her shoes and took her place next to Alex. Frank always wanted her place to be next to her. They were lying side by side when Alex reached for Frank's hand and laced their fingers together. They remained that way for a while until Frank heard Alex sob. She turned on her side to face Alex and ran her fingers through Alex's hair. She didn't say a word. She didn't think Alex would welcome any words. Frank instinctively felt that Alex would appreciate her silent offer of support more than anything she might say.

When Alex's tears slowed to a trickle, she looked at Frank and whispered, "I saw my scar today."

Frank remained silent.

"It looks awful. Red. Angry. I have no nipple. No areola. No breast. It's all gone, Frank, and replaced by a hideous scar."

Alex began crying again, and all Frank could do was kiss Alex's forehead, letting her lips linger on her skin. She hadn't felt this helpless since Toni died. She wanted to take Alex's pain away, to take the cancer away and restore Alex to her old self. But that was impossible. She could only help Alex discover her new self. Encourage her. Support her. But she had to wait for Alex to be ready to take that step. All she could do was hope that Alex would someday be receptive to her change.

They spent the next few hours holding hands, sleeping, and crying off and on. Frank realized how late it was, and she needed to get home and get some sleep. She had early shift tomorrow, which would come too quickly. She hated to wake Alex but didn't want her to wake up alone. She squeezed Alex's hand and spoke her name.

"Hmm?"

"I gotta go, baby. I have to work tomorrow."

Alex nodded and said sleepily, "Okay. Will you call me?"

Frank turned and kissed her. "Of course. Get some rest. I love you."

Alex closed her eyes and drifted off to sleep again. Frank grabbed her shoes and walked out to the living room, surprised to see Kathleen sitting on the couch staring at the television. The volume was so low Frank doubted Kathleen could even hear it. But she had a feeling she really wasn't watching it. Frank sat at the other end of the sofa and put on her shoes.

"How is she doing?"

"She said she saw her scar today for the first time."

Kathleen nodded in understanding. "I've been changing her bandages and she would keep her eyes closed the whole time. I'm surprised she chose today to see it for the first time." She covered her eyes as she started to cry. "I can't believe my little girl is going through this. Why her?"

Frank slid across the couch and gathered Kathleen in her arms. Her heart broke for Kathleen as she held her. How unfair for all of them to go through this—for anyone really. "I know. But you raised a strong woman, and she'll eventually be all right. It'll take a while, but it will happen. We just need to give her our love and support."

Kathleen leaned back and looked into Frank's eyes. "You really love her, don't you?"

"Yes, I really do."

"I'm really glad she found you, Frank. You're a wonderful person and I'm so grateful you've come into our lives."

Frank could feel the sting of tears in her eyes and blinked them back. "I'm the lucky one." She kissed Kathleen on the cheek and stood. "Get some rest and I'll see you all later."

Kathleen followed Frank to the door and she heard the click of the lock behind her. She was able to fend off the tears that had been threatening to fall the whole day. As soon as she pulled into her driveway, the tears started to fall. She slammed her hand against the steering wheel again and again at the injustice of it all. Frank hated feeling impotent, not being able to take this pain away from the Taylors. She remembered feeling the exact same way as she watched her sister wither away in front of her. There wasn't a fucking thing she could do about it.

Frank entered her empty house, and it felt strange to not have Bella greet her at the door. Julie had come to the house earlier in the day to pick up Bella and have her for a sleepover. She navigated the darkness until she found her way into the kitchen and opened the refrigerator door. Staring at the three bottles of beer Alex had left there weeks ago, Frank blinked and pulled one from the shelf. She popped the top off and gulped the entire contents down in record time. She pulled out a second bottle, intent on taking her time with this one. She went into the living room and sat on the couch. She couldn't get Alex out of her thoughts, the vacant sound of her voice as she described what she saw when her bandages were removed. Frank took a couple of gulps of the carbonated liquid and thought about Kathleen, about the pain she was experiencing that was so plain to see as she watched her daughter fight this disease. A couple of more gulps and she thought about Bruce and the look of helplessness he displayed when he looked at his little girl.

Frank finished off the rest of the beer and contemplated going to get a third but quickly decided against it. She wasn't going to use alcohol to numb her pain or help her forget the tormented look on Alex's face. She left the empty bottle on the coffee table and dragged her tired body off to bed. She prayed for a peaceful sleep but had a feeling it would be filled with visions of Alex's tears.

Alex had an appointment with the medical oncologist to discuss her different therapies, and she asked Frank to go with her. She'd had just about enough of these fucking doctor's appointments. Despite her frustration, she was grateful to have such a wonderful support system. Alex and Frank were called back to meet with the doctor, and again, they found themselves sitting across from the doctor, separated by a large desk.

"So, Alex and Frank, Dr. Moreno feels like she got all the cancer during your surgery, but we still want to do chemo to make sure we get rid of any cancer cells that might have been left behind."

"But Dr. Moreno said it hadn't spread to the lymph nodes," Frank pointed out.

"That's true, but it doesn't mean there aren't other cancer cells in Alex's body. Now, Alex, because you're premenopausal and have an invasive breast cancer, we want to be more aggressive in your treatment because premenopausal cancer tends to be more aggressive."

Alex took in everything the doctor was saying and was also aware of the increasing pressure Frank was applying to her hand. Frank's anxiety was coming through loud and clear to Alex's fingers.

"I want to warn you of some of the side effects you could experience. Nausea, hair loss, fatigue, and a decreased immune system are the most common. Because you're an ER nurse, if you want to go back to work while you're receiving chemo, I'd recommend you wear a mask at all times."

Alex guffawed. "Because breast cancer hasn't been enough, right?

Now I have to worry about a common cold or the flu? Christ." Alex ran her fingers through her hair—hair that she would soon lose.

After a few more questions and answers, Alex and Frank left the office and headed back to Alex's home. Alex changed into an old pair of scrubs while Frank made them lunch. They sat at the table and ate their sandwiches while they discussed the treatment.

"Let me know what time your appointment is for the first chemo so I can get that time off from work. Um, that is, if you want me to go with you."

Frank had been so understanding about Alex's needs. She'd given Alex time alone when she asked for it, held her hand, wiped her tears, and made her laugh. Alex had been doing her best at letting Frank know what she needed and keeping the lines of communication open. Alex reached across the table and held Frank's hand. "I appreciate that, baby, but would you mind if my mom took me the first time? I'm not sure what it is, but it's like when I'm sick I just want my mom. I revert back to being a three-year-old."

An understanding look came across Frank's face. "I get it, honey. I would like to go eventually, but I understand about your first treatment." Alex couldn't have dreamt up a better girlfriend, and she hoped she wouldn't do anything more to drive Frank away.

Alex and her mother walked through the heavy wood door and up to the counter where they were greeted by a kind-looking woman who appeared to be a little older than Frank.

"Hello. How can I help you?"

Alex was glad the woman didn't say "good morning" because in her opinion, it wasn't good at all. "I'm Alex Taylor, and this is my mom, Kathleen. I'm starting chemo today." Alex didn't detect any sympathy from this woman, and for that she was grateful. She didn't want anyone feeling sorry for her.

"Yes, Ms. Taylor. I just need you to fill out a few forms and the nurse will take you back shortly."

It didn't take Alex long to skim through the forms and sign them. They were pretty standard for any medical facility—the notice of privacy practices, arbitration, consent to medical and surgical procedures. Alex took a moment to look around. There were only two other people in the waiting room, a man and woman, probably husband and wife. The woman wore a bandana on her bald head, and Alex could feel the sting of tears in her eyes but was able to blink them back. It wouldn't be long before she too would be wearing a cover on her head.

The other couple was called back and Alex looked around the room. It was painted in calming sage green and beige, and it almost made her feel like she was in a quiet room at a spa. There were framed prints of different flowers in vases hanging on the walls to add splashes of color. Maybe next time she would have a greater appreciation for the comfort the decorator tried to instill. But all she could really focus on was the trembling of her insides. Alex wanted to retreat out the door. She didn't want to puke. She didn't want to lose her hair. Wasn't it enough she lost her breast? Now she would lose her hair? And maybe get sicker? What the hell kind of shit was this? She felt a hand on her arm, and she looked to her mom, who had an almost serene look on her face.

"I know, baby. But it will be over soon, and your hair will grow back. You will feel strong again."

Alex opened her mouth to speak but couldn't think of anything to say. How did her mom do that? Like she could read her mind? Any further thoughts were put on hold when the door opened and a tall woman with cute, short dark hair stood in the doorway smiling.

"Ms. Taylor?"

"Alex. And this is my mom, Kathleen." They approached the woman, who held her hand out to shake theirs.

"I'm Christine, and I'll be your nurse today. Come with me, please."

Alex immediately liked her. She couldn't put her finger on why, but she reminded her a little of Frank, only softer. Maybe more like Toni if she'd had short hair. She had an air of confidence about her that made Alex believe she'd be in good hands. It reminded her of the kind of confidence she tried to show her patients—people who were sick or injured and afraid. Alex would do her best to make them feel like she and her colleagues would take care of everything and they would be okay.

Christine led Alex and her mother into a private room where she took Alex's vital signs and recorded her weight and height for appropriate medication dosage. She then led them into a communal area with semi-private stations. Alex sat in a recliner while her mom sat in a chair next to her. Christine expertly inserted an IV line into Alex's arm.

"I'm going to draw some blood so we have a baseline count, then we'll begin the treatment."

Once Christine returned from the lab, she prepared the syringes with the medicines Alex would be receiving. Her doctor had explained to them that using one drug wouldn't be effective—that it was necessary to use multiple drugs that would damage the cancer cells and interfere with the growth and division of those cells. She had been given a prescription for a medication in pill form that she would have to take for five years since her cancer was hormone-receptor positive. She was set to start that when chemo ended. In the meantime, she would be receiving chemo every two weeks for the next sixteen weeks.

When Christine finished drawing the medications, she spoke to Alex and her mother. "You won't feel any pain with this, Alex, but it might feel cold for a few seconds. I can get you a blanket if you'd like."

Alex leaned her head back, closed her eyes, and took in a deep breath. She shook her head. "No, that's okay."

"If you change your mind, let me know. I'm going to begin now unless you have any questions."

"No, I'm ready." She held her mom's hand as she continued to take deep breaths in and slowly letting them out. She did her best to remain calm as the first icy jolt hit her veins. She had to remember what the doctor said. The chemo would ensure unlikely recurrence. Alex envisioned her and Frank in the park, her head in Frank's lap with the sun beating down on them, warming her, as Frank slowly ran her fingers through Alex's hair. This was her happy place. She could hear the birds sing and could see Jordan and Kirsten chasing after Aiden as he toddled along, Bella running after them. This would be the place she would visit during every treatment. She felt a grin tug at the corners of her mouth. She opened her eyes to see her mother and Christine looking at her.

"What?"

Her mother smiled. "You looked pretty peaceful just then."

"I was. I imagined me and Frank lying in a park with the sun shining down on us."

"Is Frank your boyfriend?" Christine asked as she started to inject the next vial.

"No, she's my girlfriend. Frank is short for Francesca."

Christine laughed. "Oh, that's great. Have you been together long?"

Alex thought about it. "You know, I'm not sure how long we've been together. Maybe about four or five months or so, but at times it seems longer, like forever."

"How's she handling your diagnosis?"

"She's been great despite my trying to push her away."

Christine grabbed the next vial and slowly pushed the plunger. "Why would you do that?"

"Her twin died from breast cancer a few years ago, and I was trying to spare her the pain of going through this again."

Christine glanced at Alex. "I'm assuming she stayed strong."

Alex chuckled. "Oh, yes. She's been my rock and hasn't let me get away with much. She'll be coming with me sometimes, but today I just wanted my mom with me."

Her mother smiled fondly at Alex and squeezed her hand.

Christine withdrew the final syringe. "Well, you're very lucky to have such wonderful women in your life. That's it for the medicine, Alex. I just need to take out your IV and check your vitals." Christine took her blood pressure and heart rate and entered them into her tablet. "I'm sure your doctor went over this with you, but I want to remind you that you'll probably be tired and might have some nausea. Try and get some rest. Those symptoms usually don't last for more than a day or two. We'll see you in two weeks."

Alex stood with her mother. "Thank you, Christine. You made this first treatment not horrible."

Christine rested her hand on Alex's shoulder. "I'm glad. Take care and I'll see you in a couple of weeks."

They left the center and Alex lifted her face to the sun. The first treatment wasn't as bad as she imagined it to be, and that probably had a lot to do with the pleasantness of Christine. Alex knew she'd probably feel worse tomorrow, but at least now she knew what to expect the next time.

❖

A week after her second chemo session, Alex noticed more of her hair than usual sitting on the drain as she turned off the shower. She picked up the wet, chestnut strands and felt a knot in her stomach as she realized it was beginning. She was starting to lose her hair. She knew it would happen, but it still didn't prepare her to see the thinning out. She ran her fingers through her hair and pulled more clumps out of her head. She slid down the wet tile wall until she was sitting with her knees pulled to her chest. Alex rocked herself slightly in a futile effort to comfort herself. She startled at the knock on her bathroom door.

"Baby, I wanted you to know I'm here. I let myself in."

Shit. Alex forgot Frank was coming over to have lunch. She didn't want Frank to see her this way, her scar, her clumps of hair in her hand. "Go away, Frank. I don't feel like eating lunch right now."

"Alex, what's wrong? What happened?"

"My fucking hair is falling out! That's what happened."

"I'm coming in."

"No! I don't want you to see me like this. Just leave."

"Look, you either come out here, or I'm coming in. What's it going to be?"

Why did Frank have to be so stubborn? Why couldn't she just leave her alone? Alex knew it was because Frank loved her and cared about her, but she just didn't want to deal with it right now. She took a deep breath in and let it out slowly, trying to tamp down her irritation.

"Fine, I'll come out. Just give me a few minutes." Alex stepped out of the shower and toweled herself dry. She put on her bra and slid her prosthesis into place. She had started getting her expander filled, but until she was back to her regular C cup, she would wear the prosthesis. She pulled her thick terrycloth robe off the hook and wrapped it tightly around her. She opened the door to find Frank pacing alongside Alex's bed. She stopped and looked at Alex when the door opened. Frank stood frozen, and Alex could tell Frank wasn't sure if she was welcome or not. To ease Frank's fears, and comfort herself, she slid her arms around

Frank's waist, and rested her cheek against Frank's chest. The strength and surety of Frank's arms enfolding her eased some of her anguish.

"I'm sorry, baby."

Alex felt Frank kiss the top of her head and her hands caress her back.

"What can I do?"

"I want you to shave my head."

Alex looked into Frank's eyes when Frank didn't answer.

"Are you sure?"

"My hair's starting to fall out, so we may as well jump right in. But do me a favor and call Jordan. I want her and Kirsten here when we do this."

"Of course. I'll give you some privacy to get dressed and I'll meet you in the living room."

Frank shut the door behind her and pulled her cell phone from her pocket with a shaking hand. She blinked away her tears and took deep breaths. They knew this would happen eventually, but Frank didn't think it would affect her like this. She pulled up Jordan's contact information and dialed her number.

"Hello."

"Hey, Jordan, it's Frank."

"What's going on, buddy?"

Frank took another deep breath before answering. "Alex is starting to lose her hair and she wants me to shave it for her today, but she wants you and Kirsten here."

"Oh, man, okay. Kirsten is out hiking with Brenda, but I'm expecting her back anytime now. Do you need us to bring anything? Lunch?"

"I came over to have lunch with her, so I'll make us all some sandwiches. Um, I think we need some hair clippers, though."

"Okay, we'll take care of that. How's she doing?"

"I'm not sure, honestly. She tried to kick me out when I knocked on her bathroom door to let her know I was here, but then after I told her I wasn't leaving, she came out, hugged me, and asked me to shave her head. I can't even begin to imagine how she's feeling right now."

"And how about you? How are you holding up?"

"I'm fine."

"Uh-huh. Tell me how you really are."

Frank ran her hand through her hair, then wiped away an errant tear. "It's hard, to be honest, seeing her go through this and not being able to do anything about it. But I'm trying to stay strong."

"I'm sure you are, buddy, but you don't have to be strong all the time. You can talk to me anytime."

"I appreciate it, but I'm hanging in there. Really."

"All right. But it's an open offer, Frank. Hey, Kirsten and Brenda just got here, so we'll see you soon, okay?"

"See you soon, J."

Frank turned to see Alex walk into the room dressed in jeans, a worn T-shirt, and a baseball cap. Alex came over to Frank and hugged her, laying her head on Frank's chest.

"I talked to Jordan, and Kirsten and Brenda just got back from hiking. They're going to stop and get some clippers then they'll be over. I told her I'd make us all lunch."

"I've lost my appetite. I don't want anything."

"I'm sure you don't, Alex, but you need to keep up your strength. How about I just make you some soup? Do you think you could eat that?"

Alex shrugged. "I guess so."

"That's my girl." Frank lifted Alex's chin to place a gentle kiss on her lips. "Let's go into the kitchen so I can start making lunch."

Frank set about making sandwiches and heating up soup. By the time she finished, Jordan and Kirsten had arrived. After they hugged each other, they sat at the table to eat. Kirsten handed Alex a gift bag and Alex looked at her questioningly.

"You know how much I love to shop," Kirsten said. "I saw these and I thought they'd look great on you."

Alex pulled three silk bandanas out, all in different colors and patterns. "They're beautiful, Kirsten."

"I'm glad you like them. I thought these could get you started for the days you don't want to wear a wig."

Alex leaned over and hugged Kirsten. "I love them, and I love you."

"I love you too."

Jordan cleared her throat. "Okay, enough of the mushies. Let's eat."

As they began to dig into their lunch, Jordan smiled. "Alex, your godson is starting to get into all kinds of mischief. He's obviously not listening to his moms, so I think you need to talk some sense into him."

Alex laughed. "I don't believe for one second our boy is capable of what you call mischief. What has he supposedly done?"

Jordan looked to Kirsten, who said, "Go ahead. You started it."

Jordan hung her head. "Well, I bought him some finger paints and large sheets of paper to paint. He thinks the colors of the paint look much better on his bedroom walls...and his body."

Alex covered her mouth with her hand. "Oh, no. His cute little body too?"

Kirsten nodded. "Let me tell you, it is not easy to wash finger paints off a protesting little boy." She looked over to Jordan. "Now tell her what your son did when we had company over for dinner."

Jordan chuckled. "We had Brenda and her new girlfriend over for dinner last weekend, and we thought Aiden was playing with his blocks in the living room while we cleared the table and started dishes. Turns out he went number two in his diaper, and apparently he was so proud, he took off his diaper and brought it to Brenda to show her."

Frank and Alex shook with laughter and soon had tears rolling down their faces.

"What happened?"

Kirsten replied between giggles. "Brenda told him what a big boy he was, then took him to his room to clean him up and put on a fresh diaper."

Alex put her hand over her heart. "Oh, my goodness. He's growing up so fast."

"That he is," Jordan said. "And as soon as you're up for it, he told us he wants to go to the park again with you, Frank, and Bella. He also told us that he thinks Kirsten and I deserve some time alone, so the sooner you could take him, the better."

Frank arched an eyebrow. "He said all that, did he?"

Jordan grinned. "Well, maybe not verbally, but I know how my son thinks." She winked at Alex.

"You tell that little monkey we'll be by soon to rescue him from his crazy mothers." Alex smiled. "Okay, let's get this show on the road."

Jordan grabbed Alex's hand. "You sure you're ready?"

Alex nodded. "It's inevitable, J. My hair has started to fall out, so it's time for all of it to go. It'll be one less thing I have to worry about."

Frank stood from the table. "I'll go put on some music while you guys get ready."

Kirsten followed Frank into the living room, and Frank felt her hands on her shoulders as she was looking through Alex's music selection.

"Are you okay with this, Frank?"

Frank didn't turn around, not wanting Kirsten to see the unshed tears in her eyes, and waved her hand dismissively. "Yeah, I'm fine. It's what Alex wants."

Frank felt Kirsten's hands caress her shoulders and felt the comfort Kirsten was bestowing.

"I know this has been hard for both of you, but Jordan and I really appreciate how much you're doing for her. It must bring up a lot of sorrow for you, what you went through with your sister."

Frank wiped her eyes and turned to face Kirsten and was enveloped in Kirsten's hug. All she could do was nod in agreement. Frank took in a deep breath, trying to calm her emotions. "It has, but it's not the same, you know? Toni didn't find out until it was too late. Alex was diagnosed early, and once she's done with treatment, she'll feel better. She'll be better." She gave Kirsten a watery smile. "Now how about we pick out some upbeat music?"

Kirsten nodded and selected a CD. "Here we go. This one is her favorite." Kirsten put the disc in the player, pushed the play button, and turned up the volume. She began to dance and took Frank's hand, twirling herself under Frank's arm, making Frank laugh. Kirsten kissed Frank on the cheek. "Let's go."

They danced their way back to the table and faced their chairs toward the kitchen where Alex sat facing them with a towel draped across her shoulders. Jordan had used scissors to cut more than half of Alex's hair off. Frank looked down to see Alex's hair scattered on the floor, then looked up and locked eyes on Alex's questioning ones. She grinned and nodded, and was rewarded with Alex's smile.

Once Jordan finished cutting the hair, she placed the scissors on the counter and picked up the clippers. There was a long silence, and Frank saw the trepidation on Jordan's face. She hadn't really given much thought to what Jordan must be going through, seeing Alex go through this fight. Frank felt incredibly selfish, only worried what she and Alex were feeling. Jordan and Alex had been friends since their freshman year in college, and Jordan had been a part of Alex's family for almost fifteen years. Her heart had to have been hurting to see her best friend, the godmother of her son, go through this. Frank started to stand when Jordan began to cry, but was restrained by a soft hand on her arm. She looked to Kirsten, who barely shook her head. Frank looked at Alex pleadingly.

Alex stood and faced Jordan, who now covered her face with her free hand. Alex pulled Jordan's hand away. "Hey, tough girl. You have to finish the job."

Jordan continued to cry. "I can't, Al."

It amazed Frank to see how strong Alex stood in front of Jordan. Frank's heart swelled as she watched Alex kiss her chastely on the lips.

"Come on, J. I want you to do this for me. It's really all right. Please." Alex cuffed the back of Jordan's head. "You owe me."

Jordan rubbed the mark where Alex hit her and barked out a laugh. "I owe you? How do you figure?"

Alex cupped Jordan's cheek. "I had to live through seven years of you sulking after you and Kelly broke up. And if you don't remember, it was me that gave you the kick in the ass to give Kirsten a chance. How did that work out for you?"

Jordan smiled. "I guess it went okay."

Kirsten cleared her throat. "Excuse me? Just okay?"

They all laughed and Jordan blushed. "Okay, Al, I owe you. Now sit your skinny ass back down in the chair so I can finish paying off my debt."

Alex sat back down and winked at Frank and Kirsten. "That's what I thought."

It only took ten more minutes for Jordan to shave the rest of Alex's hair off. Frank looked to Alex, and she felt her heart race, threatening to explode out of her chest. She was so damned proud of her. There she sat before them, bald and beautiful, with a determined look on her face. Frank stood and walked to Alex, cupped her face, and kissed her tenderly.

"You are so beautiful."

Alex looked down, seemingly embarrassed, but Frank put her finger under her chin and guided her head up so she could look into Alex's warm brown eyes.

"You're the most beautiful, strongest, most amazing woman I have ever known, and I will keep telling you until you believe me."

Frank kissed her again, then stepped back to look at Jordan. "My turn."

"What?" all three of them asked.

Frank smiled and pulled her shoulders back. "I said it's my turn. I don't think I'll look as good as Alex bald, but I'll take a buzz cut." Frank ran her hand over her inch-and-a-half-long hair. "It's time for a cut anyway."

Alex stood before Frank and held her hands. "Baby, you don't have to do this."

Frank squeezed Alex's hands and smiled. "I know I don't *have* to. I *want* to. I'm so damned proud of you, and I want to show my support for you."

Alex threw her arms around Frank's neck and pulled her close, then whispered in her ear, "Thank you. For everything."

Frank squeezed Alex close, then let go and looked into her eyes. "No thanks needed, love. You'd do the same for me."

Alex nodded then kissed Frank until her knees nearly buckled.

"You heard the sarge, Jordan. Give her what she wants."

Alex took Frank's vacated chair next to Kirsten and held her hand as Jordan attached the number four guard to the clippers. Frank tuned out the sound of the buzz as she kept her eyes locked on Alex. They shared a knowing grin as Jordan ran the clippers through Frank's hair. Frank hadn't planned on buzzing her hair, but Alex had shown such courage through her fight so far that Frank felt like this was a good way to show her solidarity. She really wanted Alex to feel that she was in this with her, in sickness and in health.

Chapter Twenty-nine

Alex was a little more than halfway through her chemo regimen and becoming more agitated as the weeks went on. She was tired of the nausea, the fatigue, the looks of pity in strangers' eyes whenever she went out in public. Even when she wore her wig it didn't look or feel right to her, so she normally just wore one of the bandanas Kirsten gave her. She woke up full of piss and vinegar, knowing what she had to go through after she received her chemo later that morning.

She cried as she showered, letting the tears mix with the water and flow down the drain. She moved slowly as she dressed and wrapped her bandana around her bald head. There were times, like today, when she just wanted to fuck it all and quit her treatment, but she knew what the consequences would be if she did. Alex knew the chance of recurrence was greater if she didn't complete her treatment. So she continued like a soldier marching to battle. She managed to eat a piece of dry toast for breakfast even though she knew it would be coming back up later. She hadn't made it through a single chemo session where she didn't violently vomit later that day. Her body even had the nerve to gain weight despite her lack of appetite. She used to love to eat; she loved the taste of food. Now she ate to survive. Her clothes no longer fit her or showed her curves. Hell, she no longer had curves. She felt fat and frumpy and unattractive. She couldn't believe Frank still wanted to be with her.

The knock on her front door indicated Frank had arrived at take her to her appointment. They had been getting along so well, and Frank was being very patient with her. Alex hadn't wanted much intimacy, but Frank seemed to understand and accept it. When Alex answered the door, Frank leaned in to kiss her hello, but Alex turned her cheek at the last second. With the mood she was in, Alex would have to try hard to even be cordial.

"Let me grab my purse and we can go."

Alex saw the hurt in Frank's eyes, and she felt bad for reacting the way she did, but she just couldn't seem to help herself with the way she was feeling. Before she was diagnosed, she was happy, playful, positive, and sexual. She now felt none of those most of the time. Yes, she was grateful to be alive because as she saw firsthand in the ER, there was always someone worse off. But every now and then, she couldn't shake her funk and tended to take it out on those closest to her. Unfortunately for Frank, she was now in the line of fire.

She attempted to make amends once they were in Frank's truck by reaching across the center console and holding Frank's hand.

"So, tell me about this place. Are the people nice?"

"Yeah, they've all been pleasant and attentive. Christine, the nurse I've been working with, reminds me a little of how I imagine Toni would be. She's been asking when you'd be coming with me."

"Did you tell her I've been wanting to but you wouldn't let me?"

Frank's attempt at humor didn't reach Alex, and it just made her more agitated. She silently counted to ten to calm herself down. When she felt more at ease, she looked over at Frank and saw her staring straight ahead. She had a contemplative look on her face.

"What are you thinking about?" Alex asked as she rubbed Frank's hand with her thumb.

"I was thinking about Toni and the times I spent with her while she was getting treatment. The people we dealt with were also wonderful. I was just wondering what would make someone want to work in oncology. Or hospice, for that matter. When we realized Toni wasn't going to get better, and she decided to go on hospice, everyone we dealt with, from the admissions, to the social worker, to the nurses— everyone made us feel like…I don't know how to say this…almost like we didn't have to worry about anything except spending our remaining time together. Those people are angels walking this earth."

Alex blinked back her tears and took a deep breath. "It's hard to say why people do what they do. It's some sort of calling, I guess. Speaking for myself, I chose to work in the ER because I thought it's what my personality and skills were best suited for. How about you? What made you become a cop?"

Frank was silent for a few moments before answering. "Honestly, I don't know. It's something I always wanted to be when I was growing up. I liked trying to right the wrongs and help people who needed help. Now, I like the fact that I belong to a larger family—one that's by choice and not by blood."

Alex nodded. "I can see that about you. Your honor and nobility make you the perfect person to be out patrolling our streets. I think my compassion and diligence makes me the perfect person to be a nurse in the ER."

They arrived at the clinic and waited for Christine to bring them back. Alex tried to rein in her annoyance at Frank's bouncing knee. Maybe it wasn't such a good idea to bring Frank to chemo with her. She was still trying to spare Frank the feelings of losing her sister this might bring back to the surface, but Frank kept asking to take her, and Alex finally relented. Thankfully, they didn't have to wait long before Christine came to get them.

"Hey! There's my favorite nurse."

Christine's upbeat attitude made Alex smile, and she greeted her with a hug. "Hey there. Christine, this is Frank."

Christine offered her hand. "Ah, the infamous Frank. I'm so glad to finally meet you. I was beginning to think Alex had made you up," she said with a laugh.

"Good to meet you too. I've heard a lot about you, and I want to thank you for taking such good care of my girl."

Alex's breath caught when Frank called Alex "her girl." She hoped that Frank was strong enough to want to stay with her. Conversely, Alex hoped she was strong enough to eventually reveal her new self to Frank. Currently, she had no sexual desire, and she knew that had a little to do with her treatment. But a lot had to do with her self-image. In her eyes, she was disfigured, no longer whole. She'd been considering going to counseling with a therapist who had experience working with other women who had similar issues, but she hadn't revealed this to anyone just yet. She wanted to complete her chemo and reconstruction before she took anything else on.

Alex took her place in the brown leather recliner and kept quiet as Christine and Frank conversed through her treatment. Frank gave

Christine a brief synopsis of what her sister went through and her experience with the treatment. Alex was grateful that she was left out of the conversation. She closed her eyes and drowned out the sound of their voices as she went to her happy place in her mind and Christine continued to exchange one syringe for another. The time passed quickly, and before she knew it, she was saying good-bye to Christine, saying she would see her in a couple of weeks.

Frank was surprisingly quiet on the ride home. Alex had been accurate that Christine reminded her of Toni. Christine's positive outlook and her demeanor were reminiscent of Toni. Frank had tried hard to pay attention to Christine, but she always had awareness of Alex and what she was going through. She would divert her attention to Alex and see her with her eyes closed, into herself, accepting the medications given through her IV. It felt as if Frank had been transported back three years when she would sit by Toni's side through her treatment. Frank thought she had done fairly well staying in the present for the most part.

When they got back to Alex's, Frank asked her if she wanted any tea or toast, but Alex declined.

"Can I get you a blanket? Do you want to lie down?"

Alex shook her head and went to sit on the couch. When Frank sat next to her, Alex jumped up and hurried to the bathroom. Frank followed and rubbed Alex's back as she hovered over the toilet. When Alex stopped, she rested her forehead on her arm.

"Can I get you anything? A glass of water?"

Alex shook her head.

"A cold washcloth?"

Alex shook her head again.

"Didn't the doctor give you anything to combat your nausea? They should have given you something."

"Frank, just shut up and leave me alone," Alex moaned.

Frank ran her fingers over her scalp and blew out a forceful breath. "Goddamn it, Toni! Why won't you let me help you?"

Alex looked up and glared at Frank. "What did you call me?"

Frank scrunched her eyebrows together, confused. "What are you talking about?"

Alex narrowed her eyes and spoke in a low, menacing voice. "You called me Toni."

"What? No, I didn't."

Alex shook her head and closed her eyes. "I knew you were staying with me out of obligation. I fucking knew it. You stayed with me so you could help me the way you couldn't help Toni."

Frank held up her hands to placate Alex. "That's not true. I love you and you know it."

"No, I think you love the idea of being able to help me through this, to see me survive. You want to be my hero, my savior, but I don't need that and I don't need you. Get out."

"Please, Alex, can't we talk about this? Let me explain."

"There's nothing to explain. Get the hell out. I don't ever want to see you again."

Alex pushed Frank out of the bathroom and slammed the door.

Frank stood there stunned, staring at the closed door that separated her and Alex, the love of her life, the woman who just kicked her out of her house, and a sudden coldness ran through Frank's veins. She stumbled into the living room, not exactly sure what had just happened, and plopped down on the couch. She ran her hands over her scalp, trying to figure out what the hell she said to majorly piss off Alex. She said Frank called her Toni, but was that it? Was that why Alex kicked her out? Alex had been a bit surly all morning and stayed pretty quiet. The whole experience that day reminded Frank of when she would go with Toni to her treatments. She remembered how Toni would become verbally combative when she would come home from chemo. Frank hadn't exactly been sure if it was because Toni was scared, not feeling well, or something else. And meeting Christine today, whose personality and looks reminded Frank of Toni. No wonder she called Alex by her sister's name. Toni had been in her thoughts all day, and it had brought up so many memories.

Frank didn't want to leave Alex alone, but she also knew better than to try to force things with her right now. Alex probably wasn't in the mood to hear any explanation Frank could come up with. She dialed Kathleen's number, since Jordan and Kirsten were at work.

"Hi, Kathleen. It's Frank. Would you mind coming over and looking after Alex?"

"What's wrong? Is she okay?"

"Well, she's throwing up, but she kicked me out of the house, and I don't want to leave her alone. I also don't want to make her more upset by staying here."

"I'll be right over."

Frank shoved her phone back in her pocket and dropped her head in her hands. She honestly didn't know what to do about Alex. Frank loved her and would do anything to prove it to her. But how? What more could she do? Alex obviously didn't believe her or trust what Frank told her to be true. Frank couldn't force Alex to believe her either. She believed that she could have spent the rest of her life loving Alex, that they could have been happy together. She still believed that—if only Alex would come around. The only thing Frank felt she could do at this point was let Alex have her space and figure out what she wanted.

Frank heard the front door open and turned to see Kathleen. She sat next to Frank on the couch and placed her hand on Frank's knee.

"What did my daughter do?"

Frank told her about their morning, how quiet Alex had been, how Frank tried to help, and when she got frustrated, she accidentally called Alex Toni.

"She thinks I'm staying with her out of obligation, Kathleen, but I swear I'm not. I honestly love her, and I want to help her in any way I can."

"I know you do, honey. I don't know how she got it in her head that that's why you're with her. If it means anything, her dad and I adore you and love the way you treat our daughter. Do you want me to talk to her?"

Frank shook her head. "I'll give her the space she wants right now. I didn't want to leave her alone with how sick she is right now, but I didn't want to upset her more." Frank leaned over and kissed Kathleen on the cheek. "Tell her I'll call her later, and you call me if you need me."

Alex was rinsing her mouth out when there was a knock on the door. "I told you to leave. I don't want you here."

The door opened and Alex saw her mom in the mirror's reflection. "Mom, what are you doing here?"

"Hey, honey. How are you feeling?"

"Awful. This is one of the things I hate most—the nausea and fatigue." Alex slipped past her mom and lay down on her bed. She asked again, "What are you doing here?"

"Frank called me to come over and keep an eye on you."

"Is she still here?"

"No, she just left. She thought it would be best if she weren't here."

Alex sighed. "I knew she'd run when it got tough."

Her mother sat next to Alex and looked her in the eyes. "More like you chased her off. Why do you insist on treating her so badly?"

Alex sat up and raised her voice. "What are you talking about? I didn't chase her off. If she really loved me, she would have stayed."

Her mother stood. "Cut the crap, Alex. You've been chasing her off ever since you were diagnosed. All she's been doing is trying to take care of you, and you keep treating her horribly. Your father and I did not raise you to treat people like that, especially ones you supposedly love."

"I never said I loved her."

"Oh, baby, you didn't have to. It's written all over your face. I see it in your eyes. I've never seen that look in your eyes with anyone else. Why do you continally push her away?"

"I don't want her to be with me because she feels sorry for me. I want her to be with me because she loves me."

"Why do you think she doesn't love you?"

"Mom, she called me Toni today."

"That's it? That's your whole reasoning?"

Alex looked down, avoiding her mother's gaze. Now that she thought about it, it did sound pretty ridiculous. Why was she behaving so irrationally? She could use the fact that her life had been turned upside down in the past few months, but that didn't explain why she wasn't treating other people the way she was treating Frank.

"I don't know why I'm treating her like crap, Mom." Alex broke down and started to cry. This wasn't who she was. She wasn't an asshole. She was a compassionate person who normally put other people's needs before her own. She wasn't used to being dependent on others to take care of her, but that's exactly what happened. She depended on others to take her to chemo, take care of her when she was sick or fatigued. But she had to keep in mind that this would soon be over. She only had a few more chemo treatments, then she could undergo her reconstruction and resume her normal life. Who was she kidding? Her life would never be like it was before the diagnosis. She would just have to find her new normal. She continued to cry as her mom held her, but her tears weren't for self-pity—they were for Frank.

She deserved someone better than Alex, someone who would show their appreciation and love.

❖

Frank got in her truck and left Alex's place, not knowing exactly where she was going. Things between her and Alex had been better lately, which was why Alex's behavior today threw Frank for a loop. Frank's head was spinning, her stomach was grumbling since she hadn't had anything to eat, and she certainly didn't have an appetite now. After driving all over town, she found herself sitting in the parking lot of the Joint. She didn't like to drink when she was upset, but she figured one little drink wouldn't hurt. She went inside and took a seat at the end of the bar. The bartender came over, and Frank ordered a shot of tequila with a beer chaser. After she threw back the shot, she placed the glass upside down on the bar and picked up her bottle of beer to take a drink. A hand on her shoulder made her turn around.

"Christ, Robbins, shouldn't you be on patrol?"

"We just finished our shift, Sarge, and a couple of the guys and I decided to get a drink. Do you want to join us?"

Frank checked her watch. Damn. When did it get to be four thirty? "No, thanks. I just came in for a quick drink."

"You okay, Sarge? You look pretty upset."

"I'm fine, Robbins. Go back to your table and I'll see you later."

Frank turned her back to Robbins, dismissing him back to his table.

"Paul, can I get another shot?"

Frank had her head down on her arms, which were crossed on top of the bar. She again felt a hand on her shoulder, but didn't bother lifting her head. "I told you I'm fine, Robbins." She wondered why her words sounded slurred.

"He didn't think you were fine, so he texted me."

Frank lifted her head when she heard Katie's voice, and she threw her arms around her.

"Katie! Come have a drink with me."

"I think you've had enough to drink, Frank. Let me take you home."

"I've only had a couple. I'm fine."

"Well, Paul said you've had five shots and three beers. I think it's time to go."

Frank felt her face get hot and she started crying. "She kicked me out, Katie. Alex kicked me out and won't let me help her."

"Let's go home and we can talk about it, buddy. Do you think you can walk on your own?"

Frank shook her head and felt the room start to spin. She thought she might vomit and held her hand over her stomach. When the wave of nausea passed, she put her arm around Katie's shoulders.

"Help me out to my truck."

"No way. We'll come back and get it tomorrow. I'll take you home. And if you puke in my car, I'm kicking your ass."

Frank spent the drive home staring out the window, her head bobbing with every bump in the road, willing herself not to throw up. Katie hadn't said a word to her once she got Frank in the car. Now she had the two most important women in her life angry with her. She wondered how the day got so cluster-fucked. They pulled into Frank's driveway, and Katie came around to help her out of the car and inside her house.

After Bella greeted them, Frank went to sit on the couch while Katie fed Bella. Katie came in and sat next to Frank and handed her a glass of water and some aspirin.

"So, what was so bad today that made you want to go to a bar and get drunk?"

"I didn't mean to get drunk. I don't know what happened today. I took Alex to her chemo appointment, and I guess that's when it happened. Her nurse reminded me so much of Toni, and the whole time, I felt like I was back three years ago when Toni was getting her treatment."

"What happened with Alex? You said at the bar she threw you out?"

"She started getting sick, and I tried to help her. She yelled at me to leave her alone, and I guess I called her Toni by mistake. Then she accused me of staying with her out of obligation and not love. She told me to get out of her house." Frank leaned her head on the back of the couch and looked to the ceiling as if she'd find the answers written there. "I called her mom to come stay with her, and when Kathleen got there, I left. I kept driving around until I ended up at the bar."

"So you decided to drown your sorrows in a bottle of tequila. Nice, Frank. I thought you didn't want to be like your parents."

"I don't. I'm not."

"That's where you're headed. You've had your share of stress, and you're trying to numb your pain with alcohol. Exactly what your parents did. Exactly what you said you'd never do."

"I swear, Katie, this is the only time I've done this. I've been seeing Dr. Cook, and she's been helping me deal with Alex's illness."

"Well, you need to talk to her about today. Because you're fucking crazy if you think I'm going to stand by and watch you become a drunk."

Frank was sobbing and trying to catch her breath. Her whole body shook as she tried to speak. "I-I-I p-promise, K-K-Katie. P-p-please don't b-be mad at m-me."

Katie wrapped her arms around Frank. "I'm not mad at you, but I am worried about you. You've been dealing with a lot, and I want to make sure you stay safe. You're my best friend and I love you. I don't want to lose you."

Frank squeezed Katie tightly. "I love you too. I'm sorry I worried you."

"I forgive you. Just don't let it happen again."

Frank laughed. "I'll try not to."

"Good. Now let's get you into bed. I'm going to stay in the guest room tonight just in case you need me. In the morning, I'll take you to get your truck and you can go talk to Dr. Cook. Once that's over, you can see about getting your girl to talk to you again."

Katie escorted Frank to her room and helped her take off her shoes and get into bed.

"I'll be in the guest room if you need me."

"Okay. Thanks, Katie. Love you."

Frank was asleep before Katie even turned off the lights.

Chapter Thirty

Frank read the text over and over but still didn't want to comprehend the meaning. Was Alex breaking up with her? It had been four days since Alex kicked her out. Frank had called a few times and left messages, but didn't hear back from Alex until today. Frank was so excited to see Alex's name pop up on her phone, but it quickly turned into a lump in her throat when she read the message.

I'm sorry I was such a jerk. You deserve better than me. I need some time to myself. I hope you understand. Take care of yourself.

Frank had met with Dr. Cook the day after she tied one on, and it had been an emotional session. They talked about Alex, Toni, her parents, and why she felt the need to drink. Dr. Cook thought it would be beneficial to add an extra session every week to make sure Frank wouldn't be using alcohol as a crutch. She was grateful for the extra session that was scheduled for that day. She would definitely need to talk to Dr. Cook about this text.

Part of her wanted to drive over to Alex's and ask her what the hell was going on. The other part wanted to keep her pride intact and not pursue it any further. She'd never been one to chase after women, but then again, she'd never been with a woman like Alex. Before Alex had been diagnosed, she was a different person. She laughed a lot, was friendly to anyone she came in contact with, loved to have a good time, and loved with her whole heart. One of the many things Frank loved about Alex was how tender she was with Aiden, how she always took Bella into consideration, and liked to do things to include her, like go to the park or dog beach.

Their sexual relationship was also off the charts. Frank had never experienced the level of intimacy she shared with Alex with anyone else. They were always in sync with what the other needed, whether it was slow and tender, or fast and hard. But regardless of their sexual chemistry, they had so much more than that. They hadn't had sex since before Alex's mastectomy. Frank hadn't even seen Alex naked since the surgery, but that didn't really matter to her. Sure, she missed making love with Alex, but she would have been content to never again have sex if she just had the opportunity to spend her life loving and being loved by Alex.

She picked up her phone to call Alex but just as quickly put it back down. As much as she hated to do it, she was going to give Alex the time and space she said she needed. Frank was just going to have to keep busy in the meantime. She hadn't had much time to spend with Katie outside of work. Maybe she and Katie could get together after work one night and grab a beer. Maybe she'd take a few days off work and take Bella camping. She'd been so focused on Alex's well-being that she hadn't really done anything for herself. Not that she minded. Alex and her treatment were Frank's primary concern. It still was, but Alex had made it known that Frank was no longer welcome in that aspect.

Basketball season had ended two weeks ago, but maybe Frank would play when it started back up. She got along well with her teammates and liked hanging out with them after the games. She also wanted to keep her friendship with Jordan, but she wondered if Jordan would pick sides. If she did, it would obviously be Alex's side Jordan would stay on. Frank really liked spending time with Jordan and Kirsten, and she had really bonded with Aiden. There were times when she and Aiden would be playing, and Frank imagined her and Alex having a kid or two of their own.

Frank wiped away the tears that started to fall. Not only was she losing Alex, she was losing everyone associated with Alex that she had come to care about, including Alex's parents. Frank mourned the loss of Bruce and Kathleen, who had essentially become like surrogate parents to her. They showed her more love and respect than her own parents had when they were still in her life. They welcomed her into their family, and just as quickly, she was now out of it.

Bella jumped up onto the couch and licked Frank's face, taking away the tears on her warm tongue. Frank hugged her dog, her constant companion, until the tears stopped falling.

"Don't worry, girl. We'll eventually get over Alex, and we'll move on to the rest of our lives." If only she could believe her own words.

Chapter Thirty-one

"Thank you for meeting with me, Dr. Meyer. Dr. Moreno highly recommended you. She thought maybe you'd be able to help me." Alex walked with Dr. Meyer back to her office and was invited to have a seat in one of two wingback chairs. The room was utilitarian but comfortable at the same time. She liked that they would be sitting fairly close to each other, like they were visiting in someone's living room. It didn't feel like she was being seen by a psychologist.

"I appreciate hearing that, Alex. Why don't you tell me a little about yourself and your family, then a little about your work, things you like to do for fun. Then we'll talk about why you're here. I want to know if you've ever had therapy before and what your expectations are from seeing me."

Alex discussed her parents, her relationship with Jordan, Kirsten, and Aiden. She talked about nursing in the ER and how she couldn't wait to get back. She told the doctor that she enjoyed dancing and spending time with Aiden. She almost mentioned that going to the park with Frank and Bella was also a favorite activity, but she stopped herself before the words came out. "I haven't had therapy before, so I'm not sure exactly what to expect. I guess I just want help in changing my attitude."

"It sounds like you have a wonderful support system with your family and friends. Let's talk about what you want me to help you with."

Alex took a deep breath and looked down at her hands. "I was diagnosed with breast cancer about three months ago. After going over my options, I had a mastectomy of my left breast, had an expander put in, and started chemotherapy. Once I'm done with chemo, I'll have breast reconstruction surgery and start hormone therapy."

"How's that going for you?"

Alex looked up expecting to see pity in the doctor's eyes but instead saw compassion and curiosity. "I get sick after each chemo treatment, and I'm pretty tired for a couple of days, but then my energy level returns until my next treatment. Thankfully, I have only two more to go through. I'd have to say that the nausea, fatigue, and hair loss have been the worst part about this."

"What about the loss of your breast? Wasn't that difficult for you?"

Alex blinked slowly, almost outraged that she would even ask that. "Of course it's been difficult."

"I was just wondering because that's usually the answer I get from women who come to see me—that losing their breast and seeing the scars were the hardest thing for them to handle."

Alex ran her hand along her thighs and closed her eyes. "I'm sorry. I meant the hardest thing about chemo was the nausea, fatigue, and hair loss."

"Do you have a significant other, Alex? It wasn't clear to me when you talked about your support system if you have one."

The question took Alex by surprise, and she felt a heavy feeling in her stomach. "I did, but we broke up last week."

"What contributed to the breakup? Were they not being supportive?"

"No, she was very supportive. Sometimes I felt like she was too supportive, like I was feeling smothered."

Dr. Meyer nodded. "Okay. How are you feeling about it now?"

Alex thought for a moment before answering. "I was upset with her so I broke up with her, but now I feel bad that I reacted so quickly. That's part of the reason I'm here. I've been treating her unfairly, and I want to figure out why."

"Well, Alex, it seems like there are a lot of complicated issues going on. There are a lot of layers happening. Cancer has its own relationship with the person around grief. It can change your sense of self. That can disturb your well-being and can affect your ability to maintain relationships. What do you know about grief and loss and mourning?"

"I see it all the time as an ER nurse. People die all the time and I see it, but I'm not attached to those people. They are people I haven't formally met. They're brought into my ER and I do my best to save them, but we can't save them all."

Dr. Meyer nodded and remained silent.

"I love Frank, but I'm afraid for her to go through this again. She lost her twin sister to breast cancer a few years back, and I'm afraid to let her go through this again with me. I'm afraid to let her get attached to me, and I'm afraid of getting attached to her because what if I need her and she can't handle it after all? What if she bails? And even though I've given her the option to just going back to being friends, she swears that she loves me and wants to be with me. But what if she doesn't? What if she realizes that she doesn't really want to be with me? That she just wants to help me because she couldn't help her sister?" Alex felt the tears sting her eyes and wiped them away with the tissue Dr. Meyer handed her.

"Well," Dr. Meyer began, "you're in a sticky situation because you're dealing with your own mortality. There isn't anything more vulnerable than that. So, why would you want anyone close? Why would you want to be more emotionally exposed than you already are? Your subconscious may be fairly protective, trying to keep you aware of that. As a nurse, you're very good at focusing on other people, and it would be very odd for your innate ability to focus on yourself."

Alex agreed. "It's been very hard to let people take care of me when I'm used to taking care of others. That role reversal has me all mixed up." Alex laughed as she pointed to her head.

Dr. Meyer smiled. "I can see that. You may be having sadness, anger, and hostility toward the people closest to you. If you're aggravated and irritable and explosive, and you're acting out of character, do you think you're being defensive because you don't want to be vulnerable? Or are you just in general not used to being on the other side of things?"

"Yeah, I think it's the vulnerability that I feel," Alex said. "That if I allow myself, I can see spending the rest of my life with Frank. But if I allow myself to go that far, to give myself completely over to her, and she bails, I don't know…I mean, haven't I been through enough already? I mean, honestly, I've been diagnosed with breast cancer. I've lost essentially what I think of as the essence of my femininity, and I don't think I could tolerate losing," Alex hesitated, "the love of my life. Because that's what she is. She's the love of my life. But I thought it would be easier for me if I was the one to break it off rather than be the one to be broken up with."

Dr. Meyer nodded, and the look in her eyes softened. "And how's that working out for you?"

Alex shook her head. "It sucks."

"I bet it does. So, you're just trying to be protective?"

"Yes. I'm trying to be very protective of myself."

"Do you think there's any mixed message, or ambivalence? Has she been there for you? Participating in your care?"

"She's been wanting to participate more, but I haven't let her. I've been keeping her at bay because I thought that would protect her from having to relive what she went through with Toni. I reluctantly allowed her to take me to chemo the day we broke up."

"Let me ask you something. What makes it okay for you to care of other people and not allow the same thing for yourself? What makes that okay?"

Alex paused then answered. "When I'm taking care of other people, that puts me more in control. I feel like I'm not in control when I let people take care of me because I'm not at my strongest right now."

"How scary that must be for you. Cancer does that, though. People with illnesses are not in control of their bodies. They have to develop a new relationship with their self. You have to get to know your new body. You have to get to know your new self, which can be terrifying. It would make sense that you're being temperamental, to say the least, with a significant relationship. However, it also seems like you show your true emotion with her. She's the one you get angry with. She's the one that you're raging toward. She's the one you're projecting with. She gets the brunt of it all. That suggests that she's also the safest person for you."

Alex shook her head slightly, confused with Dr. Meyer's observation. "I feel like my parents and best friends are the safest people for me."

Dr. Meyer nodded as if she understood. "But are you being completely open with them? You're not taking your anger out on them; you're taking it out on Frank. Could it be because you trust her to be able to handle that?"

Alex remained silent, not knowing the answer.

"Share with me a little how you feel about her not being there."

Alex started to cry, and it was a few minutes before she could answer. "I miss her. I miss everything about her when she's not around. She's so honorable and noble, which makes her great as an officer. She's strong, she's confident, and she's the white knight in shining armor. You know? That's her field. She tries to swoop in and save the day. But I want her to be with me because she wants to, not because she feels she has to save me. And that's how I feel sometimes—that because she wasn't able to save her sister, this might be her second chance."

"Hmm. That's interesting. Have you told her this?"

The silence from Alex made them both chuckle until Alex said, "No, I haven't."

"Well, I think that might warrant a conversation. You're in a very fragile state, and you deserve as much information as you could possibly get. It isn't fair to yourself, or Frank, to make a decision without all of the information. Clearly, the two of you are very connected, and you want the support. I hear a lot of ambivalence. You want the support, but you're scared of it at the same time. You deserve to know what's what. Does she really want to be there for you? Or does it have nothing to do with you, that she's trying to correct something from the past? Do you feel like you can talk with her? Or is it still too scary?"

"I feel like I can, but it is scary. And I don't want to have that conversation with her until I have a better grip on me. I want to make sure that I'm working to better myself physically and emotionally. Because if I'm always thinking I'm less of a woman than I was before, I'll be afraid to show my whole new self to her."

Dr. Meyer smiled and put down her pen and pad of paper on the small table next to her chair. "I think that's a good plan and also a good place to leave until next week when we meet again. In the meantime, I want you to have daily talks with yourself in the morning when you wake up and at night before you go to bed. They don't have to be long talks, just greet yourself with a daily affirmation or what you want positive to happen that day. At night, talk about how that affirmation came true, and if it didn't, remind yourself of something else good that happened in your day."

"Okay. Thank you, and I'll see you next week."

Alex staggered out to her car and got behind the wheel where she leaned her head back against the headrest and closed her eyes. She was exhausted. She'd never been to counseling before and didn't really know what to expect, but she felt better getting everything off her chest. Her mom kept telling her that she was treating Frank poorly, and Alex agreed, but it was a relief to talk to an impartial person who validated how Alex was feeling, not telling her she shouldn't be acting a certain way.

Alex thought about what she and Dr. Meyer talked about. Maybe Frank was the one she trusted most. After all, it was Frank that, in essence, knew what Alex was going through because of what her sister went through. Maybe Alex felt that Frank could handle her irritability and irrational behavior. But that didn't mean Frank should have to deal with that from her. Alex had a lot of work to do on herself before she could try to talk to Frank. She just hoped it wouldn't be too late and there would still be a chance to get back together.

CHAPTER THIRTY-TWO

Frank entered the women's locker room at the station after her shift and started to disrobe. She was just about to head to the showers when Katie came in.

"What's up, Frank?"

"Hey, bud. Just going to jump in the shower. What's up with you?"

"I was wondering if you didn't have any plans, you could come over for dinner. Michelle's making her famous lasagna tonight."

Frank thought about the offer and accepted. "I have to take Bella out for a walk, then I'll come by."

"Why don't you bring her over and we'll walk her together while Michelle finishes up dinner?"

Frank laughed. "Won't your girlfriend want you to help?"

"Nah. She says I just get in her way, so I've been instructed to stay out of the kitchen when she cooks. She allows me in after the meal so I can do the cleanup."

"That sounds fair. I'll be over around five."

Frank took her shower and drove home to get Bella. She had noticed a changed demeanor in her dog, almost like she was depressed. She didn't greet Frank at the door with her usual enthusiastic tail wag. If Frank had to guess, she'd say Bella missed Alex. Hell, Frank sure did. She couldn't believe it had been three weeks since they broke up. Time seemed to slow since then, and she wondered if anything would return to normal again. There were so many times Frank wanted to call or text Alex. When something funny happened at work, she wanted to text. When she was really missing Alex, she wanted to call just to hear her voice. But she held strong and didn't give in to her desires. Jordan had texted her a couple of times to check in, but Frank didn't really know what to say, so she texted back that she was fine and busy with work. What could she say to Alex's best friend? That she missed her and wished Alex would pull her head out of her ass and talk to her?

When Frank and Bella arrived at Katie and Michelle's, Frank put her bag down in the coat closet and went into the kitchen to say hello to Michelle. After they hugged and Frank handed her a bottle of wine, Frank, Katie, and Bella went for a stroll around the neighborhood.

"So, how're you really doing, Frank?"

"I'm doing okay. Talking with Dr. Cook is helping, especially with the extra session each week."

"I'm glad she's helping. You know, you really scared me that night you got drunk. And after what happened to you after Toni died, I didn't feel I could leave you alone. I was afraid of what might happen."

Frank dropped her chin to her chest and hunched her shoulders. She felt ashamed for having put her best friend through that in the first place, to be afraid for Frank's life. Toni's death and the estrangement with her parents made Frank want to end her own life. She had lost her entire family in a matter of days and she seriously considered putting the muzzle of her gun in her mouth and pulling the trigger. If Katie hadn't knocked on Frank's door when she did, Frank's life probably would have ended that night. Katie and Frank were the only ones who knew that story. Katie promised Frank she wouldn't tell anyone, and Frank trusted her. She trusted Katie with her life. It was Katie who demanded Frank seek psychological help, and she had been with Frank when she adopted Bella. Katie probably knew Frank would never put her life in jeopardy when there was someone or something depending on her. Katie and Bella had saved Frank's life.

"I'm sorry, Katie. I didn't mean to drink that much, and if it makes a difference, I haven't had anything to drink since that day."

"I understand, but you've been dealing with a lot of shit—Alex's diagnosis and treatment, your breakup. I'm worried about you and I want you to know that I'm here for you."

Frank wrapped her arm around Katie's shoulders and pulled her in close for a hug. "I know, and I'm sorry I worried you. It's been rough. When Alex was diagnosed, I wasn't sure if I'd be able to handle it, if it would bring up too many memories of losing Toni. But it helped that I was able to talk to Dr. Cook about things I was worried about.

"It wasn't until the time I took Alex to her chemo that Toni came flooding back into my thoughts. Alex was in a bad mood that morning when I picked her up, just like Toni would be. Remember? She'd yell at us, call us names, but we knew she did it because she was scared. I'm not sure why Alex was angry with me that day. Her nurse reminded me a little of my sister, so that also didn't help. I just can't believe she'd think I would stay with her out of obligation."

"Doesn't she know how much you love her?"

"I've told her many times, Katie, but I guess she never believed me. Or maybe she doesn't love me enough to trust me. She's never said she loved me, but I thought she did even though she never said the words."

"Christ, Frank. I'm sorry about all this. Is there anything I can do?"

"Not really. I mean, I'm not going to push her to try to talk to me. I just miss her so fucking much. I know this isn't really her that's behaving this way. She's had a lot to deal with, and I just wanted to love her and be there for her, be with her."

"Yeah, it doesn't sound like her. That time the four of us got together for dinner, I had a really great time talking to her. Michelle and I kept saying how perfect she was for you and how you'd finally found the one."

"I thought so too. I really pictured us spending the rest of our life together."

"I really hope for both of your sakes that she comes around and is willing to talk to you about what happened."

"So do I, buddy."

Alex and Jordan had taken a seat in their favorite diner, one they frequently went to while they were in college. Once they ordered their lunch, Jordan asked Alex how she'd been feeling since her chemotherapy had ended.

"I'm feeling better and my hair is starting to grow back. I'm glad to be over the nausea and fatigue as well."

"How's counseling going? Do you like your therapist?"

"I do like her and I feel it's really helping. I'm doing my homework she's given me, and my attitude is getting better. Every morning when I wake up, I lie in bed and say an affirmation. Sometimes they're so silly, but they seem to work. This morning, I affirmed that I was going to rock the new scarf that Kirsten bought me last week. I can't wait until I don't have to wear them anymore, even though they're beautiful. Pretty soon, I'm going to be affirming that I'm going to have a great hair day." Alex laughed. "It's probably because of therapy and being finished with chemo, but I'm becoming more positive and less mopey. I couldn't stand myself being so whiney, but I just couldn't seem to pull myself out of it."

Jordan reached across the table and held her hand. "We completely understood, but we were really worried about you. I can't begin to know what you were going through and how you were feeling. We were all so grateful that the cancer was gone, but we weren't the ones going through all the treatment."

Alex squeezed Jordan's hand and smiled. "I know and I appreciate everyone's support, but I felt this was my journey to go through and obviously I had some lessons to learn. I may not know all of them yet but I believe I will someday."

"And what about Frank? Is she one of your lessons?"

"I'm not sure what you mean."

"Come on, Al. We all saw it."

Alex avoided Jordan's gaze. "Saw what?"

Jordan sighed. "We saw how the two of you fell in love. We saw how you two completed the other. Then you were diagnosed and the more she tried to help you, the more you pushed her away. Did you ever figure out why you did that?"

Alex fiddled with the straw in her iced tea before she finally answered. "Yes, I figured it out with the help of Dr. Meyer." Alex paused when the waitress set down their plates. "There was a culmination of things. I wanted to spare her going through this again with someone she loved. I didn't know how to let her take care of me. But I think the biggest factor was I was scared. I was falling in love with her, and I was frightened she would leave. I didn't trust her to stay so I tried to put distance between us. I tried to step back."

"How do you feel about it now? Do you still not trust her?"

"Actually, it's not that I didn't exactly trust her, but I didn't trust myself to allow her into my life completely and allow myself to be vulnerable with her. I'm getting better, but I'm still not comfortable with my body, and I'm not ready to show my body to anyone." Alex threw a fry at Jordan and smirked. "Not even you."

Jordan feigned rejection by putting her hand over her chest and widening her eyes, then laughed. "I don't want to see you naked anyway."

Alex threw her head back and laughed. "You wanted to when we were younger and you were in love with me."

"That's true, but now I'm happily married and only interested in seeing my wife naked."

Alex looked down to her lap then looked at Jordan. "Do you think Frank would want to see me naked?"

"Do you want her to?"

Alex shrugged. "Not yet, but maybe after I'm recovered from my reconstruction. Have you talked to her lately?"

"Not really. Just a couple of short conversations. She's shut down, Al. When I try to ask her how she's doing or if she wants to talk about anything, she says no and says she's doing okay, then finds an excuse to get off the phone. And with basketball season over, I haven't seen her."

"Oh. So you don't know if she's seeing anyone?"

"I don't know, Al, but I doubt it. She was completely in love with you, so I don't think she's gotten over you yet. She's not the type to start dating someone when she's still in love with you. The big question is, are you going to call her so you can apologize?"

Alex threw another fry at her. "I want to, but I'm not ready. I have my reconstructive surgery next week, and I still have some work to do before I'm comfortable with myself. I want to be able to give Frank all of me, not just part of me. You know what I mean?"

"I do, but I have a feeling that Frank would be happy with what you can give her now, so don't wait too long. I'd hate for you to lose her completely because you were dragging your feet."

"I know, but I can't rush this. I won't be good for either of us unless I feel good about my new self."

"How are you feeling about your surgery? This is it, right?"

"Yeah, I'm feeling pretty good actually. I've been getting my expander filled while I went through chemo, but I couldn't have the implant put in until I was finished with my treatment. My plastic surgeon said I'll be in the hospital for just a day, and I should be ready to go back to work in about six weeks, but I'm going to talk to Valerie and see if she has any light duty for me so I can go back to work sooner. I'm going nuts not being able to work, and I really miss my friends at the hospital."

"I know you do. Just don't push yourself too hard, okay?"

"I promise."

CHAPTER THIRTY-THREE

I can't fucking believe this!"

"Hang on, Sarge. We'll have you at the hospital in no time."

Frank mentally slapped herself for getting tackled by Officer Robbins again. What were the odds that she would get tackled twice by the same officer while chasing a suspect? She recalled the last time when she was chasing a meth head, she got caught between the perp and Robbins, and ended up in the ER with a cracked rib. The pain sucked, but it led to her and Alex dating. Now it was her shoulder. She didn't think it was dislocated, but the pain was intense enough to not want to move her arm. She declined an ambulance but had one of her officers drive her.

She wondered if Alex was back to work yet. Not a day went by when she didn't think about or miss Alex. Frank thought Alex was done with chemo and probably had her reconstruction by now. She wanted to call her, to check in, but she didn't want to do anything that would upset Alex, so she continued to stay away. When Jordan would text her, she didn't ask about Alex. She didn't want to put her in an awkward position. Frank just continued to think positive and healing thoughts for Alex and her family.

They arrived at the hospital, and Frank registered at the admitting desk. Because of her uniform and because most everyone in the ER knew her, she didn't have to wait long before being shown to a cubicle. As she tottered through the ER, she looked for any sign of Alex and was sorely disappointed not to see her. The nurse, Nancy, was someone Frank knew, and she was grateful she'd be taken care of by a friend. After giving Nancy a brief explanation of how her injury occurred, she took off her uniform shirt and Kevlar vest but remained in her undershirt.

Once her vitals were taken, the x-ray technician came in and took shots of her shoulder. Now she'd have to wait a while until the doctor could read the films and diagnose her. She sat on the table and scrolled through her emails on her phone, then switched over to her solitaire app to help pass the time. When the curtain was pulled back, she looked up and gasped, surprised to see Alex standing there. Frank was unable to blink, afraid if she did, Alex would disappear. Neither of them moved, and Frank took in a deep breath when she realized she forgot to breathe. God, Alex was beautiful. She had gained a little bit of weight, but Frank didn't care. In fact, in Frank's eyes, it made Alex even more gorgeous. She couldn't believe it had been almost four months since they'd seen each other. Alex's hair was growing out. It was only a couple of inches long, but there was some sort of product in it. It was spiked and looked absolutely adorable on her. Frank wanted nothing more than to wrap her arms around her, but fear and apprehension kept her where she was.

Alex closed the curtain behind her, and she scanned Frank from head to toe, making her feel as if she was being caressed by Alex's chocolate brown eyes.

"Still finding excuses to see me, Sarge?"

Frank grinned. "I had to do something to get you to notice me." She looked down and wiped her eyes before the tears could fall, then looked at the woman she was still in love with. "You look great, Alex. How are you feeling?"

Alex crossed her arms over her chest before she answered. "I'm feeling better. I'm not tired anymore since chemo ended." She pulled a lock of her hair. "It's starting to grow back."

"I noticed. That style looks really cute on you."

"Thank you. I was thinking of keeping it short. Not quite this short, but I like how easy it is to take care of." Alex closed her eyes and took a deep breath. "So, how have you been?"

Frank shrugged and looked away. "I'm all right. Keeping busy with work and taking care of Bella. You know." She shrugged again.

Alex stepped closer and put her hand on Frank's knee. Frank felt the rush of heat flow through her body as it always had when they touched.

"Frank, I'm so sorry for the way I behaved. Would you...can we get together soon to talk? I have so much to tell you and say to you, but I need more time than a few minutes at work. Please? I can come to your place. I'd love to see Bella." Alex looked apprehensive yet hopeful with her eyebrows raised and her eyes widened. Frank realized at that moment that no matter how much time they spent apart, Frank was still powerless to Alex and would hang the moon for her if she could.

"I'd like that. Bella's missed you." Frank placed her hand over Alex's and rubbed it with her thumb. "I've missed you."

Alex let out a shaky breath and smiled. "I'll call you to see when you're free. Would that be okay?"

Frank nodded and once again resisted the urge to pull Alex into her body and kiss her senseless, kiss her until she said she wanted Frank back, then kiss her some more. She felt the blood rush through her body and had to calm her breathing. "I'm looking forward to it."

Alex started to back away slowly, never once looking away from Frank, until she ran into the curtain behind her. "Okay, good. If I don't see you before you leave, I'll call soon."

And then she was gone. Back to work. Taking care of patients. But she wasn't *gone* gone. For the first time in longer than she could remember, Frank finally felt hopeful for her future. Not just her future, but her future with Alex. She hoped she wasn't imagining Alex's behavior. She seemed happy to see Frank, to still have feelings for her. She could only hope that when they talked again that Alex would tell Frank that she wanted to get back together.

The curtain slid through the metal grooves in the ceiling, but this time it was the doctor, and Frank had to swallow her disappointment.

"Hey, Frank. You just can't seem to keep out of trouble, can you?"

Frank laughed and shook his hand. "I swear, Doc, I think some days Robbins has it out for me."

"Well, the good news is nothing's broken or dislocated. The bad news is that your arm is going to be sore for a week or two. Here's a prescription for some pain medication if you want it. Take it easy for a few days and follow up with your work's clinic doctor. You should be okay for full duty in about a week."

"Thanks, Doc. I appreciate it."

"No problem. Try to stay out of trouble."

Frank finished dressing and looked for Alex when she stepped out of the cubicle but didn't see her. She did see Nancy at the nurses' station, though, and walked over to her.

"Hey, is Alex around?"

"Sorry, Frank, but she just went in with a trauma. Do you want me to leave her a message?"

"Nah. Just tell her we'll talk soon. Thanks for everything, Nancy."

"You're welcome. Stay safe, Frank."

Frank waved as she walked out the door feeling lighter and more hopeful than she had in a long time. "Let's get back to the station, Anderson. I have a ton of paperwork to fill out."

Chapter Thirty-four

Bella kept whining as Frank continued to pace nervously around her house. She really wanted to go for a long run to burn off her excessive energy, but her shoulder pain wouldn't allow it. Alex would be there anytime so they could talk. Frank had no idea if they were going to get back together or go their separate ways. She hoped it was the former. Her life hadn't been the same since they broke up, and she knew it was because Alex completed her. Despite the breast cancer diagnosis, Frank would live through it again if it meant she could be with Alex. Her stomach was in a ball of knots and felt like it was on fire. When she heard the knock on her door, she swallowed back the bile she felt creeping up her throat.

She opened the door to find Alex shyly smiling at her. She wasn't sure how to greet her. What she really wanted to do was throw her arms around Alex and never again let her go, but instead she just stepped aside to let Alex in. Bella ran to Alex and uncharacteristically jumped on her. Alex laughed and allowed Bella to lick her face.

"There's my sweet girl. Oh, I missed you so much."

"As you can tell, she's missed you too. Bella, down."

Bella sat but continued to wag her tail, obviously thrilled to see Alex again.

"Can I get you something to drink?"

"Just water will be fine."

"Go ahead and have a seat," Frank said as she pointed to the living room. "I'll be back in a moment." Frank took the opportunity to take some deep breaths and try to slow her racing heart. She returned to the living room to find Bella up on the couch with her head in Alex's lap and Alex stroking Bella's soft black ear through her fingers. Both looked extremely content, and Frank took a mental snapshot to keep forever in her mind. She set Alex's glass on the coffee table in front of her and took a seat in her recliner next to the couch.

"You look great."

"How are you?"

They both spoke at once then laughed. Frank hadn't been this nervous in longer than she could remember, so she gave her standard answer whenever anyone asked how she was. "I'm doing okay. Keeping busy. How about you? How are you feeling?"

Alex continued to stroke Bella's ear and didn't immediately look at Frank. "I'm feeling better now that most of my treatment is done. I just have to take my hormone therapy for the next five years, but at least the chemo and reconstruction are finished."

Frank nodded, not knowing exactly what to say. "Well, hopefully, the worst part is over."

Alex shook her head. "See, the thing is, I thought the cancer and treatment was the worst thing that could happen to me, but it turns out losing you was far worse than the disease." When Alex looked at Frank with tears in her eyes, Frank thought her heart might break.

"I…what do you mean?" Frank asked.

"I was so caught up in fighting the disease and protecting you from having to go through it again, and protecting myself in case you decided not to go through it again."

"Alex, slow down. You're not making any sense."

"I kept trying to protect you. I didn't want you to have to take care of someone you love with cancer again. That's why I kept giving you the opportunity to leave, but you insisted on staying."

"I wanted to help you and be there for you because I love you, Alex."

"I know. But then I tried to protect myself from you leaving. I was trying not to fall in love with you because if you decided to leave me, I didn't know if I could survive that too. That's why I kicked you out of my house that day. I thought I saw it on your face, the uncertainty, and then you called me Toni and I just lost it."

"Alex, I want to explain that."

Alex held up her hand and Frank stopped talking. "No, you don't have to. Just let me finish, please."

Frank leaned forward with her elbows on her knees.

"But what I realized once you were gone is that as afraid as I was of losing you, I had never felt safer than when you were around. That with your quiet strength, I felt everything would be okay because you would do everything in your power to make sure of it.

"Then I wanted to talk to you, ask for your forgiveness, but I wanted to be better before I did that. I needed to rediscover my self-esteem. I had to make myself better mentally to be the woman you deserve. I've been seeing a therapist, and she's been helping me accept the new me, working on my attitude and outlook. I'm still not where I want to be, but seeing you in the hospital, I realized I didn't want to live another day without you in my life. I still have some work to do, especially accepting my new body, but if you'd be willing, and if you could be patient with me, I'd like for us to start over." Alex gently moved Bella's head off her lap, knelt in front of Frank, and took Frank's hands in hers. "Frank, I love you and I want us to try again. Will you please forgive me and take me back?"

Frank shook her head and stood, bringing Alex with her. She wrapped her arms around Alex's waist and looked into her eyes. "There's nothing to forgive, Alex. I love you, and I want to be with you for the rest of my life. I've waited my whole life for you, and I won't pressure you or rush you into anything you're not comfortable with. If and when you're ready to make love, you let me know. Until then, I'm perfectly content to hold your hand, hug you, and kiss you. All that matters to me is that we're together."

Alex wrapped her arms around Frank's neck and stood on her toes. "I love you so much." She pulled Frank's head lower, closed her eyes, and whispered, "Kiss me."

CHAPTER THIRTY-FIVE

"Come in, Alex. How did your week go?"

Alex walked into her therapist's office and sat in the chair she always sat in during their weekly sessions. Alex smiled. "My week was wonderfully unexpected."

Dr. Meyer mirrored her smile. "How so?"

"I ran into Frank in the ER. She had hurt her shoulder and came in for an exam." Alex continued to tell Dr. Meyer of their conversation. "I went to her house on Saturday and I told her how I'd felt during the treatment, how I was afraid of losing her but also how much I missed her. I finally told her I love her and wanted us to get back together."

"How did that go?"

Alex beamed. "Great. She said she loved me too and couldn't imagine her life without me. I was honest with her about my body issues and that I was working on becoming more comfortable. She was very understanding and said she'd be patient with me."

"That sounds like you both had a positive conversation."

Alex nodded. "We did, but it makes me want to work harder to become more comfortable showing her my whole self. How do I do that?"

Dr. Meyer laughed. "Impatient much?"

"I know, but I missed Frank and I feel that if I can expose myself fully, it will prove to her that I do trust her."

"Has she indicated that that's an issue for her? Or are you doing that projection thing again?"

Alex looked down and mumbled, "I guess I'm projecting again."

"Hey, it's all right for you to work hard on improving your self-esteem, but it needs to be for you and not anyone else. You're still fragile and vulnerable so it's great that Frank wants to be patient with you. Do you believe her?"

"Yes," Alex said quickly and confidently.

"I hear the urgency. You want to get back to yourself. You want to share your life with her and you want your body to be included. That's a respectful thing—not only to you but to the relationship."

"What do I have to do to get there? That's what I really want to work on because it's not fair to Frank or myself to deny both of us this opportunity because I can't get past my scars. I want to get past it; I just don't know how."

"There are things you can do to become more comfortable with your body, but it's going to be a process, Alex. It won't change overnight. You have to be patient and allow your mind and body to reconnect."

"How do I get to that point? I mean, it's still hard for me to look at myself naked in the mirror. I try not to look at myself below the shoulders. I have a reconstructed left breast that looks nothing like my right one, and I have an angry red scar that's a constant reminder of my disease."

"Or you can see it as a constant reminder of the battle you fought and won. It doesn't have to be a sign of disease or weakness. It can be a sign of your strength. The strength it took for you to make tough decisions to do what would be best for you. You fought that battle, Alex, and you won. You don't have to rush it, though. You want to be gentle and compassionate with yourself. Imagine yourself as a patient. How would you approach yourself? You would need to apply the same thing to yourself. Create a little bit of distance. You have permission to talk to yourself and not be crazy." Dr. Meyer laughed along with Alex. "You have the advantage because you're a nurse. What would you say to a patient who was looking at their wound for the first time, if their body had shifted, what would you tell them?"

Alex nodded in understanding.

"Limit your time. Pick a quiet time, maybe wake up a few minutes earlier and greet yourself to a new day because you're a survivor. What was all the fighting for? To have another day. Make a gesture, say a prayer, talk to the universe, whatever makes you comfortable. Acknowledge that gift of a day. Say thank you to your body. The conversation should last for only two minutes. You're doing it as you're looking at yourself in the mirror. Say 'hello, body. I don't know you, or I kind of think you're ugly,' or whatever comes to your mind. You're having the conversation face-to-face, and then you cover up, you close the conversation, and you go through your morning routine. You create this every day. Your body will start talking back to you, the more you get comfortable with it. You may be surprised. She may tell you off."

Alex laughed, acknowledging her therapist's strange sense of humor.

"She may cry."

Alex nodded. "She should cry. I've cried enough."

Dr. Meyer smiled. "You're going to say good-bye to your old body and hello to the new one. And the most important thing to remember, Alex, is to keep the line of communication open. Frank seems to me, from what you've said, very patient and understanding, and has your best interest at heart. Keep her in the loop. Don't shut her out."

"I understand. Is there anything else?"

"One more thing. Touch yourself. Your new body, your new breast may have different sensations. Find out what you feel, what feels good, what doesn't, so you can let Frank know. You need to know yourself before you can share it with anyone else. The way you made love before might not feel the same now, so it will help her to let her know what feels good to you now."

"Got it. Thank you, Dr. Meyer. I'll see you next week." Alex left feeling better than she had in months. She was anxious to get started on her new homework assignment.

❖

Alex went home, poured herself a glass of wine, and went into her bedroom. She sat on her bed and looked at herself in the mirror. Fully clothed, Alex looked normal, like the old Alex only with a cute short hairstyle. Since her change in attitude, she was more positive and like the old Alex out in public or at work. At home, when she was naked, that was a different story. The plastic surgeon had done a great job reconstructing her breast, but it was shaped differently from her right. Not her doctor's fault. That was just how it went when there was an original breast and a reconstructed one. Then there was the scar.

The scar that looked like someone took a red Sharpie and drew a line horizontally across her breast. *And let's not forget that there is no nipple or areola.*

Alex took a big gulp of wine and began to undress in front of the mirror. She removed her bra and stared at her reconstructed breast. Her breathing shallowed as she looked in the mirror. She was tempted to cover herself back up, but she had—needed—to continue. Dr. Meyer said to only take a couple of minutes to do this, but Alex needed more time. The longer she stared, the angrier she became. She took another drink from her wine, closed her eyes, and took a deep breath. She opened her eyes, looked at herself again in the mirror, pointed at her reflected breast, and clenched her jaw.

"You! You have been the cause of nothing but misery for me in the past six months. You turned my life upside down. You made me sick. You took my hair. You took my breast. You took away my femininity, my sexuality, but I'm telling you that you don't get to keep it."

Alex felt her heart pound in her chest and her nostrils flare. "You tried to take away my life, but I fought you and I won. I fucking won!"

She threw a pillow at her reflection in the mirror. Alex wiped away the tears that had spilled down her cheeks, pulled her shoulders back, and pointed again. "I won, and I will continue to fight until you're just an afterthought. Fuck you, cancer."

CHAPTER THIRTY-SIX

It had been almost a month since Alex and Frank got back together. It had been a month of rediscovery for them both. Alex had been meeting with her therapist every week, she had been doing her homework to become more comfortable with her body, and she had joined a support group of younger survivors, women around her age who had been diagnosed with breast cancer. Frank had also found a group to join for significant others of cancer survivors. The entire journey had been important for them both. But the journey was continuing, and Alex and Frank still had more to learn, more to grow.

Alex answered the door and found Frank and Bella standing on the other side of the threshold. She had invited Frank over for dinner, but didn't want the evening cut short so she told her to bring Bella along. She had chicken baking in the oven, vegetables steaming on the stove, and wine breathing on the counter. Bella greeted her with some licks to the face and then Alex kissed Frank.

When they had first gotten back together, Alex felt anxious about intimacy, but Frank had squashed those concerns. By talking openly, each expressing their concerns and fears, they were able to slowly explore. They still hadn't made love, and Alex still hadn't undressed in front of Frank, but she was becoming more comfortable with the thought. One night during a bout of sexy kissing, Alex took Frank's hand and guided it to her reconstructed breast. Instead of seeing repulsion in Frank's eyes, she saw only love and affection. Frank's reaction made Alex more comfortable, and slowly her hesitations began to fall. Each time they were together, they explored a little more, and Alex was relieved that her libido was finally returning.

After they ate dinner, they sat on the couch to watch a movie. The movie had just barely started when they began to kiss. Alex climbed onto Frank's lap and started to move against her. Frank's lips parted, and Alex took the opportunity to slide her tongue in. She felt Frank's hands slip under her shirt and caress her back. The light scratching of Frank's short fingernails on Alex's skin produced a flood of wetness in Alex's panties. She stood and offered her hand to Frank. "Take me to bed."

Frank looked up at her. "Are you sure? I'm okay with waiting."

Alex leaned down and kissed Frank, then bit her bottom lip. "I'm done waiting. I want to show you how much I love you."

Frank smiled, turned off the television, and took Alex's hand, following her to the bedroom. Alex turned to face Frank and kissed her again, a slow, lingering kiss that was made of promises for their night, for their future. She pulled Frank's shirt over her head and dropped it on the floor, then pulled her pants down. Alex wanted Frank completely naked before she exposed herself. The hungry look in Frank's eyes emboldened Alex to begin unbuttoning her blouse.

"Baby, if you're not ready, it's okay. Really."

Alex shook her head. "I'm ready. Seeing you look at me that way makes me ready."

"What way is that?"

"Like you want me."

Frank closed the distance and put her hand over Alex's, assisting in undressing her. "I do want you. Tonight and every night for the rest of our lives."

Frank pushed Alex's shirt off her shoulders and let it drop to the floor. She stepped back to let Alex finish taking off her bra. This was the first time Frank was going to see Alex naked since her surgery, and she wanted to take all of her in. Alex unhooked her bra, then crossed her arms over her chest, not allowing the bra to fall. She looked to Frank with tears in her eyes and Frank smiled and nodded. That must have given Alex the confidence to continue, and she dropped her arms and let her bra fall to the floor. She stood still with her arms at her sides while Frank took in the sight before her. Frank had always found Alex beautiful, but now...now she found Alex amazing as well. Alex fought breast cancer and had the battle scar to prove it. To Frank, the scar was a wondrous site. It was proof showing how strong Alex was, what a fighter she was, and Frank couldn't imagine being able to love her any more than she did at that moment.

Frank stepped closer, put her hand on the back of Alex's head, and whispered against her lips, "I love you, Alex. I love you and you're my hero." Frank kissed Alex gently, lovingly, and continued to kiss down her neck, her chest, but stopped when she got to her scar. She looked up at Alex without moving away, silently asking permission to continue. When Alex gave her a slight nod, Frank kissed the scar that ran horizontally across her reconstructed breast. Frank could never see this scar as ugly or a deformity. Because of this scar, the love of her life was alive. She kissed Alex's scar one more time and held Alex's face in her hands. "Thank you for trusting me. I promise to never betray that trust and I will love you with all that I am for the rest of our lives."

Alex put her hands over Frank's and kissed her again. "I trust you with my life, with my heart, and I will spend the rest of our life loving you the way you love me. Now, take me to bed, Sarge, and show me how much you love me."

About the Author

KC Richardson attended college on a basketball scholarship, and her numerous injuries in her various sports led her to a career in physical therapy. Her love for reading and writing allows her to create characters and tell their stories. She and her wife live in Southern California, where they are trying to raise respectful fur kids.

When KC isn't torturing/fixing people, she loves spending time with her wonderful friends and family, reading, writing, kayaking, working out, and playing golf.

Books Available From Bold Strokes Books

Arrested Hearts by Holly Stratimore. A reckless cop with a secret death wish and a health nut who is afraid to die might be a perfect combination for love. (978-1-62639-809-2)

Capturing Jessica by Jane Hardee. Hyperrealist sculptor Michael tries desperately to conceal the love she holds for best friend, Jess, unaware Jess's feelings for her are changing. (978-1-62639-836-8)

Counting to Zero by AJ Quinn. NSA agent Emma Thorpe and computer hacker Paxton James must learn to trust each other as they work to stop a threat clock that's rapidly counting down to zero. (978-1-62639-783-5)

Courageous Love by KC Richardson. Two women fight a devastating disease, and their own demons, while trying to fall in love. (978-1-62639-797-2)

One More Reason to Leave Orlando by Missouri Vaun. Nash Wiley thought a threesome sounded exotic and exciting, but as it turns out the reality of sleeping with two women at the same time is just really complicated. (978-1-62639-703-3)

Pathogen by Jessica L. Webb. Can Dr. Kate Morrison navigate a deadly virus and the threat of bioterrorism, as well as her new relationship with Sergeant Andy Wyles and her own troubled past? (978-1-62639-833-7)

Rainbow Gap by Lee Lynch. Jaudon Vickers and Berry Garland, polar opposites, dream and love in this tale of lesbian lives set in Central Florida against the tapestry of societal change and the Vietnam War. (978-1-62639-799-6)

Steel and Promise by Alexa Black. Lady Nivrai's cruel desires and modified body make most of the galaxy fear her, but courtesan Cailyn Derys soon discovers the real monsters are the ones without the claws. (978-1-62639-805-4)

Swelter by D. Jackson Leigh. Teal Giovanni's mistake shines an unwanted spotlight on a small Texas ranch where August Reese is secluded until she can testify against a powerful drug kingpin. (978-1-62639-795-8)

Without Justice by Carsen Taite. Cade Kelly and Emily Sinclair must battle each other in the pursuit of justice, but can they fight their undeniable attraction outside the walls of the courtroom? (978-1-62639-560-2)

21 Questions by Mason Dixon. To find love, start by asking the right questions. (978-1-62639-724-8)

A Palette for Love by Charlotte Greene. When newly minted Ph.D. Chloé Devereaux returns to New Orleans, she doesn't expect her new job and her powerful employer—Amelia Winters—to be so appealing. (978-1-62639-758-3)

By the Dark of Her Eyes by Cameron MacElvee. When Brenna Taylor inherits a decrepit property haunted by tormented ghosts, Alejandra Santana must not only restore Brenna's house and property but also save her soul. (978-1-62639-834-4)

Cash Braddock by Ashley Bartlett. Cash Braddock just wants to hang with her cat, fall in love, and deal drugs. What's the problem with that? (978-1-62639-706-4)

Death by Cocktail Straw by Missouri Vaun. She just wanted to meet girls, but an outing at the local lesbian bar goes comically off the rails, landing Nash Wiley and her best pal in the ER. (978-1-62639-702-6)

Lone Ranger by VK Powell. Reporter Emma Ferguson stirs up a thirty-year-old mystery that threatens Park Ranger Carter West's family and jeopardizes any hope for a relationship between the two women. (978-1-62639-767-5)

Never Enough by Robyn Nyx. Can two women put aside their pasts to find love before it's too late? (978-1-62639-629-6)

Love on Call by Radclyffe. Ex-Army medic Glenn Archer and recent LA transplant Mariana Mateo fight their mutual desire in the face of past losses as they work together in the Rivers Community Hospital ER. (978-1-62639-843-6)

Two Souls by Kathleen Knowles. Can love blossom in the wake of tragedy? (978-1-62639-641-8)

Camp Rewind by Meghan O'Brien. A summer camp for grown-ups becomes the site of an unlikely romance between a shy, introverted divorcee and one of the Internet's most infamous cultural critics— who attends undercover. (978-1-62639-793-4)

Cross Purposes by Gina L. Dartt. In pursuit of a lost Acadian treasure, three women must work out not only the clues, but also the complicated tangle of emotion and attraction developing between them. (978-1-62639-713-2)

Imperfect Truth by C.A. Popovich. Can an imperfect truth stand in the way of love? (978-1-62639-787-3)

Life in Death by M. Ullrich. Sometimes the devastating end is your only chance for a new beginning. (978-1-62639-773-6)

Love on Liberty by MJ Williamz. Hearts collide when politics clash. (978-1-62639-639-5)

Serious Potential by Maggie Cummings. Pro golfer Tracy Allen plans to forget her ex during a visit to Bay West, a lesbian condo community in NYC, but when she meets Dr. Jennifer Betsy, she gets more than she bargained for. (978-1-62639-633-3)

Taste by Kris Bryant. Accomplished chef Taryn has walked away from her promising career in the city's top restaurant to devote her life to her six-year-old daughter and is content until Ki Blake comes along. (978-1-62639-718-7)

Valley of Fire by Missouri Vaun. Taken captive in a desert outpost after their small aircraft is hijacked, Ava and her captivating passenger discover things about each other and themselves that will change them both forever. (978-1-62639-496-4)

The Second Wave by Jean Copeland. Can star-crossed lovers have a second chance after decades apart, or does the love of a lifetime only happen once? (978-1-62639-830-6)

Coils by Barbara Ann Wright. A modern young woman follows her aunt into the Greek Underworld and makes a pact with Medusa to win her freedom by killing a hero of legend. (978-1-62639-598-5)

Courting the Countess by Jenny Frame. When relationship-phobic Lady Henrietta Knight starts to care about housekeeper Annie Brannigan and her daughter, can she overcome her fears and promise Annie the forever that she demands? (978-1-62639-785-9)

Dapper by Jenny Frame. Amelia Honey meets the mysterious Byron De Brek and is faced with her darkest fantasies, but will her strict moral upbringing stop her from exploring what she truly wants? (978-1-62639-898-6)

Delayed Gratification: The Honeymoon by Meghan O'Brien. A dream European honeymoon turns into a winter storm nightmare involving a delayed flight, a ditched rental car, and eventually, a surprisingly happy ending. (978-1-62639-766-8)

For Money or Love by Heather Blackmore. Jessica Spaulding must choose between ignoring the truth to keep everything she has, and doing the right thing only to lose it all—including the woman she loves. (978-1-62639-756-9)

Hooked by Jaime Maddox. With the help of sexy Detective Mac Calabrese, Dr. Jessica Benson is working hard to overcome her past, but they may not be enough to stop a murderer. (978-1-62639-689-0)

Lands End by Jackie D. Public relations superstar Amy Kline is dealing with a media nightmare, and the last thing she expects is for restaurateur Lena Michaels to change everything, but she will. (978-1-62639-739-2)

Bitter Root by Laydin Michaels. Small town chef Adi Bergeron is hiding something, and Griffith McNaulty is going to find out what it is even if it gets her killed. (978-1-62639-656-2)

Capturing Forever by Erin Dutton. When family pulls Jacqueline and Casey back together, will the lessons learned in eight years apart be enough to mend the mistakes of the past? (978-1-62639-631-9)

Deception by VK Powell. DEA Agent Colby Vincent and Attorney Adena Weber are embroiled in a drug investigation involving homeless veterans and an attraction that could destroy them both. (978-1-62639-596-1)

Dyre: A Knight of Spirit and Shadows by Rachel E. Bailey. With the abduction of her queen, werewolf-bodyguard Des must follow the kidnappers' trail to Europe, where her queen—and a battle unlike any Des has ever waged—awaits her. (978-1-62639-664-7)

First Position by Melissa Brayden. Love and rivalry take center stage for Anastasia Mikhelson and Natalie Frederico in one of the most prestigious ballet companies in the nation. (978-1-62639-602-9)

Best Laid Plans by Jan Gayle. Nicky and Lauren are meant for each other, but Nicky's haunting past and Lauren's societal fears threaten to derail all possibilities of a relationship. (978-1-62639-658-6)

Exchange by CF Frizzell. When Shay Maguire rode into rural Montana, she never expected to meet the woman of her dreams—or to learn Mel Baker was held hostage by legal agreement to her right-wing father. (978-1-62639-679-1)

Just Enough Light by AJ Quinn. Will a serial killer's return to Colorado destroy Kellen Ryan and Dana Kingston's chance at love, or can the search-and-rescue team save themselves? (978-1-62639-685-2)